Mamang Dai is a poet and novelist born in Pasighat, Arunachal Pradesh. A former journalist and a Padma Shri awardee, Dai is the author of two collections of poems and works of fiction and non-fiction including the novel *The Black Hill* that received the Sahitya Akademi Award 2017, in English.

Dai lives in Itanagar, Arunachal Pradesh.

ESCAPING THE LAND

MAMANG DAI

SPEAKING
TIGER

SPEAKING TIGER BOOKS LLP
125A, Ground Floor, Shahpur Jat, near Asiad Village,
New Delhi 110049

First published by Speaking Tiger Books 2021

ISBN: 978-93-5447-067-7
eISBN: 978-93-5447-075-2

10 9 8 7 6 5 4 3 2 1

Typeset in Minion Regular by SÜRYA, New Delhi
Printed at ...

For my parents Odi and Matin Dai
A tribute to the pioneering
men and women & veterans of the NEFA days.

‘It is time to walk barefoot into the onions
And watercress, midstream into the lilies.
Today we must shut out the mineral gaze of the world,
Kneel to life and water
Simplicity, greener than we ever imagined.’

—*Runaway Sun*,
Pablo Neruda

Book One

TIME

The house of calendars

The house stood on a hill covered with bamboo thickets. It was raised on concrete pillars twelve feet above the ground and looked slightly askew, as if ferocious winds had buffeted it. The old wooden boards slanted to the left, though looking up from the sloping path to the house, the pointed dome of the hill behind the house and the triangular ridging of the roof appeared to be joined in a perfect line. More hills loomed behind.

An old cane sofa, a table and a couple of stools were placed haphazardly on the veranda. No one seemed to be about. The front door was wide open. I walked in. Bright sunlight spilled in through thin cotton curtains and the emptiness inside the house gave it an air of a transit camp. I knew this was the old part of the house. I had been here before but this visit was coming after a gap of many years. I noticed a new extension that jutted out on a slope overlooking a clump of trees surrounded by rice fields.

'Hello, hello!' I called out, not worried by the absence of people because I knew someone would come round by and by. I peered out of the window. A path below to the right led to a lake and a zoo, and the road on the left was the national highway that skirted a big hotel and turned in towards the city of Itanagar. From this intersection another road ran straight through the mountains to Gohpur town in Assam.

A pile of books was stacked in one corner and the wooden boards of this room were tacked with calendars in horizontal layers of bright colours. There were pictures of flowers, lakes, gushing waterfalls, gods and goddesses, the sacred heart of Jesus, lilies, Japanese art, sea birds, snowflakes, everything; and they came with the printed names of shops, agencies, student unions, arms dealers, cement mixers and a host of other companies who had taken the trouble to print out these pictures for all the years that had come and gone. A number of dates were circled in green ink. Perhaps they were important dates. What had been so important, I wondered. Where had the owner of the house come by this great collection?

'Ah, everywhere I went, every time I bought something in every small town, I was given a calendar. I don't know why,' said the owner of the house. He was an elderly man in his mid-fifties who had come in from working outside somewhere in the big compound. 'I thought I would put them up like this,' he said. 'Pity to throw them away. Anyway, they brighten up the place, don't you think?

'Yes, but what are these dates—all circled?'

'Well, they are just marks. March—May—summer—winter—a reminder of time for an aging politician, that's all. Tell me, how are you?'

'I am working on a project. That's what I came to tell you.'

'You look happy,' he said.

I was feeling happy. I was starting work on something that interested me, and it felt good to be sitting drinking tea on the veranda. 'I wanted to ask you some questions,' I said.

'Oh, like what kind of questions?'

'Questions about you, politics...your life...'

'Hmm...What is there to tell? You can ask anyone here about me and they will tell you more than I would ever be able to! What *don't* people know about politicians?'

This was true. No one was better known than Lutor, the veteran politician with his long and successful career in politics since the formation of the state. Children shouted his name and women's faces broke into smiles when he entered a village. Men spoke of him with evident camaraderie and he was welcomed wherever he went.

'I have some good friends, that is all,' he said, sipping tea in between answering my questions about his political career. He laughed when I pointed out that everyone spoke about him as if he had extraordinary powers to predict the future. Yes, he knew about that but he disputed that he had any powers. 'Look at me,' he said, 'do you think I look any different from the man next door?'

No, he looked like any one of my uncles with a familiar, dependable face, but I didn't say anything. I had an idea of Lutor's reticence and I knew this was his way of making conversation to deflect interest away from himself. Nothing about him gave any sign of his extraordinary influence on the lives of men and women in the villages. But I knew something of his past and I shared an association with some of the characters in a story from long ago when everything had been different and full of possibilities.

That evening, I opened the windows of my small study and stared out at the hills. Everything was still. I looked around the room. There was the table. The lamp. The pen. I rummaged through a pile of papers until I found an old journal marked 'NEFA NOTEBOOK.' Other than a few entries in a clear, slanting hand there was little else in the book except a photo of a young man sitting on a stone with one arm resting on his knee as if posing for some artistic effect. In the background was a bamboo hut, slightly out of focus. I began flicking through the pages. A piece of paper fell out. I picked it up carefully, knowing what it was. It was a blank sheet folded in two that held a piece of pressed fern. I stared at it. How old was this piece of memorabilia? It was almost withered away, but here it was—these things that had been nudging at me all these years to look again at this green life offering food, shelter, medicine; and explore the secrets of their buried, invisible roots.

Now the brown memento was so old and stiff it was ready to fall apart if I touched it too much. It could go into the fire and that would be that. The lives of people in every village and district had changed since the time this piece of fern had been so carefully pressed in between the thin pages of a book. There were new roads and new towns growing faster than anyone could have imagined. Yet the land remained the same. Nothing could change the outline of the hills. In the dry winter months, the jungle could be pushed back but the next summer would always see the return of wild creepers flaunting their monstrous beauty and clinging to the swooning trees. No work force with hundreds of men and machinery and giant excavators could dig away the trees and rocks and fling the insidious vine into a permanent death. I held the photo and continued to gaze out. I could feel the chill settling on my shoulders. Something was tugging at my heart. I hit the light switch and the small lamp made a yellow pool of light on the table. I thought about Lutor and the things he had said about the mountains and how they were always there, rearing up over our lives. But now I sensed something else. A lake was hidden somewhere and a small wave was curling and lifting, as if to peel back the surface, beginning with a corner, there—along the quiet edge of water. Was it true what Lutor had said, that everyone was born with an original obsession? From what age did anyone begin to realise this? Was it from the time a person could dream?

No, Lutor had said. It was after the first setback, or even very late, maybe after several setbacks. It was the time when you realised life can fool you and you have to fight back. Then you find out which way your heart lies and after some time, suddenly, the rules of the game are trespassed. The common guidelines no longer apply. Instinct takes over and we act according to our memory of the original obsession.

The original obsession

The original obsession was a dream of a knife blade. Everything that happened began from there, from the time when there was a war and the world changed, and a knife began to cut through the canvas, sometimes with serrated edges, sometimes covering the distance between two points in a single stroke. But most of the time it was a slow gnawing, with blunt edges.

Once, a man dreamed he dived into the river and saw, resting on the sand, a gleaming knife. Lomey carried it up firmly gripped between his teeth. Shortly afterwards he was blessed with a son. Ignoring his wife's pleas, he did not stay home to celebrate this birth. Instead, he joined a band of warriors who were already setting out to avenge the murder of a great chief of the area. He was among the chosen, known for his courage and daring. His friends were waiting for him.

In October 1953, a party of 165 men accompanied by an armed platoon of Assam Rifles had been attacked in a small village called Aching mori in the remote valley of the Subansiri river somewhere deep in the mountains beyond Assam. Forty-seven people including the commandant and twenty-seven Assam Rifle jawans had been killed. They were men sent by the government to survey the area beyond the established post of a place called Along. The band of warriors did not attach importance to this. Their mission was to avenge the murder of the chief who had accompanied the ill-fated column as Head Interpreter. In the wilderness beyond their own village, he had been captured by unknown tribesmen and brutally tortured before he was killed. The men wanted a name. Who had killed their chief? It had taken them several months of secret meetings and investigations to gather information from other villagers about what had happened. And now they thought they had something. They were restless and eager to set out before anyone got wind of their intentions. The route was uncertain and they would be stalking a dangerous prey.

They marched into forests dripping with perpetual rain. An icy wind made them crouch against one another. The men stopped all speech and began to move like animals breathing without a sound, their eyes restless and their bodies alert for sudden attack. It was fight, or die. They knew they could not turn back now. The serrated leaves of wild cane swayed soundlessly as they passed by with faces set like imperturbable masks. Sometimes, ferns with lips and eyes caressed them. Then Lomey, the father of the newborn child, remembered his son like a searing flash and smiled at the small patches of sunlight that floated like magic pools before them in that fearful forest.

One morning, they crawled up a steep hill of mud and decay and saw below them the sleeping village. It huddled in the stillness like ancient stones rolled together, and Lomey felt his heart exploding.

'Remember, we want only one…' His friend Dinu whispered in his ear.

Lomey felt mockery rising up like a black wave. It would

be impossible, he knew that. They would be fighting in close combat, eye to eye, teeth to teeth. He remembered his dream of a knife blade.

In the subsequent slaughter the village was razed. Its inhabitants fled screaming into the jungle. Lomey himself did not know whether he was still breathing or whether all that was happening around him—the screaming men and women, the contortion of bodies and the death cries of rage and vengeance—was another dream. When the fighting began all his movements obeyed another instinct. His hands moved with exquisite speed and accuracy, his mind became a flame of blazing ferocity. He cut a man on the shoulder. As he fell clutching his arm, Lomey brought his sword down in a full arcing stroke on the fallen man's head.

When Dinu shouted that they had the man they wanted he suddenly remembered where he was, and wiping his sword hastily on the man he had struck down he rushed forward to join the others.

'We are not cowards. We have come all this way and we have achieved our goal,' he thought.

What followed was another dream. Their village was a distance of eight days. The element of surprise was gone and men of the enemy village would be stalking them now. They would have to double their speed and hack their way through a new trail to confuse them. The man they had taken prisoner spat on the food they gave him. He wanted to die. They wanted him alive. Only in the village could the true and final act of revenge be enacted. The entire village must witness his slow death. Only then would the spirit of the dead elder be truly avenged. The captive stared back at them with narrow, glittering eyes. He showed no fear. He uttered not a word. But on the fifth night he cried out loudly and they could not stop him. When Dinu hit him on the head he snapped around sharply and tried to bite him. Then he continued his piercing cry opening his mouth wider and wider like a mad beast. The terrible sound echoed around the forest. The men watched him with hate and mounting desperation. He was a mighty foe. They understood that if they untied his hands he would tear open his chest and show them his heart beating with equal rage and derision.

When they reached their village, they found soldiers with guns waiting for them. The new government would not permit tribal feuds and the soldiers had come with orders to seize the captive and the men who had captured him. It was the order of the new sarkari. The whole village fell silent. There would be no punishment. The new sarkari niyom, rules, would now look after everything.

'Our time is over,' Lomey told his wife that night. Runners were carrying the news of their unimaginable triumph to distant villages. He himself had put his thumbprint on a number of sheets dotted with black, unknown lines. In the administrative post of Along, the officer he had faced when declaring his name and clan had looked at him with a mixture of fear and loathing.

'We have put the seal on our fate. It is out of our hands,' Dinu said. Dinu had accompanied the warriors because his friend Kitem had also been killed in Aching mori.

Both Dinu and Lomey were political interpreters. Their job was to liaise between the officers and the tribesmen. They were men appointed on the basis of their standing and influence in their community to translate the meaning of 'sarkari'. They spoke a mixture of dialect, Hindi and Assamese. Sometimes it happened that another interpreter was needed to interpret the interpreters. Nevertheless, they were the pioneers who travelled to hundreds of villages to negotiate among warring tribes and organise meetings to pave the way for settled administration. But now, times were changing. The traditional institutions of village headmen and tribal interpreters was being overtaken by a new administration and Dinu and his household were already preparing to leave Along and return to their hometown of Pasighat.

'Yes,' Lomey thought. 'My thumbprint that is like no other man's on earth is being carried away on a sheet of paper. The new sarkari has reached us. Others will decide what will happen now.' He heard his child wailing. He had named him Lutor. His wife's footsteps shook the bamboo as she moved about the house. Lomey listened. 'I will be reborn in my son,' he said to himself.

The new government was a group of officers struggling to draw a cohesive map of the country's frontiers in post-Independence India. They were handpicked men, drawn from the army and from All India Service cadres, eager to travel and face any challenge, but here in the remote frontier they were discovering that the mountainous land stretching northwards from Assam to the Tibetan plateau was a blank of unexplored territory. In the hill town of Shillong, the administrative capital, news of this murder and vengeance in the hills caused pandemonium among the new officers recruited to handle the administration of this frontier.

Where is this place? they asked.

The name Aching mori was on everyone's lips. Big books and maps were consulted. In British India records the early history of the region was a perplexing series of revisions, notifications and Acts that generally emerged out of punitive expeditions following a killing or a skirmish when strangers entered tribal territory, or when tribes made raiding forays into the Assam plains. When the British discovered tea and oil in the Brahmaputra valley they drew a line under the provisions of the Bengal Eastern Frontier Regulation, 1873, to protect their commercial interests and establish the limits of British territory. This was notified as the Inner Line. Transferred on the ground this line was littered with references to hundreds of starting points, numbered masonry pillars, patrol paths, junctions, towns, rivers and confluences. British subjects were prohibited from going beyond this Inner Line without a pass into the Hills area demarcated as the North East Frontier Tracts of Assam.

Some of the officers thought the Aching mori incident had happened in the Abor hills.

Where?

Don't you remember the Abor war?

The Komsing case?

This was a reference to the single, well-known Komsing case of 1911 when a British political officer had crossed the Inner Line on a survey mission into the Abor hills. His name was Noel Williamson. He had explored Abor country before but this time he wanted to travel further upstream along the Siang River and he was carrying gifts for the villagers. He was accompanied by a colleague, Dr. Gregorson, a tea garden doctor, and everything would have gone well if not for the meeting with some tribesman along the way. There was an altercation, the outcome of which was that Dr. Gregorson was killed in a camp where he had stayed behind, while Williamson and his party of men were attacked and killed in the village of Komsing. This had resulted in the punitive Abor Expedition of 1911 when

British troops marched into the Siang valley. The Abor had been defeated and forced to sue for peace with the surrender of thousands of war arrows, war kits and swords along with the return of any property belonging to Williamson and Dr. Gregorson. A permanent post with an assistant political officer was established in a place called Pasighat on the banks of the river Siang, setting in motion a series of policy revisions vis-à-vis the tribes of the frontier, and opening the doors to exploration of the region. The Government of India also seized this opportunity to send survey missions into the hills to propose a suitable frontier line between India and Tibet. In 1914, the Hills area was renamed as the Frontier Tracts. The same year, a delegation led by Sir Henry McMahon of the India government was negotiating the Simla Accord to demarcate the country's northern boundary, by which the Frontier Tracts were effectively wedged in between the Inner and the Outer Line on the crest of the Himalayas.

Did it happen there again, in the Abor hills?

No, no, this is way beyond.

Where?

We'll soon find out.

The new Republic could not have known then that there would be still more murders, deaths of government agents and soldiers, and the accounts of terrified survivors bringing their reports before a stunned circle of officers labouring to shape the wilderness into a comprehensive administrative map. History was being written in slow, laborious stages wavering between friendship and enmity, fear and trust; and just as the Komsing incident of 1911 resulted in so many changes in the region, similarly, in 1953, the Aching mori incident was to have far-reaching and enduring repercussions.

One of the decisions taken by the government then was to rename the Frontier Tracts. Following the Aching mori case, in January 1954, the remaining tracts were demarcated as the North-East Frontier Agency (NEFA). The 'agency' meant that the NEFA would be administered by the president through the governor of Assam as his agent, under the general supervision and control of the Ministry of External Affairs. The tracts were divided into frontier divisions and simultaneously a new administrative cadre called the Indian Frontier Administrative Service was created with recruits for this cadre to be drawn from the All India Services, and other service cadres of Assam.

This piece of news gave hope to a shy, young man who was then studying in Shillong. His name was Lipun, and he was twenty-four years old. It was his photograph that lay on my desk. My mother used to talk about him. He was the mysterious grand uncle who had been raised by one of my mother's paternal aunts after his parents died when he was a young boy. Most of the time the only thing I had heard said about Lipun was that he was somewhere, far away. By sheer dint of hard work Lipun had won a government stipend and he was one among the first batch of tribal men favoured to move out of the NEFA and complete their studies in Shillong. They lived in a building called the NEFA hostel which was a large private bungalow taken on rent by the NEFA administration's Department of Education. They received a stipend of sixty rupees of which fifty-five went into Mess charges. The news of the Aching mori incident filled them with fear and consternation. It also gave rise to some heated discussion.

'What got into those people. Why do such a thing?' said Darin, a fellow student. 'Now the government will react and we are all going to suffer.'

'Who are these people?' Lipun asked.

'I heard it happened up in Tagin country, in the Subansiri area.'

Where was that? Lipun realised how little he knew of the mountains and valleys beyond his hometown. Darin and he were from Pasighat. At the time towns like Pasighat and Along in the Abor Hills were the comparatively better-known parts of NEFA by their proximity to the big towns of Assam along the Brahmaputra river. There were tribes living in the next valley but they did not communicate with each other, thought Lipun. In school they were instructed in the Assamese language and Lipun knew his teachers who came from Assam, but about his own land and people he had little or no knowledge at all.

It was the same with the officers who were outraged, more so because no one had a clue about this region and the people who had perpetrated the crime. The Abor and Mishmi Hills carved out from the old Sadiya Frontier Tract were by now somewhat familiar territory, but this was only a small part of a vast land that lay like a brooding, sleeping giant. A lone Dakota aircraft was despatched to conduct an aerial survey of the spot. There was even some talk of bombing the place and setting the jungle alight to burn out the villagers just like the British had done in the Abor war of 1911.

'The government must take action. The tribes do not understand goodwill and kindness. They are ungovernable and they deserve to be punished!' This was the thinking among some of the officers regarding the Aching mori case.

Lipun felt his heart wince at the harsh words. Perhaps the people of Aching mori had been afraid. There had been no one to explain anything to them. As far as Lipun was aware everyone who had come into their land had come as strangers.

'We will send soldiers,' Lipun heard the officers saying. Others were saying they must establish contact with the tribesmen. 'We don't want to send out punitive expeditions like the British. What if we handle it like this—we'll send out columns of men with officers and try to surround the area.'

He knew they were spreading out charts and confabulating at great length. The name of that little village far away in the hills began to sound like a war zone. Perhaps I could be of some help, he wondered to himself. He felt caught between a feeling of great humiliation and a pitying love for his homeland. It was so unknown. There was nothing there, only row upon row of mountains, all those ranges covered with the densest, greenest forest one could ever imagine. Where were the people? He marvelled at the tenacity of all those small villages clinging to the mountain as if the mountain and the poor huts sloping down in close, tightly packed rows were bound together forever.

It was with these mixed feelings that Lipun entered the office of a senior officer who summoned him one day and said, 'Well, how about it?'

How about what? He stood stiffly trying not to look at the stern but handsome man who was signing some papers. They were papers concerning an appointment and first posting for Lipun.

'How about going to Along?'

He struggled with an image of thatch houses in a small place lost in the enormous jungle. Along was the place that had been selected by the government as base camp for their troops to march up into the village of Aching mori. He was being sent as a junior government official with a starting salary of one hundred and seventy-five rupees a month plus thirteen rupees ration money.

'How about it?'

Yes, how about it? Why not? Perhaps he could be of help. Perhaps he could travel up into the Tagin area too. If those villagers saw him as a fellow tribesman, they might welcome him and they could talk about a lot of things. All this was to prove wrong but Lipun could not know about this then. Time had its method. Everything happened in stages and the land was the wide canvas over which the days and months rolled without a warning signal or a murmur, just as he marched into the wilderness, crossing rivers and hundreds of miles to reach the town of Dibrugarh where his bedding, camp equipment and his tin trunk were roughly loaded on to a Dakota aircraft that carried him straight to the small landing strip in Along.

In different circumstances, Lipun's arrival would have been greeted with some fanfare. He was, after all, one of the first local men representing the government, doing sarkari work. There was Dinu whom he knew from Pasighat, but there was little time to sit together and talk. As it was, Lipun took up his duties quietly even as the town was being turned topsy-turvy with the arrival of a host of strangers and the visit of the advisor to the governor of Assam. The Aching mori incident was uppermost in everyone's minds and in a pincer drive, columns of soldiers surrounded the ill-fated village and captured seven men who were said to be the culprits of the 1953 attack.

One cause for happiness in this confusing time was the birth of Dinu's daughter. She arrived squirming and wailing one November dawn. The house was empty as if everyone had retreated into a glum silence with the arrival of more officers and more soldiers. Everyone was talking about new names for the area, new divisions and new rules that were being imposed on them. Both Dinu and Lomey were caught up in this whirlwind and there was very little time for family matters.

'Quick, we must give a name to this poor child,' said Gagil. She was Dinu's sister and she was the only one attending the birth in the small, empty house. Her eyes brimmed over with tears as she looked at the angry red face of the infant. The wind was roaring down the gorge and rattling the rusty tin roof and making the doors creak and whine as if they were mourning something. She heard footsteps. It was a young boy bringing a message from Dinu saying that he and his party would be unable to reach the town before nightfall. Then the old midwife looked around her and said, 'Listen to that wind! We can't wait for them. Otherwise the wind might claim the baby. Hurry, think of something. Call her O-me, meaning daughter, or why not Mukseng, mist and cloud, since it's so cold!'

'No, no, none of the old names,' the exhausted mother had waved her hand.

'Why, if you want something new give the little one an aying name!' cried the midwife. 'Why not call her N-E-PH-A or something, whatever it is that everyone is talking about now?'

No one said anything then and that was how Dinu's

daughter was named Nefa-Ome, daughter of NEFA, shortened to plain Nefa, just as many young men and women were named after the incidents and changes that were taking place when they were born, like Mac (McMahon line), Gandhi, Assam, Bharat, and Stilwell, after General Joseph Stilwell of the famous Stilwell Road of World War II vintage.

When Lutor was five years old, his father died. Soon after, Lutor's mother attached great importance to a dream of a serpent that she saw visiting the house. Early one morning she unlocked the door of the granary and gasped when she saw a deep hollow in the largest mound of rice. Now she understood her dream. Stepping back slowly she whispered, 'If you are hungry we will give you food. Do not bring harm to our family.'

It was the season of heavy rains. The earth was churned to slush and no one ventured out, not even to work in the fields. One dark evening Lutor came upon a flying fox staring at him from its perch on the wooden rafter in a corner of the hut. In the faint light filtering in through the open door behind him there was the dark creature, rain-wet and alive, watching him. Lutor held his breath. He could not utter a sound. The room became an enclosure that hummed with the sound of water. He saw the big leaves breaking. The canopy of forest crashed down and he inhaled the wind heavy with the odour of crushed fern and wild chestnut. The liquid eyes of the animal shone like gold and Lutor stood transfixed.

Later, much later, the family would wonder how and

when the creature had come in. The old people who had been sitting on the veranda all day had seen nothing. Perhaps it was the ghost of a relative. Perhaps it was another dream. Whatever it was, when it had happened there had been no time for thought. Lutor's uncle had rushed in shouting loudly and struck the creature with a heavy pole. The furry animal fell to the floor without a sound and did not move again. Lutor shuddered. He had seen the look of the falling animal. It seemed to smile at him with great tenderness as if to say:

'It is alright. Do not be afraid. I have seen you.'

After the visitation, as his mother used to call it, Lutor remembered that he had fallen very ill. The medical officer pronounced a case of severe malaria but no one believed him. The health centre was a ramshackle hut of bamboo and diagnosis was often arbitrary, simply going by external symptoms that in Lutor's case was a fever that seemed to be burning up his body. He did not have a single shivering fit that everyone knew was a symptom of malaria. His mother kept him at home and gave him black tea mixed with a little opium. Lutor lay inert and fell into a coma for three days. He woke only when his mother tied a piece of ginger on a black thread around his neck. Lying still with his eyes closed he remembered a dream as if someone had been trying to speak to him.

He saw a boy perched on a rock skimming stones on the river. The expert twist of his wrist flung the stones making them escape, leaping over the water into the distance beyond his vision. The widening ripples fascinated him. He stared at the water and crouched, dreaming all afternoon while the sun circled the trees and dazzled the water. His back burned. He glanced quickly around him and then jumped in casually, feet first, hitting the water with a loud splash. Turning, somersaulting underwater, he opened his eyes and saw the current rushing past him while he held his breath, staring and staring until he could hear his heartbeat beating in his head above the sound of the rushing current and he had to surface at last, gasping for air. Resting his arms on the rock he tried to peer again into the swift water. He always imagined a shining knife lying on the river bed. He knew about his father's dream of a knife blade. At first it had frightened him, but now, as a young man, it fascinated him and he wanted to transfer that dream into the moment and unravel its symbols. In a wondrous glide he would dive in deep and pick it up with his teeth. Then he would rise up and wade out of the river with the blade clenched between his teeth just like the legendary warrior whom everyone had known and admired. He watched as a bird skimmed the water then rose high into the sky. He sat still and waited. All alone he watched the bird's silent dive, swoop, swirl, and then the swift disappearance. Instinct! The only way to live life was by instinct. The bird's longing stayed in his soul. He clenched the knife blade and all the burning, hushed afternoons were lodged forever in his soul like a first encounter with himself.

The NEFA days

Lipun arrived as if fate had appointed him to be there at this specific moment to become the guardian of the boy. People said at the time that Lutor's mother had been born with the powers of a shaman. She was a woman from the northern hills, and though she had never demonstrated her powers, it was believed that her clan people offered sacrifice and prayed to the spirits to take away this power from her and transfer it to someone else. Sometimes a shaman would dance and roll naked on the ground in a trance and this was the reason for the woman's relatives to beg the spirits to remove this powerful gift. It was transferred to her brother who in later years was to become famous throughout the land as the rainman.

People said that a few years before leaving their village the rainman had been seized with a bout of madness that lasted for ten days. He crept into a hut and refused to eat or speak. He signalled for things to be brought to him because no one could understand what he was saying. They said a spirit had entered him and he was speaking the language of the gods. Then one burning summer day when the crops were shrivelling in the field, he had emerged out of the dark, closed hut and pointed to the sky. The frightened relatives looked up and saw nothing. It was a blank, empty space shimmering with the heat of the sun. Then the rainman spoke. He said he would fetch the sun and carry it away.

A long ladder of bamboo was constructed with more than a hundred steps. People stood in a circle as this ladder was lifted and held upright by supporting wooden posts. An assistant shaman, the miri irging, was chosen from the Daji clan. He was the man fated to climb this amazing structure.

'I am ready to obey,' said the young man. He put his foot on the first rung and tested it with a thumping movement of his feet. He smiled.

Everything was still and no one said a word. The rainman had looked at him with no expression in his eyes. The young man seemed to hesitate for a fraction of a second. He knew of mystery and magic but now he could not fathom the moment. It was as though a mystical power was moving his body upwards and ever upwards without his will or power to resist. The villagers gathered in the spot were a crowd of eyes and faces that bent backwards as they looked up to follow the disappearing figure climbing up to the sky. Now he was gone from view. Still they tilted their heads back awaiting something, all except the rainman who sat idly with one leg extended and his head bent over some drawings he was making in the dust with a stick. Suddenly, as if an arrow had been shot from the sky a flame of fire streaked down and fell in their midst. There was a smell of burning and a sizzle of flame. The villagers, as if hypnotised, could only rear back, silent, aghast, their eyes bulging in horror as they looked on the burnt, blackened body of the young assistant. The rainman stopped his scribbling and let the stick drop from his hands. The awestruck assembly heard the rumble of thunder. Another deep growl followed and suddenly the croaking of frogs and shrill cries of insects and unseen birds filled the air as a wind started up, bringing with it big, pelting drops of rain. Had the young man stolen the sun for a moment and carried it in his body to allow rain to spring out of hidden clouds? What had the rainman done? Had he sacrificed a human being to fetch the sun and carry it away in his burnt body? Was there an enmity between him and his disciple? Who was to know, least of all ask about these things? The villagers ran to their houses to get out of the rain. Only the rainman was left in the empty clearing. Those who dared look back saw him cut the ropes of the supporting poles, letting the ladder slide to the ground where it lay shining in the rain. All this had happened long ago but everyone still believed it.

They said that the rainman could make fish jump out of the water in a silvery shoal and that his touch could make a dry rock weep water. But as far as Lutor knew his uncle performed no more miracles and chose to live quietly instead. He told Lutor stories and said the flying fox is enchanted by fire. 'Light a fire in the jungle and he is sure to arrive, circling overhead to gaze at the bright glow. They are mesmerised by the smoke, and after man has gone, the flying fox descends and licks the ashes clean. Perhaps it is the taste of salt.'

When Lutor's mother died and Lipun received orders to move to a new posting, the rainman agreed to Lipun's offer that Lutor should accompany him and study in school. It was then that the young Lutor saw the rainman smile at him for the first time and suddenly his boyish heart had been filled with a sense of well being.

In 1959, Lipun was posted to an outpost called Anini.

At first there was some confusion. Where was this place? No one knew for certain. It must be across the Abroka mountains in the east, said Lutor's uncle. This was a region of high passes covered in snow. Across these mountains lay the land of the Idu people who sometimes appeared in their villages to trade in wool, war coats, musk and yeast to brew rice beer.

No, it is to the west, someone said, but Lutor's uncle was right. It was a new subdivision in the land of the Idu. Lipun was being sent as a government officer and his instructions were to hold public meetings, maintain law and order and look after agricultural development and supply of drinking water. He was to report to the political officer in the town of Roing.

'I know Roing,' Lipun said, but beyond that he did not know anything else. His friends offered sketchy information. 'It's somewhere near Tibet,' they said. 'It is the hardest trek in NEFA. If I were you I would quit!'

But this was the last thing on Lipun's mind. He looked at maps and traced the thick pencilled line of the river. There it is, he cried, pointing to a small dot that marked the town of Roing in the foothills between the mountains and the plains. 'But it is fourteen days' foot march from Roing to Anini!'

He looked at the young Lutor who already had a hawkish, inquisitive air about him, and decided to start out early in the New Year, as if delaying his departure by a month would be enough time for the boy to grow up and make the long journey with him.

It was a wild, breathtaking journey. They crossed the Brahmaputra river in a ferry boat heaving with people, goats and squawking chickens and landed with their faces wind burnt, dry, and coarse as the river sand. The landing ghat and the towns of Assam were shifting dreams that appeared and retreated every year as the river changed course and swallowed everything in its way.

'The town of Sadiya used to be here!' exclaimed Lipun, jumping off the boat and spreading out his arms. The famous Sadiya where he had studied in the government school before the massive earthquake of 1950 had flushed it away forever. 'There used to be flowering trees from here right up to the political officer's bungalow—and a row of pine trees up to the Assam Rifles camp and another row of trees up to the hospital building…'

In the blinding light of the open sandy space Lutor saw the trees standing before him like illuminated sentinels holding spears of leaves.

'And here, the British officers used to come up on to the boats and examine everyone for their papers. If there was no Inner Line permit you were prohibited to disembark and quickly sent back on the same boat.'

Lutor saw a big, beefy man in a sola topee standing on the shore, scrutinising the bedraggled group with blue flashing eyes. The image turned into a straight-backed Lipun plunging ahead and pulling him on. No. There were no more strangers here. Lipun was in charge, and he was fixed in his goal to march forward and befriend people that he had never met before. They made a wide detour of the river, hopping on to smaller boats and floating through more ferry crossings until suddenly, one day, Lipun announced that they were near the town of Roing. They were on the back of a converted World War II jeep and Lutor was blinded with dust and sun. In Roing a strong, handsome man stepped forward to receive them. His name was Singa, he said, and he would be their guide.

Lipun was very excited. He had a tendency to be friendly and talkative with porters, drivers and men in his camp, but Lutor noticed that whenever he was in the presence of an officer from Shillong or Delhi he withdrew and seemed unwilling to communicate. It was the same with Singa. The big man with his fringed hair tied back in a knot spoke barely half a dozen words throughout the fourteen days they struggled up and slid down mountains.

'Now we know the difference between a hill and a mountain,' panted Lipun.

Singa said nothing but he pushed, cajoled, lifted, and carried the stumbling Lutor into the next camp and the next as lightly as a feather. The approach to Anini started from the Dibang river valley through a wild landscape of ugly, sloping mountains scarred with deep gashes gouged out by the calamitous earthquake of 1950. They reared up higher and higher in a continuous chain and Lutor thought they would never reach their destination but continue climbing up and crawling down until they died. One day they reached a wide, boulder-strewn place. Singa signalled for them to be silent. A swift-flowing stream cut across their path and feathery white pumi grass glinted like a waving sea before them. All around them Lutor saw scarred mountains rearing up like ugly apparitions, as if they were wounded or angry about something. They were like midgets standing a few inches tall compared to the height of the towering peaks above them and young as he was, Lutor sensed that the mountains were scowling. It was a place of flash floods and landslides, Singa said, and many people had been killed here by falling rocks. Just the previous year a team of engineers and forty men were buried under a landslide in that very spot while crossing a stream to look at a new road alignment to link the hills with the plains. The avalanche of boulders hurtled down with such force that in a second all trace of an accident was wiped out, except for scattered grains of ration dal on the rocks. In 1948, another landslide had wiped out a whole village where a British political officer was holding a meeting. It was the village of Minyutang across the next stream. They were sitting in the sun, talking, when suddenly a landslide swept down and buried the village and the men without a trace. Singa said killer avalanches were triggered by loud noise or rifle shots aimed at birds or monkeys. 'It is not good to disturb the spirit of stones,' he said.

The time in Anini passed as in a dream. Lutor saw snow for the first time and jumped out of his bamboo cot in surprise. One day he saw three burly men in long, red robes and long boots talking to Lipun. Who were they? Lutor felt his heart beating fast in fear, not knowing about Chinese incursions in Tibet just across the border from where they were.

'They are Khampa men of Eastern Tibet,' Lipun told him. They wanted to know if the local administration would allow them to stay in Anini. It was the year of flight and movement when in the following month the Dalai Lama of Tibet would successfully be escorted into India, not via Anini but at Tawang in the western part of NEFA by a band of loyal bodyguards just like the burly men that terrified Lutor.

Open up the land. Bring it into the mainstream. Let the new government reach every tribe and village. 'Any person from outside who goes there as an official must show respect and understanding for tribal ways. Otherwise, he is a misfit.

In post-Independence India, this was the thinking behind the Third Policy for NEFA, an in-between approach between the British policy of 'leave them alone', and extreme assimilation or detribalisation. It was a dream of the NEFA administration that if properly applied, this policy was the best method for full integration of the tribal people with the rest of the country. It was coupled with a Forward Policy to push northwards closer to the McMahon Line to secure the country's border along this frontier. These were the days of duty and exploration. Lipun would unfold his NEFA map and jab at the pencilled line of the river. There! He would find the small dot that marked a place from where they would begin another journey. 'Northward, east or west, what does it matter? It is our land. Come on,' he cried, and Lutor would be riding with his mentor along precarious mountain roads to remote habitations whose names had meant nothing to him at the time. The call for officers for NEFA had received an overwhelming response from every corner of the country. 'Why do you want to go there,' despairing relatives might have cried, 'do you want to make your wife a widow?'

NEFA was a cruel place where officers, soldiers and priests had been attacked and killed, and tribal chiefs and villagers had lost their lives in endless hostilities. There were no roads, no electricity, no towns, shops, nothing; yet men came forward, lured by a sense of adventure and a willingness to serve.

'Look, there!' Lutor saw a dense canopy of trees spread out below them. Their new destination lay somewhere beyond that forest. Lipun was always pointing and he was always looking. They trekked through sunlit forests of oak and rhododendron and followed primitive tracks walking under trees that blotted out the sun. Suddenly they were in a green cave of buried vegetation that rose in clouds of moist, hot air. The trampled ferns on the side of the path shook with thousands of leeches aroused by the scent of blood and bigger, striped leeches fell on them from the branches of trees. Lipun smoked his bidis non-stop and rubbed crushed tobacco leaf on Lutor's legs saying the smell would drive away the unwelcome creatures. But there were bigger dangers. Herds of wild elephants roamed freely and left their tracks everywhere. Lipun signalled for silence when the guides followed their footprints as this eased the labour of finding their route, while swarms of gnats, dim-dams, flew into their eyes and mouth and left small hard bites that turned into itching sores. Lutor felt grateful for the line of porters and escorts accompanying them. After the Aching mori incident the NEFA administration had issued a general security alert instructing all officers to be accompanied by security escorts.

'It is quite unnecessary,' Lipun had said. 'What about an attack by wild elephants, huh?'

For the first time in the history of NEFA a new directive had also been issued to build fences around office quarters and campsites. But it was impossible to follow these rules to the letter in the wild tangle of jungle and sand banks of rivers where they halted for the night. They lit big fires instead and Lipun sat up at night, as if to keep watch, talking with the porters who were drawn from the ALC, the Agency Labour Corps, some of whom were tribal men earning money for the first time in their lives. Sometimes Lutor woke up and peered through the cracks of their bamboo shelter. He saw firelight and the faces of men looking at the flames, and he saw the face of Lipun, so thin and determined, slapping away at gnats and insects and sitting with his small frame leaning close to the fire in a typical pose that was to become a fixed image that Lutor would carry forever in his heart.

In some outposts law and order was maintained through a police battalion, but most of the time disputes were negotiated by the officer-in-charge through public meetings held in open fields. On many days Lutor watched the assembled men fearfully. In the hot sun voices grew vociferous. Sometimes a man would jump up and draw his sword, glaring around at the assembled kinsmen who had come to broker peace. Government officers like Lipun were the new arbitrators. Sometimes the distant drone of approaching aircraft would make them look skywards and suddenly everyone, the villagers and officers, would be running to the DZ, the dropping zone, with cries of joy and excitement. Stand back! Stand back! Everything was air dropped and the crowd watched in fascination as parachutes unfurled like giant butterflies and bags of rice and sugar and live goats, 'meat on the hoof', slanted earthwards. All these precious items were stored in the Central Procurement Organisation godowns where the agricultural inspector would measure and weigh the goods and fold away the parachutes for future use. Sometimes a bag of rice or a goat would miss the cleared space and disappear into the forest. Sometimes the Assam Rifles men would throw a party and suddenly produce mutton curry sizzling with gravy and onions that would delight everyone and make them burst into song. Lipun and his friends made jokes and said they were unlearning everything that they had been taught. 'To hell with instructions,' they shouted. 'We are the Non-Essential Fellows Association. Long Live N-E-F-A!'

Time was rolling on and slowly Lutor became aware of

a sweet relationship that existed here where everyone, to a man, shared a camaraderie that spread into the hearts of the people they were making contact with for the first time. They were deep in the Kameng Frontier. Lutor walked with a spring in his step and barely attended school. Instead, he spent his time climbing hills and eating hard, green fruit. He was happy, but he had no friends and when the wind moaned at night he thought his life would end here buried under the mountain, in the place of wild elephants.

'Don't worry,' Lipun consoled him. 'We'll be moving on soon. There are many more places to visit.' Lipun, after all, was an officer, and he knew many forces were at work changing the land, but even he could not have foretold the extent of change awaiting them and how it would shape and direct their lives.

The hills are safe for us

When he was nine years old, Lutor had fallen in love. He was running through an endless forest with people who were all running in silence. Desperation and fear was written on every face and Lipun was shepherding the group carrying his old gun and a gunny bag full of papers. A baby was crying and Lutor heard a man's voice say, 'If that baby doesn't stop crying I'll throw him over the cliff.' A woman sniffled. Her feet were swollen and she could not move another step. Lutor clutched a small bag of potatoes and stayed close to Lipun who now carried the woman's baby on his back. 'Move, move,' he cried. 'Silence! Silence!'

It was November of 1962, and one by one every post in the frontier was being abandoned before an advancing Chinese army. No one knew from which side this army was approaching but government wireless telegrams ordered officers to burn buildings, banks, houses, every scrap of food and every drop of medicine and Evacuate! Evacuate!

At first, Lipun had protested. 'Stay in your villages,' he told the villagers. 'Stay quiet and don't move around. The hills are safe for us.'

For weeks he had been hearing sporadic news of Chinese and Indian troop build-up in the frontier, and wondered if the country was at war. He stayed close to his crackling transistor and muttered the names of posts—Tawang, Sela ridge, Walong, Kibithoo, Dhola post, but no one had come to tell them anything and it was the sudden arrival of the order that had caused panic. He ignored the orders to burn down government offices and ration godowns, but told the people there to take whatever they could and retreat into their interior villages. The hills are safe! He urged them on. The hills are safe!

Lutor heard the name B-o-m-d-i-l-a and thought it was a nearby place but Lipun said it would take eight days to get there. He had looked at Lutor and at the bedraggled group of men and women and wondered if he could wait it out in one of the villages, but Bomdila was the Divisional headquarters and it was his duty to report to his senior officer there. An alternate route was to leave the hills and head straight for Assam where they heard everyone had fled. But Lipun's aim was to return to Pasighat after he had met the deputy commissioner in Bomdila. He decided to march to Bomdila so that he could gain firsthand information of what was happening. They were marching at full speed when early one morning they saw someone with a lantern approaching their makeshift camp. Three Assam Rifles jawans had come with another wireless message that Bomdila had fallen to the enemy. The message came from Tezpur in Assam because everyone had already fled Bomdila. The news spread like wildfire. In the absence of communication from civilian or military authorities the NEFA population was left to cope on their own and everywhere people were running back to their villages or towards Assam to reach the safety of the Brahmaputra valley.

Lipun decided to follow a jungle trail to a base camp called Seijosa in the foothills near Assam. He pointed in a southerly direction. It would take them a week to reach there, he said, if they walked fast and if they were not devoured by wild animals or attacked by elephants. Everyone else—officers, interpreters and dak runners—had fled. In one abandoned outpost they met an Assam Rifles jemadar who was the only person left in the debris of smoke blackened buildings and scruffy-looking street dogs. He had lit a big fire and was boiling tea. He offered Lutor a steaming tin mug and when Lutor refused he was surprised to hear Lipun scolding him and telling him to drink it up at once. Lipun and the jemadar chatted for a while, then the man bade them goodbye with a stiff salute and wished them safe journey. He said he would remain in his post. Reports reached them now that heavy fighting was going on in the western Tawang-Sela sector and Lutor wondered what would happen if they were taken prisoner. No one, least of all Lipun, could know at the time that a silent, mass evacuation of a population of civilians, government and army personnel, and soldiers was taking place, all pulling back southwards from the snow-covered battlefields of Tawang, Sela, Jaswantgarh and Nuranang, and in the trijunction with Myanmar on the Dong plateau east of the Lohit river. Many of the troops had lost contact with battalion headquarters and were straggling and starving, wounded and snow blinded in abandoned posts, still carrying their rifles and radios and living off wild roots and jungle leaves.

For Lipun it was a nightmare of travelling in the dark through dense jungle with the constant fear of encountering wild elephants. It was bitterly cold. They were afraid to light a fire in case the smoke gave their position away. Local porters threw down their belongings and fled back to their villages. All this time Lipun carried the baby on his back tied with a red cloth, and he was later to say that the greatest fear he had felt then was that the infant would start to cry. On 19th November 1962, they reached a place called Itakhola in Assam. It was an old market town and the Assam government had set up a camp here to receive the hordes of people fleeing from the hills.

Lutor first saw her in this camp wearing a yellow checked frock. She was turning on one leg, then on the other and standing by her was a young woman wrapped in a big shawl. Next to her was a man in a baggy suit and a big, furry hat talking earnestly to an Assamese gentleman. In that atmosphere of despair and utter confusion, this couple and their daughter stood out like a bright, conspicuous circle of hope. Something about the lines on the man's face and the calm, waiting expression of the woman delighted the young Lutor. He felt reckless and ready to protect them.

'Hello there,' cried Lipun, going up to the man with the hat.

'Oh! Thank god, thank god you are safe,' the man answered, turning around and embracing Lipun. A broad smile creased his face. They were old friends. He was the same Darin of the NEFA hostel days in Shillong, and he was now a schoolmaster. Darin and his family were fleeing from Dirang, an old fortress town on the road to Tawang.

'Everything has been wiped out,' Darin was saying. 'Our soldiers are being massacred. They have no clothes and they don't know the area at all. It is really terrible. I think the government has miscalculated everything.'

Unknown to Lipun, a new Army Divisional headquarters had been created to command the whole of NEFA from Dirang Dzong, south of the crucial Sela ridge. But the Chinese had cut off retreat by detouring round Thembang and encircled Dirang. At a place near the Lagyala monastery overlooking the beautiful Morshing valley, retreating Indian soldiers had been ambushed by a Chinese unit in position behind Indian lines. 'I heard it came down to hand-to-hand combat and the place is littered with hundreds of Indian and Chinese dead,' said Darin. 'We grabbed what we could and fled via the Chaku route.'

For a while both men stood silent, overwhelmed by the fearful reports from the sea of people around them. Lutor stood waiting, stealing a sly glance at the girl and her mother. None of them were in a position to understand what had happened, not yet. They had just escaped with their lives. Their families were safe, and that was all that counted.

'We are going to stay in Tezpur,' said Darin. 'Why don't you join us? I am just getting the transport sorted out.'

Lipun considered this. Tezpur was about an hour's drive away and it would be more comfortable there, but he wanted to be in the thick of things. Some of his officers were here and there might be all sorts of final details to take care of. He would stay the night in the small rest house.

'Lutor can go,' he said. 'I will come and pick him up early tomorrow.'

Lutor felt glum and scared to be left with strangers but the girl was staring at him. She had lowered her head as if she wanted no contact with anyone, and her big round eyes looked at him with sly distaste. What funny hair she's got, he thought to himself, just to make himself feel better. Her hair was black and cut short in the bowl-shaped style of the Adi, but looked unruly. It stood up in tufts and across her forehead. Maybe her mother, or she, had pinned the front locks down with a row of clips. Two gaudy earrings dangled from her ears giving her a strange, grown-up vampish look. Just when her father and Lipun had dashed away with the Assamese official to see about a vehicle, and her mother's gaze was turned away, two young boys passed close by pushing a cycle and tinkling the bell. One of them stopped and, bending down a little, made a face at the girl. 'Ch-Ing-Ch-ONG! CH-ING CH-ONG! he said. The girl's leg shot out and she gave him a kick.

'Hoi!' he cried out, alarmed. Her mother turned around and the two boys walked away quickly. The girl's face was red and angry. Lutor felt admiration rising up in his heart and he grinned at her. She glared back at him and began to tug at her mother in a great show of impatience while all the time looking at Lutor out of the corner of her eye. Lutor was smitten. Her name was Umsi and in the present moment of uncertainty there was a larger plan for her—she was going to go away to boarding school in Shillong, if everything went according to plan, of course.

Everyone is running to Shillong, thought Lutor, as they ploughed through an uncomfortable dinner that night. Umsi's mother did not come out of her room so the father, Umsi and Lutor dined in a cold, draughty dining room where many people were hurriedly eating rice and a weak, watery dal as if this would be their last meal. The news was out that the Chinese were within fifty kilometres of Tezpur and everyone should dig trenches. Then they said everyone should evacuate. No one knew what was happening and it was a mad rush to the river where the ferries plied day and night taking a frightened population across into south Assam. There was wild talk of burning all the tea gardens and the town already appeared scarred and battered as smoke billowed out of grey buildings where they were burning currency notes in the State Bank compound and dumping coins into ponds.

'Eat your food properly,' Umsi's father was saying. He was a big, laconic man and Lutor was glad to be with him on this terrible night. He understood that they were fleeing from the same Kameng Division and this fact alone made him feel as if he knew this family intimately. 'All the tea garden people have already left for Calcutta on charter flights,' the father was saying, 'but we, we will continue here. Just watch, there will be a ceasefire tomorrow. I am sure of it. Now eat your food properly.'

Lutor learned that Umsi's brother Kellan was already studying in Shillong. He heard Umsi's father saying: 'Education is important. So many things are happening in the world. You must study, otherwise you will be left behind. We are parents with no gold and silver, but whatever we have we are putting it all together to send you to school.' He was speaking for the benefit of his daughter who was paying no attention. Her eyelids were drooping and Lutor was grateful for his good fortune in studying in village schools where they could smoke Capstan and Panama and No.10 cigarettes under the trees.

Lipun came to fetch him very early the next morning saying they might get a lift on a truck to the railway station, so hurry up, we have to leave immediately. Umsi would be going to Shillong where her father would give his report and await the outcome of everything that was happening. Lipun said he would submit his report later and that he anyway had nothing to report except pandemonium. After that who knew what would happen. It was a war, but for the young officers it was almost routine to face such upheavals, live among unknown people, take orders and travel hundreds of miles, always on the move from one ramshackle hut in one settlement to another.

No one was up yet that morning when Lutor left, but just as he climbed on and Lipun tried to push the pedals that seemed to be suddenly weighted down, the window curtain fluttered and Lutor saw Umsi's face pressed flat against the glass. He thought she was smiling and that she even rubbed her hand on the glass as if she was waving. Lutor suddenly felt he wanted to stay one more day but Lipun heaved strongly and they pedalled away.

The end of solitude

In the aftermath of the border war that ended with a unilateral ceasefire on the day Umsi's father had predicted, the Frontier Divisions of NEFA were changed to plain, simple 'Districts', each one named after a river. A few years later, the control of NEFA was transferred from the Ministry of External Affairs to the Home Ministry. Civilian administration limped back into the hills though everywhere people still talked about another Chinese attack, saying they would be sure to return.

In Pasighat, Lipun and Lutor were the proverbial itinerant travellers who were at last reunited with family and friends. Everyone wanted to hear Lipun's account of the war. There are jottings and tour records of this time in the NEFA notebook, and it was probably during these brief visits to Pasighat that Lipun had left his books with my mother, that were now in my possession. He told everyone that the worst part of the war was over, but no one was convinced. Pasighat was hundreds of miles away from the border yet Lipun found ferrymen working day and night to take people across to the safety of the river towns of Assam. After the initial pandemonium following the news of the Chinese attack, every administrative centre in NEFA had become a ghost town. In the Pasighat hospital the scene was chaotic. The old, infirm, blind and bedridden mustered enough strength to exit the building, and consumptive patients coughing their lungs out shouted for relatives to carry them back to their home villages. It was old Dinu of the frontier days who would not budge. 'Let them come,' he said. 'We'll see what happens! Why is everyone running away?' But even he was terrified that Lipun and Darin and other boys from Pasighat would have to return to far-flung outposts that had been captured by the Chinese, and who knew what might happen again.

In such a climate of fear and distrust, army officers returning to their stations in Tenga valley and the Tawang-Sela sector carried packets of sweets to distribute to children running beside their vehicles. The Central Reserve Police Force also took up their duties again in the NEFA. One evening, in the outpost of Chayengtajo in the Kameng hills, the young jawans were getting ready to play volleyball. There was nothing else to do to pass the time. Every evening they put up the net and took sides hoping physical activity would tire them out enough to make sleep arrive swiftly and carry them into another dawn. The jungle hummed and the evening was hot and humid. 'Chalo! Chalo!' they called their friends.

The evening began, slowly at first, and then picked up speed as the young men got into the game, playing to win. It was a flurry of movement and voices, and some of the men, panting with the exertions, thought their teammates had jumped on them for fun. Their eyes were blinded with sweat. The salt taste of blood mingled with the cries of pain. It was the pain that surprised them and struck terror into their hearts. A group of tribesmen carrying swords were running amuck in the field. All their guns had been stashed away and they were dressed lightly, only in shorts and vests. Nine jawans were killed. Their barrack was burnt to the ground and the administrative officer in charge, a man from Assam, was killed in his house. Bodies lay strewn on the ground and the house of the officer burned all through the night.

A great silence descended on the place. The attackers disappeared. The scent of death hung over the black field. It was many days before news of the attack reached the authorities. Nine soldiers! It was unthinkable. There was shock and rage. Who were these people who rose up suddenly and killed people who came to their land even while they took gifts, and accepted the rice and salt of the government?

'Bomb the place,' someone suggested.

Just like in the case of Aching mori there was agreement and disagreement. The government in New Delhi was struggling with its own teething problems and the recent Chinese attack had made everyone jittery. It was Lipun's first appointing officer who raised his name again.

'He is a local man. No one else can go there. Maybe they will talk to him. Let's try it like this…'

This time Lipun went alone. He was returning to the Kameng hills and marching to take up residence in a two-room hut. The villagers stared at him. He looked like them. He was no outsider.

'You are just like us.'

'Yes.'

Some of them had heard of him. 'Jai Hind!' they greeted him. The chief of the village was a grand old man who called his people around him to talk to Lipun. They laid their sticks on the ground and said: 'Look! This was the dark cloud! The soldiers were the dark cloud! They were coming to make us into slaves!'

'No!' Lipun argued. 'Look at you. What is wrong with that woman there? Why is your son ill all the time? Why are your eyes going blind? It is not ghosts. It is not spirits. It is disease! These things happen everywhere. People are cured by doctors who give you medicines. If you let the government come here your people will be healthier and happier. I promise you no one will steal your land. No one will turn you into slaves. If the Chinese come again the government will protect you. If they come again, where will you go? What will you do? Where are your fields? Where is your rice and salt? How long will you live like this?'

These were the interminable days and nights when Lipun travelled cross country from one village to another. The house he lived in was on a ridge and on clear days he could see the snow-capped peak of Gorichen like a shining shield rearing upwards into the icy ridges of Sela pass. Sometimes he thought: Who knows where this will lead us? Here I am sitting and talking about development and education. Faraway, senior officers were perhaps thinking about the same things. There was a definite Tribal Policy and they too would be watching how things were developing or not developing. Maybe someone is sincere. Maybe the people will respond in a way that will enable us to make a difference. Who knows? It is a long way, even for us.

He coughed badly and his guides would not allow him to carry anything. They were awed by this gaunt, serious man who sat with them day after day and night after night trying to resolve their differences. They brought him gifts of newly laid eggs and Lipun looked at the hard, lined faces of men and women and children dressed in scraps of clothing who didn't know anything about the rest of the world; no, not even about India or China. They lived their lives as they always had, in this swathe of land dangerous with death and disease. Yet they survived. The jungle is our garden! they cried. And Lipun thought: Everywhere the knots are tied. And we cannot untie them now. This is life. We carry on hoping our efforts will benefit someone.

He wrote copious notes in his tour diary, but these were written to make the days meaningful. He was talking to himself and he would not submit these notes to the authorities as required.

Learning:
What are the things we have heard?
That New Delhi is the capital of India.
We are Indians.
New Delhi is very far away.
NEFA is a part of India.
It is very hilly.
We belong to a Scheduled Tribe.
I am a tribal officer.

And before this,
What did we hear before this?
There is the land of Kojum-Koja.
It was a famous civilization.
We came from there.
When we die,
We will be recognised by our ancestors.
A shower of leaves falling
from sacred trees will show us the way.

We own this land so that we may rest here.
NEFA is the land of the fittest survivors.

All this time, Lutor waited in Pasighat. He was re-united with his uncle, the rainman. He missed Lipun, but Lipun's old friend Darin arrived as if to make up for his absence—and as if time had decided that Lutor and Umsi should meet again in Pasighat on the banks of the Siang river.

Umsi's brother, Kellan, led a gang of boys who were in the habit of pelting the town with stones. His father said Kellan had been named after a British officer, O'Callaghan, who had started the school in Pasighat, but the name had been mispronounced and just as well, because Kellan showed no respect for study. The bowl of a town, hot and steaming in the circle of forest echoed to their wild shrieks of Cowboys and Injuns as Kellan ran whooping down the dusty road in full-throated battlecry, shouting, 'death to the palefaces.' Umsi had no friends of her own. She followed her brother blindly and became his most loyal soldier.

In one corner of the town the Sibo Korong stream stretched and curled into a deep, green pond. Wild grass grew in dense clumps glazing the landscape with a shimmering copper glow that rippled and scattered seed when the wind blew down the gorge. An old elephant apple tree marked this secluded spot. Sometimes the fruit, green and hard as a cannon ball, fell with a thud and turned rusty brown until the children found them and Kellan suggested they would make good missiles.

The green space gave them freedom. The tree offered shade and no one came there to fish or hunt. It was their portion of the river. A protruding rock half submerged in the water became the diving board for them to jump into the green water. Kellan and his friends guarded this place and stalked the banks like lions. No strangers were allowed. But this was where Lutor surprised them with a loud shout and a running dive, arms outstretched to embrace the water. At that moment another boy with a plain, brown face and small, lidless eyes full of mirth jumped out at the onlookers and splashed into the water after Lutor. His name was Rudar and he was Lutor's single ally. Kellan marshalled his forces and they all jumped into the water yelling at the tops of their voices to frighten away the intruders, but they were friends after that.

Umsi, as Lutor knew from the first time that he had seen her in that dreadful camp in Assam, had joined her brother in school in Shillong, but the Darin family was in Pasighat every winter during the school vacation. They brought red apples and cartons of cakes, bread and bakery items, things that Lutor had never seen before, and once, Umsi gave him cubes of hard cheese strung like a necklace that he swung around and hung up on a nail before chewing them up bit by bit. In return he raided the neighbour's garden for oranges, and like the river their lives flowed together without a thought for where they were heading. It was the happiest time of his life.

Sometimes he tried to impress her with Adi words, thinking she learnt only English in school. 'You know what that is?' he would say, pointing up to the cloudy trail of the Milky Way in the sky.

'It is the winter-summer divide *di-giin diyu ri-su*!' she would answer unexpectedly. 'You think I don't know these things?'

She must have heard it from her grandmother, he would think, quite pleased that she hadn't become all English.

'And that star there?' It was her question now.

He would gaze up intently at the star near the moon and say, after a long pause, 'Is it the moon's sister?'

'It is her maid,' she would laugh. 'It is always there in attendance to her. Don't you know that, you ignorant crocodile?'

'How should I? I'm so busy looking at you I have no time to look up.'

'You liar, *yao*, *yadma*!' Umsi would shout, laughing.

One windy March day when Umsi was away in her Shillong school, Lutor stood looking at the Siang river emerging out of the hills like a green snake. A high embankment of boulders had been raised and his uncle had performed the ritual ceremony for this capricious river that flooded every summer, drowned people and gobbled away pieces of the town. The tall poles of bamboo weighted down with baskets of sacrificial food offerings bent low over the water as if whispering to unseen spirits. Lutor had helped carry the stones with the villagers and the barricade had been reinforced with steel mesh. Now he heard the thin gurgling voice of the river and felt a premonition. He was restless with waiting and he wanted to be on his way, somewhere, doing work that would fill him with a sense of wellbeing.

The rainman was saying: 'I have looked at this river since I was a child. Twenty years ago, you and Lipun went across the river. Before that it was narrower. Now, look at it. How many times it has changed course—expanding, like time.

This is the way history is told. I can see change. I can predict war and sorrow. I can see the end of solitude. Now we are waiting, but all these things are written in our destiny and no one can change them. But whatever may happen you must realise your place: In between the world of spirits and men, hanging by a thread—the soul of man! Whatever you do, don't deceive yourself.'

It was on that March night that the town of Pasighat was startled by a fierce wind wailing down the river gorge. It echoed around the town and made a young woman peer out anxiously in the dead of night. Her name was Gagil, the same young woman who had been there when Nefa was born, and she was keeping a lookout for her brother Dinu who had gone on his last official tour as interpreter with the new district officer on a village visit. The lantern swung in her hand as the wind gathered force and started mooing into her ears. It was a dreadful sound and she did not hear the shouts of men until they were right before her eyes. They seemed to be shouting and signalling but she could hear nothing. She stared at a stretcher rocking and swaying down the road and suddenly the lamp fell from her hand and everything was plunged into darkness. Someone shouted from the opposite house and Gagil recognised the sound of her sister-in-law, who was now calling in a voice louder than the wind. This broke the spell and she began shouting to wake up the household even as she rushed across the road to her brother's house.

The party of men had been returning to Pasighat. They were crossing the Sille stream when the wires holding the suspension bridge over the stream snapped and they were suddenly thrown down on to the dry riverbed below. One porter died on the spot, everyone had serious injuries and the officer had been driven in the single jeep straight to the general hospital. Dinu had refused to be taken there and so the men had brought him home. The rainman was holding up the stretcher and he looked as if he was carrying the burden of a thousand years on his shoulder. For the men of his generation Dinu was the lion of frontier days, the last of a breed of men like Lutor's father Lomey, and all the other great ancestors who had already passed away. Now the rainman lifted the broken body carefully and set to work as if a demon had entered him. He shouted rapid orders to one and all, told them to keep all visitors out of the way and shouted instructions to Gagil. Then the rainman tied the riidin creeper thread around Dinu's wrists and braided more twine into his hair, and for the first time Lutor heard the rainman chanting loudly in a language no one could understand. Lutor thought he was challenging the gods and asking them to take his life instead if it was a life they wanted. His loud, resonant voice filled the house with a strange melody. The household stayed awake all night moving swiftly and silently and talking in whispers to everyone who came to visit. The women boiled herbs that turned the colour of tea and the rainman broke bits of beeswax and poured honey into the mixture. He spooned this concoction into Dinu's mouth for three days and nights and Dinu vomited blood. 'It is a good sign,' the rainman said. 'The clotted blood is flowing again.' He burnt more beeswax and blew smoke into Dinu's ears, all the time whispering something. Lutor understood that only the greatest shamans could do this. The rainman was travelling between earth and sky. He was calling all the spirits who protect man, reminding them of an ancient relationship and their benevolence to mankind in the past. Dinu lay hovering between life and death until early one dawn the rainman woke the tired household and told them that Dinu would be alright. A few days later he allowed Dinu to be airlifted to the hospital in Dibrugarh where Lipun had already arrived on hearing the news. Dinu recovered but had his leg in plaster for many months. Lipun supported him throughout this period and they returned to Pasighat together. Lutor watched as the two of them, Lipun and Dinu went for long, slow walks in the open fields around the house. The doctors said it was a miracle that Dinu did not die. He walked with a limp and his eyesight was failing, but he was still strong and when Lipun asked for his daughter Nefa's hand in marriage, the old man readily gave his blessings. Lipun was thirty-eight when he married the seventeen-year-old Nefa. Everyone had assumed that Lipun was a confirmed bachelor so the news was greeted with some surprise, but people came from near and far to wish the couple good health and joy.

For Lutor it was the year of the outcast when he was finally set adrift. It seemed the present stirred itself and demanded change in a cycle of every ten years or so. A decade after the flight from the Chinese another war was fought in the region, this time for the liberation of Bangladesh. International aid poured in and Shillong was flooded with relief goods of food, canned milk, and piles of clothes. The air raid alarms sounded regularly and frightened and thrilled senior girls in school like Umsi, who ran into bunkers and said loud prayers every night begging everyone to forgive them and wishing even the tyrannical teachers goodbye: *'see you in heaven, miss!'*

It was also the end years of the North East Frontier Agency. One cold January morning Lipun and Lutor stood with thousands of people dressed in colourful traditional costume who lined the small airfield in the beautiful Ziro plateau. They were gathered to greet Prime Minister Indira Gandhi who unveiled an illuminated map of a new Union Territory with the brand new name of Arunachal Pradesh—Land of the Dawn Lit Mountains.

The NEFA secretariat in Shillong that was Lipun's head office was also poised to shift to a new place that had been earmarked as the capital for Arunachal Pradesh. Pasighat had been the first choice but the local elders had refused to give land fearing that development would bring strangers, pimps and prostitutes, and all manner of disease into their land. The government had finally selected a site in the central foothills. This was the beginning of Itanagar, extending up from the original site of Naharlagun by the Pachin river to the villages of Poma and Jote surrounded by tropical evergreen forests with hidden lakes and remnants of an old brick fort from which the place took its name. The town planners fell to their work with enthusiasm and planted rows of flowering Bauhinia trees all the way from the new check gate up to Naharlagun. The first houses were wide and spacious with big compounds and kitchen gardens. Small shops sprang up and an industrial unit was opened.

When Lipun was posted to the new capital, Lutor was in his final year in University. He met Umsi and heard that she was going to enrol in a Delhi college. 'Don't go away. Stay near me,' he said to her earnestly. He sensed that if she left everything would change. He even thought of following her to Delhi but his mentor Lipun was gently pushing him into another arena that the old veteran of frontier days assessed as necessary for an emerging state. By the summer, when

Lipun and Nefa left for the new capital town, the dry river where Dinu had fallen was already a swirling torrent of green water.

Lutor plunged into youth activities and worked on a constitution for a fledgling Student's Union that took birth at this time. The face of his friend Rudar beamed out at him. 'Look, here it is!' It was a newsletter printed in the state and it had their names in it. 'We better get down to work,' Rudar said, looking closely at the paper and pointing to the article about the Adi branch of the Student's Union. They had started something and this would be the forum to launch their long cherished dreams for a bright future.

On 20th February 1987, Prime Minister Rajiv Gandhi visited Itanagar to formally inaugurate the birth of a full-fledged state. The town's Indira Gandhi Park was a sea of people waving flags to celebrate the landmark occasion. For Lutor it was a time of mixed feelings. He had cause to celebrate his success in becoming a politician of the state but as he stood facing the milling crowd he was filled with an unaccountable emotion of overwhelming joy and a deep sense of loss. How the years had gone! Step by step the state had moved in its long journey of constitutional and administrative growth. The NEFA days were gone forever. Now, Arunachal Pradesh was the twenty-fourth state of the country.

Book Two

MEMORY

The corners of our lives

A light rain at night had soaked the earth and Itanagar was cold and deserted as Lutor drove out of his house. He was starting his journey very early. The streetlights were still burning and a few sleepy dogs curled up tight by the shuttered shops did not bother to turn their heads as his car sped past. It was an old habit, to travel early or late at night because the roads were empty then and Lutor felt he could sleep if he wanted to, or stay awake and think, if there was anything to think about. He was puzzling over an urgent call he had received from his friend Rudar in Pasighat.

Someone had been killed and no one could identify the dead man. The body had been found seated upright against a tree with a bullet wound to the head, hidden in the cane thickets that covered the hillside near the Sigar stream. The killer had tried to gouge out the victim's eyes and brains. It was the stench that had drawn a passer-by to the spot and the brutal murder had left a scent of death hanging over the area.

'You can make this a fact-finding mission,' Rudar had said. They were heading into an election year and he had convened a meeting to give Lutor's tour a specific purpose. Then he had whispered that an old friend, Kellan, was also coming to Pasighat to meet him. This was the puzzling bit.

For a moment Lutor felt a wave of trepidation as images from a distant past flashed through his mind. Kellan was an old friend but the last time Lutor had seen him was many years ago when Kellan was leaving for Tirap district in his new posting as the District Forest Officer. Lutor had lost track of the man in the unrelenting whirl of politics that he had plunged himself into. Now he was coming to Pasighat and the way Rudar had conveyed the news to him hinted at some specific purpose that he did not know about yet.

What could it be? Rudar had never been one for secrecy. He was a lifelong friend and political ally since the time they had started their political careers as young public leaders supporting a regional party when the state held its first elections to a thirty-member house. However, their victory was shortlived as the government fell the next year. After a two-month period of President's Rule when the state's first regional party chief minister was deposed by the ruling United National Congress (UNC) Lutor had launched his regional All-NEFA Peoples' Party (ANP). It was a protest against the overbearing tactics of national parties but he had had few takers. 'It is political suicide,' everyone had said. 'The Congress is the party for our state.' But Rudar had stayed with him and helped him win victory for the ANP in Pasighat. They had worked hard together to build up support for a pan-Arunachal movement with the support of friends from other districts, until in the last decade the ANP had suffered defeat to his arch rival, Tanik, and everything had turned into a riddle.

In the chaos of political life and learning to toe the line as a Congress-ruled state, something unprecedented had happened. An old issue had erupted and united everyone in a momentous decision that was hereafter to be referred to as the people's referendum rally. Thousands of people thronged to attend this meeting called to discuss the growing presence of refugees and illegal settlers in the state. An imposing village elder stood up and said that the NEFA administration had been duped into allowing a few Chakma families to live in the state. 'Once there were four families, now there are sixty-four thousand of them! They are encroaching on our land, killing our animals and destroying our forests. What is the Centre doing for us?' Others followed with more or less the same words and sentiment. Quit Arunachal! It was the unanimous decision.

In the crowd, Lutor watched as a tall thin man took the podium. Who was he? Some people whispered that his name was Tasong, and that he was Tanik's uncle. He had silenced the crowd with a peremptory movement of his hands. His voice was harsh and his words fell like an intonement. 'Look at me,' he had said. 'I have been struggling with this problem since my student days. Now it is too much to bear.' He pointed to Tanik sitting with his colleagues. 'Look, here are our veteran leaders. All their pleas with the Centre have fallen on deaf ears. Who will tolerate this stepmotherly treatment? I call on you, people of the state, let us renounce our allegiance to the Centre and become our own party. Tanik, your leader is ready to proclaim a new party for the state—the United Peoples' Party of Arunachal!'

It was an unthinkable feat. Lutor had immediately realised what this declaration portended and how Tanik was going to achieve the impossible and become the unopposed leader of the party.

Tanik began by evoking memories of a land clear and pure as the sun and moon. In a direct reference to Lutor he said, 'The NEFA party have also tried their best, but till today we are facing the same problems. We must find another way. The land belongs to us. The Centre's treatment of our heartfelt appeals is insulting. Arunachal is a sleeping giant and now we are awakening from our sleep. We are ready to go our own way and be the masters of our destiny!' Tanik's words rolled over the enraptured crowd. He was the leader they wanted. His handsome face radiated energy and love and Lutor too felt spellbound by the emotion in the man's voice as he pointed skywards and said, 'The mighty sun is witness to this historic day!' There was the sound of clapping like an explosion of thunder and suddenly a new break-away party, the UPPA was born.

Lutor's friend and senior politician Aohun of Anini had said, 'You and I know it is a gimmick. Tanik has never lifted a finger on the refugee settlement issue. It is the students who have been spearheading this movement, but Tanik wants out. This is electoral posturing. His position is shaky and he is pre-empting a move by the Party to remove him. Clever man! Let's see what the Centre does.'

'Nothing…the Centre does nothing,' Lutor could have told him that then, but in the climate of euphoria and high expectation who could say anything?

The year had marked a turning point. Since then, politics in the state had turned into a tug-of-war between communities whereby anyone could pull the rug from under an opponent provided there was enough money to buy a majority. New leaders emerged, a new breed of political strongmen full of ambition and plenty of money took over the reins of government, but these were brief, ephemeral periods, as if the state was testing the waters and sniffing which way the wind was blowing in New Delhi. In fact, Tanik had already staged a comeback when he had challenged New Delhi with an offer: Say you will take me back. I am the only leader capable of holding all the communities together. You can't do without me.

And that's how it had been. In a well-publicised merger Tanik was welcomed back into the UNC and everyone cheered for Tanik and the Congress party.

'It's a hangover from NEFA days, since the days of ration sorties, salt and rice,' said Aohun. 'Our people are ready to vote UNC as the party of the tribal people.' He was furious that the Centre had created a situation where infighting was sure to erupt within the party. He had stuck with the Congress and retained his position as party president and Tanik, seizing the moment had made him a minister with the home portfolio, but it was an uneasy alliance. The party was in disarray. Lutor's ANP party was also considerably weakened even though he was voted back to power from his Sirum-Pigo seat and he was still hanging in there.

Lutor remembered all this as he drove slowly, taking in the surrounding landscape. He had been on this road so many times before. Once he had marched with Lipun through all these places. And look! Now everything was different. A journey of walking for ten days in the NEFA days could now be covered in six hours. He knew that when he reached Pasighat there would be people to receive him. Rudar would have organised everything and these days the public were well geared to receive politicians. He would be surrounded by party workers and lobbyists bringing gifts and petitions. 'This time the regional party will win! We need funds. You must contest again.' He could say yes, or he could say no.

A feeling of great weariness pressed down on him. He lit a cigarette.

The sun was already sinking behind the hills when he reached the police check post at Ruksin. The place was bustling with country buses and three-wheelers belching fumes and a cacophony of sound as pedestrians ran in and out between passing vehicles. Soon he had passed Dibu Korong and the saw mill area and crossed the municipal gate announcing the entry into Pasighat. It was Pasighat city now, but he still thought of it as Pigo-Pasighat, the old name of his hometown from where he had won every election from his Assembly seat of Sirum Pigo. He saw the landmark statue of Mahatma Gandhi at the centre of the market. God knows who had done the job, but the statue hadn't quite come out right. The figure was chalky white and disproportionately small compared to the oversized circumference of the pedestal. He drove on along the road skirting the airfield and the new stadium, feeling his spirits lift as he took in the familiar sights. He could hear the river as he approached the house of his uncle on the banks of the Siang in the middle of a last remaining patch of teak forest. All along this stretch new construction had changed the landscape, but here it was still peaceful. His uncle was away, but Rudar was waiting for him.

The first thing he said was, 'Look what I got.' He pulled out a bottle of apong and beamed at his friend saying, 'Welcome drink! A-ha, welcome drink!' A fire was burning in the kitchen and Rudar pulled up a stool and said that Kellan would be joining them soon, but the meeting was going to be hurried because Kellan would be leaving for Tirap the same day. 'Kellan has some information but you know we can't talk on the phone these days, everything is overheard,' he said.

It was true. No matter how secretly they arranged their meetings word always got back to the rival camp about all their plans and movements. That was why they were meeting here instead of Rudar's house, even though Lutor felt that secrecy confused things. In politics if someone could not stand up and be counted it was better to write him off as a voter for the rival camp. 'Listen…' Rudar was saying when there was a brief knock and Kellan's head peeped in through the door.

'There you are!' said Rudar. 'Come in. Come in.'

Kellan stepped in. The men greeted one another.

'How have you been?'

'Good. Good,' said Kellan. He looked the same as Lutor remembered him, a little older but still with the friendly, easy humour of someone who had travelled and made friends with people in the places where he had lived. 'It's been a long time,' he said.

Kellan had been in Tirap district since his posting there more than two decades ago but his application for transfer had always been turned down. Yet he had not been unhappy. The district was lush with forest and there were many people from their own home districts camped there as timber operators. Life was comfortable. Or had been comfortable, until recently.

'Tell him,' said Rudar. 'Tell him about the bullet.'

'Wha-at?'

Kellan held up his hands. I'm only the messenger. He leaned forward and said, 'Rasa Lowang has received a bullet.'

Who, what? Rasa was an old Tirap friend and the ANP candidate for the parliamentary (East) seat. For a moment Lutor was unable to register what had been said. Kellan had said it so casually and now he was waiting for Lutor to say something.

'Tell him about the phone call,' said Rudar.

'Well, yes…some weeks ago I also received a phone call,' said Kellan. It was in the middle of the night and he had thought it was an emergency call from his wife in Pasighat. But it had been something else. A young man's voice on the phone who had simply said, 'Hello. I have been asked to tell you to pay ten lakh rupees by the end of the month. Keep the money ready.' Click.

Lutor realised that Kellan was talking about the extortion cases that were being reported from Tirap district. He had seen Intelligence Bureau reports of a group of young men taking on the role of vigilantes collecting money from timber contractors, traders, forest officials and engineers. The report stated that they were operating on behalf of the National Socialist Council of Nagaland (Khaplang group), the NSCN-K, and that they were being patronised by the Tirap politicians. Lutor knew the Tirap representatives. They were his colleagues, but they had always denied the reports of a 'fear psychosis' prevailing in the district saying these were stray incidents hyped up by the media to look like the district was being overrun by terrorist groups.

'Why should you always look for a third element?' Temat was scion of a Tirap chieftain family and a political heavyweight. He sported tailored shirts and expensive sunglasses, and he had waved aside Lutor's questions. 'Ah…so, there is some brigandage but what of it—don't worry. We will handle it. It's because our local youth are disgruntled and restless. We need to give them employment. We need a separate department with more funds for our districts to wipe out the feeling of neglect and isolation. You see, our youth are taking up arms because they don't want to take up a begging bowl.'

Kellan said all that was hogwash. All the departments in the district were paying a percentage of their salary to militant groups to leave them alone. 'It's protection money. The militants or brigands, call them what you like, know how easy it is to play this extortion game and we're seeing a silent invasion of the land. I think we are losing the two districts. No one is talking about it.'

'Yeah, but they elected their leaders. The area is stinking rich,' said Rudar. 'In fact, Pasighat and many other districts are poorer than them. And still the Tirap politicians are saying they need more money to combat unwanted elements and restore normalcy.'

'Where did Rasa find it, the bullet, I mean, how was it delivered?'

'It was left wedged into the front door of his house. It came in an envelope with a printed note signed by an area commander or political supervisor—but payable to whom exactly and how, no one knows, or it's never disclosed,' said Kellan.

'Who would have brought it, any idea?'

'None at all. It's a full-time extortion racket and there are so many organizations. A group gets hold of a few guns and they think they're an outfit. Everyone is receiving extortion notes and phone calls and bullets.'

He looked down and shook his head. 'Everyone pays up. Otherwise they disappear. People are very frightened. If you visit Tirap today you can smell fear.'

'But Rasa, why would he be a target?

Kellan shrugged. 'I think he's being watched,' he lowered his voice, 'he said he may come to meet you.' Then he added softly, 'I heard something about an Ordinance to check terrorist activity. Is it true?'

Lutor nodded slowly, staring at his friend. This was a current dilemma he was wrestling with. Tanik had come up with an idea for an Act to control criminal activity in the state. It was a tough piece of legislation modelled on a similar Act of the Maharashtra government to deal with organised crime in the state. But, Lutor wondered, it was still under wraps and yet to be placed before the State Assembly. The fact that Kellan knew about it meant someone high-up was dropping information to rake up controversy over the proposed Act.

'It might work,' said Kellan. 'On the other hand, it could be abused…Who knows, huh…? I believe it is quite draconian. But the thing is, the government must act. The local politicians believed that they could use the militant groups for their political one-upmanship, but now they too have to pay up. That's the problem. I remember my father used say, "When you dine with the devil be sure to use a long spoon."'

Dimly, Lutor heard the sound of water. It was raining. A vivid picture of Kellan's father wearing a furry hat passed before his eyes. How he wished they could sit silently for a moment. How much better it would be to sit together and talk about other things. 'I think you should move out of the place for a while. I can speak to Aohun about a transfer…' he was saying, when there was a loud knock on the door.

'We are here!'

'I'd better be going,' said Kellan.

'Stay, stay,' said Rudar, as the door opened and a group of young men entered the house.

They were led by Kamin, a young advocate, and one of Lutor's strongest supporters. He was accompanied by the brothers Orin and Kasi. Orin was a reporter running a newspaper in Itanagar and he had brought another journalist friend, Peter, from Tirap, who lived in Itanagar.

'He was not from this area. Peter thinks he was a timber operator,' said Kamin. He was talking about the dead man.

'There are lots of people floating logs downriver,' he said. 'They are operating for militant groups and they are reaching everywhere. It's timber money for arms and drugs. The big dealers are in Dibrugarh and Tinsukia but our forest officers and police are all in on it.'

The clumps of tall bamboo surrounding the place where they found the body had been smashed by gun shots. But no one had found a gun. 'Maybe the man was here on a mission and started showing off by firing a few rounds,' said Rudar. 'Maybe some big dealer felt jeopardised and had the man bumped off.'

'Or maybe the man was shooting birds,' said Orin's brother Kasi.

'Ha! With a semi-automatic weapon?' Peter turned on him.

'Well, that's what we're trying to find out, isn't it?' said Kamin.

There was a moment of silence. Outside, not far from the tightly packed room, the Siang River flattened out into the Brahmaputra and it was impossible for anyone to track drug peddlers, poachers, illegal migrants and timber operators in the ever-changing landscape of wide sandy shoals and narrow canals. Every year the river tore out chunks of land but the area was flat and fertile and new settlements had sprouted all along this strip, right down to the new site of

Anpum village, Bizari, and to Paglam from where ferry boats plied to ghats in Assam.

In the days of the British Raj when the railway had come into Assam, every small town on the route had burgeoned into thriving towns dealing in coal and tea. People had poured in from other parts of the country to set up as traders, tea merchants, and oil companies. Now there were drug lords and arms dealers.

'It must have something to do with the factional rivalry of armed groups,' said Peter. 'Everyone says there is no trouble. But no one is going to Tirap. Ask anyone. Everyone is avoiding the place. Who would argue with the barrel of a gun?'

'This is because our politicians are involved in the cover-up,' said Kamin.

'Even the doctors are running away,' said Peter. 'In the hospital patients are sometimes given a half kilo of rice. Ha ha! They have to cook their own food or eat raw rice while waiting for someone to treat them. People go to hospitals to get healed, but here they go to hospital to die!'

'We were better off in the NEFA days,' said Rudar, muttering to himself under his breath. 'Even enemies are treated across borders.'

Lutor looked at his friend. Kellan was staying out of the discussion. Now he said, 'You may not know how things have changed. The militants are gaining ground with something called Operation Salvation, helping villagers with sanitation and health care. It's an offer you can't refuse.' He stood up. 'Well, and now I have to get going. I'm not the politician. Good luck everyone.' He shook hands all around.

'You'll miss the ferry, I am sure of it,' said Rudar. 'You should leave tomorrow.'

'Oh no, I have booked one,' said Kellan, laughing. 'Anyway, I have to go and visit the family.' Then he added, 'You know, my sister is here in Pasighat.'

This piece of news hit Lutor like a bolt of lightning. Suddenly he felt everything around him had changed but Kamin and his friends continued as if nothing had happened after this startling disclosure made by Kellan about his sister being in Pasighat.

Lutor heard them as if in a dream. What was Kamin talking about? It was a private member resolution to move for separation of the two districts of Tirap and Changlang from the rest of the state into a Union Territory. All the legislators of the two districts supported the demand. It is a democratic demand, they said. There is no pressure from terrorist groups or any tactic to merge with greater Nagalim. We only want to facilitate central assistance to ensure jobs and a better future for our new generation.

Ah, but the villagers are so poor and frightened...Lutor tried to focus his thoughts. Who will protect them? How can we end their isolation from the rest of the state...Ha! Isolation within isolation...what a state of affairs! The Centre could afford to ignore their cries and pacify them with a display of funds that put everyone under a spell. The lure of easy money!

He heard Kamin saying the ANP had to win the Lok Sabha seat. Yes, then the party would have a forum to expose the politician-underground nexus, that is, if anybody listened, because the state had only two seats and in the numbers game this was negligible. But Kamin was smart and tough. He had filed a Public Interest Litigation charging Tanik with corrupt practice and catapulting himself into the chief minister's chair with the backing of militants. As a result of this, a CBI investigation was currently ongoing but it was dragging on. When had anything reached a clear conclusion here, thought Lutor, his attention wavering in and out of the conversation. Everyone was still talking politics, assessing the possibilities of candidates and exchanging stories about long journeys, the state of their vehicles, the condition of the roads and most important of all, funds. They were all bitterly aware how a regional party would always be strapped for funds. Gone were the days of the sedate Agency Council and innocent electioneering. Now everything depended on money, power and aggression. The evening waned. They were joined by more people; rice wine was poured out until at last Lutor heard his friend Rudar saying that at this rate they would be unfit for the meeting the next day.

When at last the house was quiet again, past midnight, Lutor went out and stood on the veranda. He saw patches of light flashing through the trees and wondered if it was the light from a late ferryboat. Rain, small towns…He had looked on this scene so many times before but now he felt he was seeing it all again for the first time. Something was happening. The light and the wind seemed to be talking to him: All this is permanent. Even if the leaves fall and winter breaks the twigs, even if summer drowns the roads and pulls down the hills, they will emerge again and look like this. Just as you are looking at it now, just like so many other eyes will look at it again. Time sways and alters the past, but in every lifetime such moments will return, alive again with thoughts of youth and beauty. And this will be generated by the land. Yes, thought Lutor, there was the desire to win, to offer something and be a leader, but something else was returning to him from more than half a lifetime ago and he was afraid that after all these years, after the years of political struggle an angel would look at him again and turn his gaze in another direction.

'I wanted to live quietly, as a family man,' he had once said, a long time ago.

'You? No one would believe that. You cannot sit still in one place even for a day,' Rudar had said. Rudar was the realistic campaigner. Now he had stepped out quietly and appeared to be looking hard at the dim scenery. He had heard Kellan's words and seen Lutor's start of surprise on hearing that Umsi was in Pasighat. The two friends stood together silently, leaning on the balustrade. Rudar spoke first. 'So,' he said, without turning his head, 'what's happening?' When Lutor didn't answer he went in and returned with a mug of tea. 'Tell me if you want it blacker,' he said, and walked back in.

Lutor was lost in thought. He could not believe what he had heard. Umsi was in Pasighat! Kellan's words whirled around in his head. It was but yesterday that Kellan was escorting Umsi to New Delhi where she was going to join college. 'Do you want to come with us?' he had asked.

'Oh no, no…' Lutor's reaction had been instinctive. He had never travelled to the city and he was afraid. He muttered some words of encouragement. In his heart he felt regret that Umsi was going so far away. She could have studied in Shillong, nearby, he thought, but he felt a bit reassured when he heard that she would be admitted into a hostel. Umsi, of course, had been radiant. Write to me, she said. Yes, he had promised. But he was no letter writer.

He found paper but the pen stayed stiff in his hand and his mind became numb. Instead it was Umsi who overwhelmed him with news of the college, her room, the streets and cafes and how she and her friends scrambled to get back to the hostel before the gates were locked for the night. What is there to go roaming around, so late? Lutor had wondered. He could only imagine her reading books. Sometimes she would look up and then—maybe—she would remember him, he thought, feeling a little foolish. I'll visit her soon, he decided, but balked at the idea of travel. He could trek across mountains but could not imagine a journey by rail or air. He collected all her letters and kept them in a big plastic bag. Rudar was the only person privy to this bundle of mail.

'Let's go for a jaunt to the city,' he prodded Lutor. 'We should see Delhi!'

'Yes, yes, said Lutor, swearing they would go to Delhi, but that day never came. Instead Rudar got married. A year of work and festivities came and went, and then one spring day when the world was green and fresh, a ghostly whisper reached Lutor. Umsi was in trouble. It was about a love affair with a boy she had met in the city. Her parents were upset and there was talk that they would bring Umsi back to Pasighat. Then all was silent again.

Lutor dared not ask anyone for information. People greeted him and he thought they were laughing at him. More than anything else Lutor remembered the terror that had seized him. 'I will go to Delhi and hear it from her lips,' he decided. Umsi was not a stranger and he was not one to shy away from facing the truth, but the words remained stuck in his heart. Instead he remembered waiting and hoping that Umsi would suddenly emerge and tell him everything was alright, but it was only his friend Rudar saying that. No one came. Later, for many years he had asked himself if she had waited for him. Perhaps she had waited every day for his appearance in her home to ask for her hand in marriage, but he had hesitated, and all had been lost.

He had lost Umsi to a tea planter no one had ever met, except maybe for her brother Kellan. There was no farewell. It had happened very suddenly, Umsi's parents had been tight lipped, and since those years there had been no occasion for Lutor and Umsi's family to meet. Rudar stayed close and talked about everything except what had happened. News of Umsi had floated back to them piece by piece, a hint here, a question there, a comment; and Lutor had set his heart like stone to show no emotion. Yes, that was how it had been, he told himself now. Just like that we let everything slip out of our hands. He had failed, or not had the courage to succeed. He had not read the signs properly. But Rudar and all his friends at the time would testify that a demented Lutor had set off in search of a woman. He had an idea where she lived, in one of those fancy bungalows screened by tea bushes and tall trees. He would walk up to the door and when she opened it he would say, 'You belong to me. How can you hide from me? For what purpose?' But how could a man spend his life looking for someone, expecting her at every turning without asking directions, carrying a photo that he could whip out of his pocket and show to strangers saying, 'this woman, have you seen this woman?' How could he walk up and down by a tea garden waiting for her to appear so that he could accost her with his defeated self? He had thought about pity, love, hate, and he had wondered many times what it was that he most wanted to show her so that he could make her feel the same pain. But now it was over. He had searched for her for months and years and suddenly, one day, sitting in the back of a country bus on a blazing hot day, half dead with weariness, it dawned on him as clearly as the fierce midday sun that he had lost Umsi forever. She was someone else's wife. He fell asleep weeping, thinking that one day she too would regret her wilful action.

'You would never have been happy with her,' said Ossu, a young woman from Pasighat who was looking for work in Itanagar. They had worked together briefly on magazine work for the Students' Union newsletter. He had barely noticed her but Umsi had once accosted him. 'Everyone is talking about you and her,' she had said angrily.

Now Ossu came by his house often, just looking in, she said, to see what he was up to. He heard her words and resented her presence, but Ossu was shameless. She was a big, outspoken girl who flaunted bright clothes and stood close to him wearing a heavy, sweet perfume that nauseated him.

'If there's no child you are free,' she hinted.

Lutor wondered if she was mocking him. He looked at her and she flushed. He thought she wanted him. He moved away but was drawn back again by her persistent presence. One day sitting in his cramped study he became aware of her shifting and tidying books on the shelves. 'What are these,' she said, shaking a rolled bunch of calendars. She was turned away from him and he could see the long slope of her back and her rounded buttocks as she lifted her arms and strained to reach the top shelf.

'Here, I'll do that,' he said, not wanting her presence. He moved up to her and noticed the beads of perspiration on her upper lip. 'Here,' he took the books and calendars out of her hands and thumped them down on the floor. She did not move and he felt surrounded by her strange perfume. It was hot and heavy in the room and as he turned around to face her she moved closer, almost swooning into his arms. He felt her naked and slippery with sweat under the thin blouse that was sticking to her body. He put his arm around her roughly and had taken her there, in that small room. He thrust into her almost with rage and when she cried out under him like a grunting animal he was seized with a keen erotic pleasure that flooded his body like fire. He did not love her, no, but Ossu exercised a dark, sensual spell over him. Her coarse and blunt nature repelled him, yet when he took her like this his desire was inflamed by the thought that this was a hurtful vengeance that he was wallowing in.

Ossu bore him a son and they were married for twelve years. Lutor could not recall how those years had passed but he remembered his son and how he had looked on that one morning that was to burn a scar into his life forever. A freak accident? A punishment from the gods? Something had happened to his son. He had heard Ossu screaming and then she was running out with two young boys whom Lutor recognised as his son's friends. They were running to the river. It was nearby, just below a sloping bank of sand that gleamed white in the late afternoon sunlight.

What happened? What happened? The boys had been swimming and enjoying the day when Lutor's son had suddenly cried out as if he was being thrown out of the water. Then he sank and that was the last anyone saw of him. It was a whirlpool that had sucked him under, they said. No one had seen that spinning well of water before. Perhaps a deep current had caught him in its undertow. Such things had happened before. It was the work of the Banji spirit, the dark spirit of water. That is why, people said, our forefathers warned us never to be arrogant about water. Lutor's uncle had stayed by the river all night. 'Five days, it takes five days for a drowned body to surface,' he had said and waited, but the rainman knew this time they would never find the boy again. 'There is no one to talk to. The spirits have taken him away and departed. I can only hear a dead silence,' he said.

It was prophetic. For many years, Lutor started at the sight of floating debris and driftwood on the river bank thinking it was the body of his son. One night he tore up all the fishermen's nets in a demented fury crying out that they had entangled his son but he never found his boy again. It was a hard thing to live with. Ossu did not speak to him and they retreated from one another as though their liaison had proved cursed and fatal. One day she left and he knew she was looking for a new home. He could not blame her. She had given him a son and that was more than enough, if only he had not lost him!

An island of peace

On the day of Lutor's public meeting, the new festival ground reserved for celebrations and big gatherings was full of people. Since its growth from a settlement of scattered villages of Balek Rasam, Tigra and Roing perched on a stony hill, Pasighat had always been known for its culture of public debate. It had something to do with the influence of traditional village councils, and the innate curiosity of its denizens, and villagers from far and wide who strained to see and hear what was happening in Pasighat.

I was driving in from Itanagar. It was the festive New Year season of Aaran, a time for family get-togethers, and after my meeting with Lutor I had decided to follow up and visit all my relatives in Pasighat again. The road by the Sibo Korong bridge was jammed with vehicles and motorbikes. I couldn't resist turning in to see what was going on. Rudar hailed me even before I had alighted. 'You're here,' he cried. 'Come, come, join us!'

'I am on my way to Mirmir,' I told him.

'Okay, okay,' he said, 'but stay awhile, while I attend to a few things.'

'I'll stay here,' I said, prepared to stand by the car and look on the milling crowd even though I had not planned to attend the meeting.

Rudar was the man in charge. He had worried over this meeting convened at short notice, but now he looked around and felt pleased at the turnout. There were plenty of young men who looked a bit thuggish, he thought, but he knew if he went up and spoke to them they would respond with the confused smiles of young lads, meek as lambs. Everyone knew each other, the old recognising the young, and the young knowing the old folks well enough to be able to pick out the ubiquitous uncles and grandads to avoid. He was not surprised to see faces from Tanik's camp among the crowd. 'Well, look at the spies,' he thought, staring at them. A young man darted back and forth carrying video equipment.

'Get out of the way,' a woman called out angrily. 'We can't see anything.' She had come to hear Lutor speak. No one wanted to miss out on anything.

Lutor saw the crowd and wondered what he could say now. His thoughts were with what Kellan had told him about the troubles in Tirap and Changlang. But from here the district was far away. Could the crowd before him feel the ill wind that was slowly moving across the land? It was a big state, but not that big, after all, he thought. He had founded his party on the basis of unity and brotherhood. Their cry had been 'One Land One people.' And so it would be, it must be.

'Does anyone here know anything about the dead man?' he asked. The crowd fell silent. 'Is there no one looking for him?' No answer. The body had been found almost a week ago. The local newspaper had carried the police report with a message seeking relatives of the deceased. The man was distinctly tribal, a young man with not a scrap of identification on him. Lutor knew by now everyone in the area must surely have heard about the dead body more by word of mouth than through the newspaper, but no one had come forward to identify the dead man. It was very odd.

'How can a man be killed right here, in our forest and no one know anything about it?' Lutor said. 'Strange, is it not, that a man is killed and no relative, friend, father, not a single person knows anything at all about the dead man? No one is claiming the victim. Will the killer go scot free? We must be careless, or we are being overrun by a force that we have no knowledge about.

'I am a politician,' said Lutor. 'I go to New Delhi. I say, look, this is what is happening in Arunachal Pradesh. Our state is being overrun by extortionists and militant groups. Our villagers are living in fear. But what happens? The union government refuses to believe me. "No, no, how can it be," they say. Arunachal Pradesh is an island of peace. Arrey, don't worry so much. Concentrate on infrastructure.'

There was a titter in the back row. Hear! Hear! Someone clapped loudly.

'One man is killed here,' continued Lutor. 'In Itanagar and across the river more people are kidnapped, threatened and killed, but no one is convicted. No one knows the killers. This is the terrible silence that is falling over our land. Is the government surrendering? They say this kind of thing is happening in other states too.'

'That's because they are involved in the cover-up,' someone yelled out.

'What about our own leaders, huh?' another voice shouted.

'The government says don't worry so much,' continued Lutor. 'They will handle it. It is a *security issue.* But I want to know what is this security issue? Is it about hiding facts and not acknowledging what is common knowledge? The union government talks about border security and about China. Don't be fooled. A "security issue" is a slippery fish. The terms of reference are always changing. Yes, we are a border state but our interests for the country and the security of the state is the same. So why is a "security issue" something that we cannot talk about? Why can we not discuss what is important to us? What sort of state are we? Are we a peaceful state, or not?'

This was the beginning of a discussion that was to continue into the evening. Questions and comments flew back and forth.

'All our leaders are camped in Itanagar. Who stays in their constituency? Everyone says there is no trouble. We are peaceful. But no one is going to Tirap. Ask anyone…'

'No one is coming here, too. They come back only during election time!'

'What about our water and electricity, huh?'

'We are living in darkness!'

'Why should we support this government?'

'What kind of government is this?'

'GRP! It is the Get Rich Party—'

'Down with the UNC! Long live ANP!'

Rudar was standing near the entrance when out of the corner of his eye he saw the familiar figure of a local businessman turned politician making his way towards him. His name was Kijji Ongo. Kijji was from a village near Pasighat and he had set up a saw mill, one of the first in the area many years ago. He was a wealthy man but now he was complaining bitterly that he was dying, and happy that he was dying.

'Why, you should be happy. You are doing good business and good politics,' said Rudar.

'Why, why? My life is being eaten up by bugs and leeches! Women! They want frivolities. And their hearts are like iron. They sharpen their weapons all the time.'

This drew a smile from Rudar. Kijji was the older man but he was a free floater and a known womaniser. He was also an astute, unscrupulous politician and people said he was the prime mover behind Tanik's success. Both of them were thick as thieves. In the last elections Kijji had won against Lutor's candidate in a bitterly contested battle. People said it was the money that did it.

'I was blind,' said Kijji, shaking his head. 'I must have been under an evil spell. Ah, and they were so sweet once.' Kijji's eyes were serious. 'It's like this,' he said. 'A man has all the freedom to search but in the end he finds very little. After a while they are all the same. In the dark, and in the daylight, soft beautiful creatures with words, more words, and inevitably tears, tears!' He slapped his thighs and laughed. 'By the way, I heard Kellan was here, is it true? And where is that beautiful sister of his, Umsi?'

'What about her,' said Rudar.

Kijji stared at him. His big, florid face broke into a wide grin and he shouted, 'What about her! Ha, ha, that's a good one!' He put up his hand to his head and laughed with his eyes squeezed shut tightly. 'What about our friend Lutor's ex-sweetheart, what about her!' he said.

Rudar tried to keep a straight face. Kijji spoke as if he knew everything and maybe he did. But how could the news of Kellan's visit spread so quickly? Lutor was addressing the crowd again and Kijji became silent. He heard Lutor saying, 'You have heard that many of our own politicians are leaving the state to live in other parts of the country. They are leaving because they cannot face the trouble that has come into our land. So, good luck to them if they are tired of living here, but for me, to pack up and leave for a new destination is unthinkable. It would be writing off my entire life. If everything depends on yourself then what better place to make a life than the place where you were born? Everywhere people love their land. It is life, birth, happiness and children. It is our source of strength and our inspiration. It is life.'

Rudar shifted slightly, feeling the silence deepening.

'Good turn-out,' said Kijji. 'Lutor's still holding, huh? He hasn't changed.'

Rudar looked at Kijji. 'You haven't changed either,' he replied. Kijji laughed loudly. He pressed close to Rudar tilting his head forward as if to whisper something but his phone rang and Kijji whipped the phone to his ear with an important air. It was a relief for Rudar when he heard the scraping of chairs on the dais and Kamin announced that the meeting was over. Kijji Ongo plunged into the crowd and disappeared.

'Thank god,' thought Rudar, pushing his way through the crowd. 'Now we can proceed to the Gagil house for refreshments.'

The Gagil household

The Gagil house was one of the first concrete houses in Pasighat. The house was built in the old style with high ceilings and bay windows that the local carpenters had achieved after a great deal of labour. A wide veranda ran all the way around the house and the cement floor was worn smooth with the hands and feet of children who had learned to crawl and taken their first tottering steps in the house. It was a big, boisterous place with extended families living in its shelter since the day Gagil had stepped in as a young bride, more than five decades ago, when she married Tanmut of the Tamta clan. Everyone had grown up, gone away or died, but Gagil, who was an aunt in the maternal chain of relatives, still held sway as the grand matriarch while her husband spent his days talking with old friends and playing carom with the boys. Tanmut had been with Gagil's brother Dinu at the time of the Aching mori massacre, and like men of that generation who had thought nothing of walking for eighteen days at a stretch he was still restless for physical movement.

Today, in the house a young girl was shaking out packets of chips and popcorn into big glass bowls and instructing everyone to dress well and serve like this—from the left—

and with this spoon—and from that dish, holding it like this, bending from the waist, hair tied back, don't smile…!

Her name was Kampo and she was Gagil's granddaughter. Gagil and Tanmut had three sons and just when they thought everything was settled for all of them to become landowners and do good business, Kampo's father had turned out to be the unpredictable one. In a loud, loving family he was quiet and studious. He had wanted to join the army but in the face of stiff resistance from his parents he had opted for a degree in international relations and landed a job in Delhi with a development agency. At the time, Gagil and Tanmut were clueless about multinationals, corporate business, the UN or any other global organization. They waited, hoping their son would be diverted somehow to return home and settle down in Pasighat. Instead, Kampo's father told them about his plans to wed a Delhi girl he had been dating for some time. Her father was ex-army and had travelled in erstwhile NEFA. He had also accepted an offer for a field trip to Europe, and he told them that departure was imminent.

'He is becoming like Lipun!' Gagil had shouted. Tanmut said it was better than being in the army. Gagil bit back her angry words. 'But we haven't even seen the girl,' she said. Their eldest son travelled to Delhi and returned, saying his brother was adamant. He would not be coming home for some time. He wanted to travel and see the world. It was a time of great upheaval for the family with relatives offering advice, talking about a wedding—what's to be done now, they said, it's your son's wish. You can't turn him away. It's good if he gets married…if only he was not so far away!

Not long after this period of turmoil, news of Umsi's clandestine marriage shocked the Pasighat families.

Everyone said, 'Delhi is dangerous. Don't send your children there. They will never come back!'

Gagil and Tanmut didn't know how to react. The world was changing. In Pasighat the first tourists began to trickle in bringing a vista of other worlds. Young people talked about Bollywood stars and foreign travel and the site for a new bridge over the Siang became their stomping ground for parties with loud music and the roaring of motorbikes that shook the town like an earthquake.

It was the birth of a baby girl that changed everything. When the news reached Gagil, she was suddenly shouting on a crackling phone line and talking to her son again, 'How is the baby, how is the baby's mother, when are you coming back?'

Gagil's old friend Tibul said, 'if it's going to be an Indian name tell him, Madhuri. If it's a miglun name Elee-ja-beth.'

'Kampo,' said Gagil. Kampo, meaning beautiful.

After this long-distance ceremony when Gagil was reconciled with her son, Kampo stayed with her grandparents while the young couple travelled. 'We must woo them back,' said Gagil, talking about her son and daughter-in-law. 'After all, how long will they travel? We can offer everything here, and at least the child should speak Adi and know her relatives,' she told her silent husband. This was how Kampo joined school in Shillong where Umsi, and Nefa before her, had set the trend for sending girls to boarding school.

'The girls are coming and going so fast there's no time for our boys to marry them,' was all Tanmut said.

Kampo was nineteen years old and she liked being back in the old family home playing the hostess and shaking everyone up. Everyone was pouring into the Gagil house. 'Don't make such a fuss,' said Gagil. 'I know Lutor very well and he likes plain tribal food. All this will confuse everyone.'

'Well, we have to keep standards,' said Kampo to no one in particular. The young girls were giggling and she knew that they would get everything mixed up. 'It takes a lifetime, a lifetime!' She muttered to herself, but loudly, so that Gagil would hear. 'Maybe the young politicians like this kind of service and good food and napkins and pudding. Just for fun, why not, huh?'

'Yes, yes, and candlelight too,' the old lady replied, 'because there will be a power cut and the lights are going to go off.'

'Hah,' Kampo shook her hands in a gesture of impatience and walked off, laughing, towards the kitchen.

The lights were burning brightly and cars were parked all around the garden when I hurried up into the veranda.

'Come in, come in,' said Gagil, greeting me warmly as Ome—daughter. 'How are you? How is Itanagar?'

'Hot,' I replied. It was early March but it felt like the middle of summer. 'Everyone says it's hotter than usual.'

Tanmut came out. 'Ah, you know, the leaves of the Inji used to turn red in April. Now they are turning red in February.'

'Everything is changing,' said Gagil.

'Yes, but think of the tangom. Those burrs used to stick to our clothing at the time when they put up the big pandals during Durga puja. Now they are all over the place, even in March!'

'Okay, okay,' said Gagil, walking ahead.

'The weather is changing every year, did you notice?' continued Tanmut, whispering close behind me.

'Yes. No rain this year, but unusual snowfall in the other districts,' I told him. Tanmut seemed eager for news and conversation. 'Perhaps it's the Ice Age coming back.'

'What's that, eh?'

'The Ice Age, like the one that killed the dinosaurs,' I said, turning round to bend close to his ear.

'There you are!' cried Kampo. 'What are you talking about?'

'The Ice Age,' said her grandfather. He told me to sit while he shuffled away towards the garden.

I looked around at the old place. This was the house we had all returned to as children whenever we were in Pasighat, and Tanmut was the great uncle who would always be sitting out in the veranda talking with traders about rice, sugarcane, and machuas bringing fish from his fish ponds that they displayed in big basins, splashing and silvery in the bright light of a petromax lamp.

'Come, sit for a while,' said Gagil. 'We'll talk. Your aunt Tibul is also here. She was asking about you.'

'There's no time! cried Kampo. 'The guests will be here soon.'

'There's always time,' answered Gagil tartly. 'I have time. I'm sure Ome has time. Sit down and I'll tell you what we did before you girls were born.'

'I have time…' As far back as I could remember Gagil had always said she had time. Back then as a young mother it might have taken her a long time to adjust to a big, demanding family, but making her calculations she had made the jigsaw of her life emerge—if not entirely complete, at least as colourful pieces about to find their proper place.

Now her brow was furrowed with deep lines and she walked with a slight stoop, but anyone seeing her for the first time would still be struck by her calm face with prominent cheekbones and eyes that looked directly at you as if she could see everything. In her day she had been hailed as the perfect daughter-in-law who brought good fortune to the Tanmut house. She was stern about duty and obligation, and even now, when everyone pulled in opposite directions they were bound by her presence. In the kitchen, young girls bent over steaming pots of rice and cooked meat day and night.

Now she said, 'A house full of young girls is a happy place. Guests feel more welcome in a house where there are young daughters who will come out smiling to offer you food and snacks.'

'Ha, but everyone wants a son,' said Kampo.

'Oh yes, sons are good but it's the women who make them,' said Gagil, 'and anyway who would want to come to a house full of sons with hardly a word to say to anybody?'

Kampo nudged me. 'It's just that men don't change their clan titles. That's why they think men are so important,' she said.

The first thing aunt Tibul said on seeing me was: 'Maying! There you are, my beautiful, clever girl! Why haven't you made us happy with a handsome son-in-law?'

'Come, let's get out of here,' said Kampo. 'The ponung-dance is about to start,' she called out, waving briskly to Tibul and pulling me away.

Kojum-Koja

In one corner of the garden stood a light, wooden building raised on cement pillars. This was a new, popular feature in all the houses of the town and its purpose was for providing entertainment with a local touch. A bamboo railing ran around an open platform and thatched roofing completed the picture of a gazebo that was big enough to seat dozens of people. All the activity of the house was now concentrated on this point. Bare feet stepped back and forth, scraped against bags, baskets, a torch, bamboo tubes, a baby's cap. Nothing would be lost. Every item would be accounted for and reclaimed after the excitement had died down. For now, the evening was just picking up, relatives were arriving and the bustling activity all around made everyone talk in unnaturally loud, singsong voices.

'Quick! Let's get our drink!' Kampo darted forward and grabbed two mugs of apong. The girl carrying the tray laughed and gave me a boiled egg wrapped in a leaf along with some grated ginger. This was for starters. We began sipping the sweet, potent rice beer.

A group of twenty ponung dancers were already in place, ready to start their performance. They all wore red ga-les and short, black jackets. The man leading the dance as the shaman-miri for the night had been especially invited from the village of Sigar across the river.

'I don't understand why they have to perform this dance all the time,' said Kampo.

'Aren't they grand?' said Tibul coming up to us and clutching my arm. Her thin face was crinkled with excitement. 'This is in honour of Lutor,' she said. 'He can't get a note right but he loves music and songs.'

'I am fed up of this dancing and singing,' said Kampo. 'Why do we have a ponung for every politician and VIP?'

'Because it is tradition,' replied Tibul. 'Listen! This is the one about the green enchantress floating down to earth through white clouds. She is going to teach us to dance and sing.'

Tibul was nodding her head in rhythm as the miri began chanting in a loud, clear voice. The night was swimming and shimmering in streams of memory. Before everything else there was the land of Kojum-Koja, a sacred place beyond the moon and stars. This was the first civilization from where man began his journey through the different heavens to descend into the world carrying stories of happiness and hope.

Footsteps echoed and the murmurs of men and women reached me as if from a great distance. Was that really the wind rushing in? What was the meaning of this chanting? And where did the words come from, rising and falling in this hypnotic cadence? Far away, beyond the stars, a battle was raging between the star people of Kojum-Koja and the lord of the waters. The star people had killed the son of the water king and the grief-stricken father had unleashed a fierce flood. Everything was being destroyed. What would happen to the star people now? The story was very old and vast, spreading out like the branches of an ancient tree into the land of the Engo Takar people. The miri followed the journey of the dog, faithful companion of the legendary archer brothers Nui-Gamro.

'Nui shot an arrow and the dog bounded forward!'

The miri shook his sword and a lost world came to life as the grand lady of mythology, mother Kiine Naane, source of all seed and grain was resurrected in verse. She filled the house. Her vast granary was spread out before her like a rippling sea of gold in the warm sunlight. The dog had lost his way and was now sniffing the air and approaching the great mother. She gazed at him and stretched out her hand. The dog stepped forward throwing back his ears and wagging his tail.

'How did you reach here?' she asked.

'My master was hunting the wild boar, destroyer of crops, and he shot his arrow. I gave chase and the path led me here.'

The earth mother laughed kindly.

'Here, take this back to man,' she said, and placed a grain of rice in the groove of his ear. 'Tell him it is my gift. Let his people remember me and celebrate this day in my honour.'

The world disappeared and the grain was swept away in a puff of smoke as the dog, wondering at this dream, stumbled and sped away back to the hunting grounds of his master, back to the land of Kojum-Koja, but Oh! Everything was buried under a deep and dark sea. The ancient civilization had been wiped out forever. But no! Look again! Don't lose heart! Out of this destruction something stirred and sighed. A delicate form rose out of the water like a green shoot. It was Nyanyi Mete the celestial aunt, the green enchantress! She had survived the terrible flood and floated out of the debris to bring a message of hope to mankind.

'Today is the day!' cried Tibul.

'Oh earth mother! Giver of grain! We bring you offerings to celebrate and honour you! Green enchantress of a lost world! We welcome you into our hearts, bringer of love and harmony!'

Who created these stories? The night was full of firelight and shadow, and my heart was beating in rhythm to the chanting. There was a river and there was a lake, there… curling back at the edges in a shining ripple of silver with all the sparkle of the stars fallen into it. It was dancing across the heavens and sweeping the horizon with light, fire, and dreams. I was thinking about Orion the legendary hunter fixed in the starry sky with Sirius when Kampo nudged me sharply. 'Look, look, there's Lutor.' She pointed with her chin in the direction of Lutor who was standing quite still looking at a group of people who had just arrived.

'I like the way his hair falls over his eyes, especially when he is looking so serious! He doesn't look old, does he?'

'He's not old,' I said. 'Fifties is not old for a politician, late fifties, I think.'

'He looks like a samurai, don't you think? He looks like that actor—Ken-something! Have you seen his films? An Adi samurai,' Kampo said enthusiastically, quite infatuated with Lutor. 'He's cute!'

'Sshh…don't talk so loudly. He'll hear you!'

Lutor was standing closer now to a woman wearing a chocolate-coloured blouse over a pink ga-le.

'Is that Umsi?' Kampo whispered.

'Yes, let's go and greet them.'

Umsi was with her sister-in-law, Mentiri, whose sharp eyes spotted us immediately.

'How are you? How are you?' Everyone was calling out

to each other and in this whirl of activity Mentiri's voice rose and fell saying, 'Oh no, no, I hate Itanagar. I hate the roads. I hate Tirap. That's why I don't visit my husband Kellan. Oh, the roads. The roads, they kill me.'

'They're not so bad,' said Umsi, laughing.

'That's because you don't live here,' said Mentiri gushing on, turning to me, 'you can't avoid me this time. You are coming to dinner.'

'Of course I will. But you must come to Itanagar too!'

'Umsi can go,' said Mentiri. 'I cannot tolerate these road journeys. Why don't you go to Itanagar?' she said, turning to Umsi.

'You could stay with me,' I offered.

I sensed Lutor was straining his ears to catch Umsi's reply but Mentiri gushed on with her wordy political comments. It was well known that Mentiri was a bit of a chin wag and she spouted ideas that left people without the vaguest notion of what it was that she wanted to convey. She was active in the women's movement and had political ambitions, but her comments and observations were so contradictory and garbled that no one liked to get into conversation with her. Kampo pretended to have heard someone calling her and ducked away, followed by Umsi who said she was going to meet Gagil. When Lutor saw Rudar looking at him he too jumped at the chance. 'Would you like some apong?' he asked, and before Mentiri could answer he held up his hand and said, 'I'll get one for you.'

'I'll get something too,' I said, hurrying after Lutor.

Gagil's eldest daughter-in-law, Mamo, stood at the centre of a group of women who were pouring boiling water into giant bamboo baskets filled with rice brew. They looked strange and shadowy, like whispering witches floating in a cloud of steam. Another daughter-in-law brushed past carrying a large basket and I heard her asking Lutor why he was standing alone.

'I came to get a drink for a lady,' he replied.

'I'll take care of it,' she said, throwing him a look full of friendly mischief.

I looked back at Mentiri and saw her already in conversation with another group. I was moving towards Mamo and the distillation point from where jugs of apong were being ladled out and carried to all the guests when I saw Orin coming in. He was dishevelled and obviously excited about something.

A large shadow seemed to exert attention. I was conscious of this presence and the feeling of someone's gaze on me. I turned around. At the same time Orin said: 'Oh hey, you know each other?' He introduced me to Kamin. 'You must know each other, surely,' he said.

'Oh yes, hello,' I said. I knew Kamin from college in Delhi. We had met in students' meetings, but briefly. In my friends group we thought he was too earnest and boring. Now he said, 'So you are interested in politics?'

He must have seen me in the field this morning, I thought. 'Well, no,' I said. 'I'm here to celebrate Aaran.'

Kamin said nothing and I felt relieved when Kampo passed by and waved blithely to Orin.

'Do you want anything?' I asked.

Orin looked into his mug. Kamin held his calmly and said, 'They'll be coming round this way. You don't have to do anything.'

'I'll join Mamo,' I said, turning away.

'Okay, but come back fast.'

Someone was calling my name and I saw Tanmut sitting

with his friends in the deepest corner of the house, waving his mug and calling out, 'Maying, my dear, my mug is empty! No one is looking after us!'

Mamo was laughing. 'Take this to them,' she said, handing me a full jug.

'Here, here, give it here,' said Tanmut affably, taking the jug out of my hands and happily sloshing wine into his friends' brimming cups. 'Have some more. Go on, don't be so slow! Yours! And yours! And yours! Do you know, my niece here was telling me the climate is changing? It is due to the Ice Age! Soon you will see, according to the experts, human beings will become small, shrunken creatures and the Dino-SORAI birds will be coming back! Isn't that so?'

'Is that a political forecast?' one of the old cronies asked and began to laugh loudly.

'Who knows, these days anything is possible.'

'Well, it's the Ice Age for us!'

'Did you attend Lutor's meeting today?'

'No, no. I went fishing! But I believe it was a good turnout.'

'Yes. But Tanik won't be sitting idle. That's for sure.'

'That's true...some people are like weeds that grow overnight.'

'With people like Tanik one can't be too careful. Lutor should stay undercover and then suddenly launch a movement to shake the very foundations of these hills,' said Tanmut.

'Times have changed. Loyalty is not a big thing anymore. It's money. Everything depends on money,' said his cronies.

'Yes. Everything is different now...' Tanmut agreed, moodily sipping his beer.

When they were young men, Tanmut remembered how men like Dinu, Lomey and he had stalked prey like determined lions. The sunlight was striped and blazing with their ferocity and everything was swift and soundless, the silence of the kill, the stillness of death, holding, holding, as if the universe held its breath for such violence.

In the days of inter-village feuds, after a village was burned to the ground, the victorious marauders went into the forest. They carried their bloodied daos and slashed at the undergrowth. The leaves and trees shuddered under their attack. It would be pitch dark and out of this darkness would rise the weeping spectres of men and women and their children. They drooped under the blow of sword blades and suddenly, in one voice, they would cry out for mercy. 'Aaii! Sparc us! Have mercy! Take us to your village. Take everything, oh masters of the night. Masters of the forest! Masters of war!

This was how of hundreds of families were marched back from their dead villages into their new homes. They were kept apart but they were given food and shelter and ordered to clear fields and fell trees and chop wood for building and fencing arable land. They worked hard, and in time the younger, able-bodied men were sent to look after the mithuns, gather thatch for roofing, and bring back fodder for the pigs. There were enormous wild yam that had to be dug out of steep hillsides covered with wet vegetation alive with the movement of leeches. The slave men returned torn and bleeding, and their women plucked out the bloated leeches in silence. The children scrabbled for food, the families growled, snarled, recoiled from social contact and fell asleep like the dead, with no dreams. Years passed. The captive men died. Their wives succumbed to disease and despair and the new generation of men adopted the clan title of their owners. In time they settled into a familiar routine with their master's family. They had no memory of the places they had been taken from. They did not know fire and death and they had not heard the hard oaths and demented cries of their vanquished forefathers. They were free of this burden of remembrance and they were happy ranging far into the forest away from the village and any other living being. The thought of running away never crossed their minds. Where would they run to, and for what? Life was food and breath and that was all there was. Only someone mad would try to swim across the river, or run to another village, but what would anyone get for that kind of impulse? The women whispered and did not look on the faces of the men who had captured them. He would be the great warrior and he was good enough to them, but it was ill luck to look into the eyes of a warrior. His gaze carried omens and if he was angry an accident would make a person fall off a bridge or be crushed under a stone. The warrior men were careful too. They did not want to look at the captive women. Many of them were young and flaunted a hard, lascivious beauty. In the past some young man had inevitably fallen into this pit of desire and made love to them. Then they were lost because the rigid taboos of the tribe made their offspring outcast forever and no matter how much time passed, these things were never forgotten.

All this was now a thing of the past. Since the Aching mori incident sarkari rules had banned slavery, blood feuds and head hunting among some tribes but still, Tanmut thought, there had been greater honour and valour in the old days—the frontier days when men had marched to distant villages to fight for land or celebrate a marriage alliance. What does a society do when an old practice is suddenly taken away by men who do not live with you but watch you from a distance and impose new laws with armed police? There is a space that needs to be filled, if only to carry on in some dignity towards a new way of life.

'Now the new labour force is the migrant population,' Lutor was saying. Everywhere they were being wooed, for the tea plantations and the hydro-electric power projects, public works, roads and bridges, down to the last petty traders, butchers and cobblers. They constituted an enormous vote bank and this was Tanik's winning card. Tanmut knew how every election truckloads of migrant workers were rounded up to cast their vote. He looked around hoping to catch someone's eye for another round of apong when he saw Ongat's son Kasi coming in and heard a loud voice beside him saying, 'There you are! You never come to visit us, accursed sons! Your wives never come to pay their respects. You don't know anything! Your mother, how has she brought you up?' It was old Jema airing his views about the younger generation.

I saw this delivery brought a bright flush on Kasi's face but he clamped his mouth down in a tight smile and looked at the angry uncle. Lutor was about to move forward when I heard Kamin's voice.

'Hai, what do you know about Kasi's life? If he's struggling or hungry or finding it hard to find a job and make ends meet, what do you know? Have you visited him and asked?'

Jema looked surprised. At any other time he might have laughed or spat, and been on his way, but the drink made him feel differently tonight.

'Tah! Tah! That is not my job. I am like his father. Let him answer.'

'Are you?'

'Hai! What do you mean? Speak plain.'

'Let him be,' Kasi said, sitting down now next to Kamin and rubbing his hands together.

'No, I want to ask father Jema, what have you done for him?' Kamin was looking at the old man with a serious, questioning expression.

'He's not a young child.' Jema replied. 'He should know the rules. You should know the rules.'

There were all sorts of interjections and everyone was talking at the same time—the young! The old! Tah! What are we coming to? Who gives a damn!

'Other people's sons and daughters bring gifts. They don't forget to visit their elders…'

'Well, Kasi has nothing,' Kamin said. 'So I'll bring you something. What do you want?'

'Hai! I was just reminding him of human laws of behaviour!' shouted Jema, exasperated beyond words.

'It's okay. It's okay. Let the old talk.' Everyone was muttering and cursing with mixed amusement but Kamin looked really angry.

'No! I'll tell you what I wanted. When I was a student I wanted to buy books. But no, it was not possible. There was no money and there were no books. We grew up like this, dreaming! Now I have finished that part of my life—books or no books—and we are trying to change things so that the next lot of us will be confident, more secure. Why do you talk of behaviour? We hear our fathers telling us about the migoms. Sometimes they shouted at you but even then you said 'even the spittle of the migom is development.' Tell me, is that not pathetic? We have no pride. And how can we? We don't know anything! How long is it going to take us, tell me, with your crying about the old days, crying about today's lack of behaviour? What behaviour? I tell you, we are warriors. That is the only behaviour that brings respect. Throw away your beads and all this talk about honour and past glory. Say something new!'

There was more noise after this outburst. Jema started laughing loudly and not only his cronies but old aunts and spinsters joined in the unexpected, highly interesting debate.

'The men can't hold their drink. It's disgusting,' Kampo said, making a face as she passed Lutor.

'Oh yes,' he nodded to her, suddenly noticing her young face. It was strange, now that he had seen Umsi again all his perceptions seemed to have become heightened, particularly about men and women and how they related to each other. How wonderful, how wonderful, he thought, to be meeting like this, to be among friends and relatives without doubt and pretence. Even old Jema is talking like never before. If only things could go on like this forever.

'Are we leaving tonight?' It was one of the boys who had accompanied him from Itanagar.

'Yes, of course,' he said. He looked for Umsi and saw her in the far corner talking to Gagil. He continued to look at the two women, lost in thought, until Mentiri came up to him and said what are you thinking about?

'Oh, I have to leave,' he replied, tearing his gaze away from the corner.

'What! So soon,' Mentiri exclaimed. 'We are inviting you to our place for dinner tomorrow. I mentioned it to Umsi and she said okay. Let's all meet before everyone returns to Itanagar!'

Lutor was wondering how he should respond when Rudar came up and asked him again about his programme.

'I was planning to leave tonight,' he repeated.

'Oh, but it's so late. Why don't you leave early tomorrow? The others—Maying and Umsi are planning to leave tomorrow too.' He seemed to stress a little on Umsi's name.

'Day after tomorrow,' Mentiri corrected him. 'Don't forget our dinner!'

Lutor listened, but now he had made up his mind to leave immediately. He had heard what he wanted to hear, that Umsi would be coming to Itanagar, and it was imperative that he should be there before her. Everyone complained about his sudden departure. Kamin was especially put out, saying many things needed to be discussed, but Lutor was smiling as he bade goodbye, saying they would all be meeting again soon anyway to discuss their election campaign.

He did not see Umsi again but his mind was already whirling with a thousand things he suddenly needed to do as if in honour of her impending visit, and he laughed when Rudar put in two huge bottles of black apong into his car.

'Hey,' said Rudar, standing close and swaying a little, 'don't worry. I'll escort the ladies.'

'Everything is happening in one night,' Lutor thought as he set off. His knees hurt a bit sitting bent up in these long drives but so what. Everything was returning. His whole life was at stake again. It was a new year, wasn't it? The year of the green enchantress! And a man was entitled to remember a few things even though his associates like Kamin might disagree. A simple man, that's what he had wanted to be, even though Rudar would not believe him. A simple man. How complicated was that? He felt free when he was alone. I have to prepare the house! He thought about the bare rooms. What would she think? My god, why have I lived in such a sloppy way! Now he would barely have time to tidy things up before Rudar and the Pasighat group arrived, and then who knows, she—Umsi might come to see him. 'Of course we'll meet in Itanagar,' she had said. Her self-assured manner irked him. How could she be so cool when so many years had been wasted? He wanted everything to be sleek with happiness so that when she came to the house she would be jealous. He had survived her, after all. He had built the house with the help of a few friends. One never knows about politics, better to have your own place, he had said, rejecting ministerial bungalows and the legislator's cottages. He was happier in that part of town, closer to the original village of Poma away from the concrete mess that the capital had become. What about the compound, he thought, already imagining Umsi standing there and gazing about her. The few trees he had planted had not grown. No one had tended them. She had given him a plant once, when the town was new and they were still together. Which one was that? His mind whirled desperately. It was the mountain ebony, the one by the coffee bush that he had shown her saying he would start a coffee plantation. She had laughed, saying coffee would be no good at all, but they had been happy then. Yes, this will do better, she had said, planting the thin sapling. It had grown. The bottom branches had been eaten up by bugs but it was still there. Thank god!

Once she had cooked for him—chicken in gravy with diced potatoes and grapes—she told him stiffly, though he saw only a few pale grapes sprinkled on top, and he didn't like grapes. It's more like boiled chicken and potatoes, why can't she just say that, he thought, but when she asked if he liked it he said: Delicious! Fabulous! He almost laughed out loud now thinking about this. Umsi and her peculiar little traits that he had never forgotten! Ah! Love, what is it? It is the things we never forget about another person. He was falling in love—no, he was still in love with her. From start to finish she was the green ribbon tied around his heart.

He was impatient with the car. It was his trusted Scorpio but now he felt it was old and slow. It was a dusty, bumpy ride and Lutor was staring so hard at the road, leaning forward as if willing the vehicle to move faster that he hardly registered the Banderdewa police check gate and was surprised when he crossed the landmark statue at Pehalwan Point and then suddenly, out of nowhere, as the car swung around another bend the lights of the city twinkled under a clear night sky. Itanagar!

The rainman

Time was flying. In Pasighat there were many people I had to meet but for the moment I was content to sit back and do nothing. I was in Mentiri's house and Umsi and I were in the garden with aunt Tibul who had come from Gagil's house as was her habit, moving from one house to another in the vicinity whenever she heard there were visitors. Aunt Tibul had never married but her sister Ongat had two sons, Orin and Kasi. Orin was the firstborn and Kasi was his step brother, conceived out of wedlock, people said, with a man working in the Border Roads Organisation. The man had gone away on posting and never resumed contact but Orin's father had treated the younger boy as his own. Ongat was a silent, moody woman and after the death of her husband in a hunting accident she kept to herself. It was Tibul who had raised Orin and Kasi. She had managed to do this with her small earnings from selling vegetables from her garden. She gardened with a passion and everything was laid out here—varieties of mustard leaf, aubergines, chillies, mushrooms and dried bamboo shoot in sealed packets. For all these years, Tibul had sat in the circular Pasighat market peering at customers with her long, lean face looking like a friendly hedgehog surrounded by greenery. Recently she had taken to carrying a small cloth bag slung across her chest for her new handset. A loud ringtone would make her scrabble around with one hand for the source of that sound shouting, Oi! Oi! while hurriedly pushing vegetables on to a piece of newspaper with her free hand. The young boys who prowled the market knew her and sometimes they buzzed Tibul just to hear her shout Oi! and see her bend her head at an expectant angle until they were almost upon her. 'Here, why don't you take this!' she would say then, scooping up a pile of chillies almost in anger. Now she held a small bowl of pickle that Umsi had brought from Delhi and was smacking her lips in delight.

'Aaa-s-aar! Mango pickle!

'Aa-*ch*-a-rrr,' Mentiri called out through the kitchen window. Tibul continued, 'Aa-saa-ar! What tasty things other people eat—*dopua*, yum!'

Kellan and Mentiri's son was running around in the garden carrying a big picture book. 'I'm taking him to Delhi with me,' said Umsi. 'He's going to study in school there, isn't it? She called out to the boy.

'No!' shouted the child.

Tibul looked up and said, 'Hoi, from now you must stay here. Don't go away again and live so far away!'

'What reason is there to live here?' Mentiri shouted out again.

'We can meet like this, everyday,' replied Tibul.

We all laughed. Old hometowns have a way of absorbing you in, no matter how long since your last visit, for the town people it is as if it were yesterday. This was familiar territory and both Umsi and I felt more spontaneous than we did in Delhi, or Itanagar. There was a similar curve, a pattern in our lives. We had left home, and we had travelled, though Umsi, certainly, was the real feisty, iconic beauty who had followed her dreams. There were many of us who had wanted to be like her: Romance! Travel! Wealth! But now I sensed something else. Umsi didn't say it but I suspected the total isolation of being cut off from home and relatives must have come at a cost. I had caught up with her, somewhat, when I had moved to Delhi. Umsi's husband, Karan, was from Kangra, and at the time that Umsi met him he was the manager of a tea garden in Assam. After the 1962 Indo-China border war many planters had handed over the tea gardens to their Indian assistants. By the 1980s, the tea industry had picked up again and the social life of a planter was once again centred in planters' club meetings. Umsi had met Karan at one of these get-togethers when her brother Kellan had been invited by an old school friend and Umsi's father had allowed her to go with him. Karan was a handsome, tribal-looking man who seemed to want to keep to himself and who was insanely jealous of anyone who came near Umsi. His mother had lived with him in Assam but now she was living in Palampur and neither of them wanted to return to this part of the country.

The place was changed, Umsi had said. It was already changing before we left. Every tea garden was paying a tax per kilogram of tea and this went to the coffers of militant organisations. 'At first I thought it was a grand movement,' said Umsi. 'We were very excited about the student movement and all those ideals when the Assam agitation started, but it turned sour. All the gardens and oil companies had to pay up and the extortion became threatening and violent. When my daughter was born we decided it was best to leave.'

Karan had returned to the family business in real estate and construction. After the cloistered life of a planter, Karan was restless to travel. He had shown Umsi the world in a mosaic of glittering cities and summer islands until one day, said Umsi, on a high hill facing the wild Atlantic she had suddenly come face to face with an image of a woman standing on a windy cliff wondering how she had come so far from home. A cold rain was blowing across the land and she had felt a jolt at the utter desolation of that hill and the sadness of the landscape surrounded by sea. When they passed an old stone cottage yellow with lichen something had turned in her soul. I want a home, she thought, a permanent place like this stone structure, full of pieces of history. Where is my life?

'We invent stories for ourselves,' she said, 'and at that moment I felt as if all that I had been was not the real me. Maybe I had floundered, huh?'

I wondered about that. People say the past makes us who we are. Maybe the hardest part is when somewhere along the way we come upon a truth that makes us stop in our tracks and face the stories we have carried around in our heads about who we are. Well, Umsi seemed to have made that encounter. I knew Umsi to be kind and warm hearted; she was also intelligent and passionate and I could not imagine her sitting around playing hostess and making small talk, giving parties and living a life of leisure. In Delhi we had met often and when Karan was away, we were more at ease in the big house where a cook prepared hot curries while Umsi grabbed at a bottle of bamboo shoot and spread it on our food. Sometimes she made walnut cake, stirring and singing at the top of her voice. Her daughter had been a little girl then, but now she was ready for college, said Umsi.

'Did you ever miss this place?' I asked.

'No, never!' said Umsi, laughing.

'But here we are,' I said.

'Hmm, that is the surprise,' said Umsi.

'It's the bamboo shoot,' shouted Mentiri. 'You miss the taste of bamboo shoot.' She pushed the window wide open as if to let the mouthwatering aroma of meat and bamboo shoot waft across the garden.

'It's too much politics and money here,' said Umsi, but she was smiling and looking relaxed and happy. I watched her slyly. I wondered if she could talk about Lutor and all the gossip I had picked up about their affair. But I kept my thoughts to myself. Umsi was still a mystery. Even now, sitting in the sun, I felt she was like the wind. 'I am travelling!' she had said. 'Yes, I am happy!' She had agreed to spend a few days with me in Itanagar, but Umsi had been away for so long and her movements were marked and chequered by so many lines and layers it was difficult to pinpoint the person, and if she had any desires, what were they?

'You know the rainman was here,' she said, surprising me.

What's this with the rainman, Mentiri called out again. Is it true he can do magic? Do you believe?

'You'd better believe,' said Tibul, sitting up and staring at us. 'He has very strong powers. You know you have to call him Kakii uncle. It is a very important name.'

'Oh, I don't know about Kakii's magic,' said Umsi, 'but he has something, yes…I like the name Rainman, the idea of someone sitting just like this, always being here with his honest thoughts and words. In a way his constant presence here sort of makes the life I thought or imagined I wanted possible.'

'He never travels,' said Tibul.

'Oh, he travels,' said Umsi. 'In fact, he's just back from a long tour. He's like a time traveller, I think…He believes in other roads.'

'How is he?' I asked.

'He is the same…older, but the same,' said Umsi. 'He was asking about you.'

The first person on my list of people to meet in Pasighat was the rainman. In the Delhi office where I worked everyone said now was a great opportunity to set up a biodiversity office in the state. Even the minister had pitched in saying he was aware of 'smoke signals' coming from the state that pointed to large-scale destruction of forests and the environment. Ministers are always trying to intervene, I thought, intervening with promises, intervening with funds. And my hometown always did this—it provoked the cynic in me. I was born in a place of dissent. Look at this outline—endearing outline of the hills. Look at the mountainside, scarred with rain. Look at this earth, scarred with cutting, the claws and bones of the seasons; the failure of development. What did politicians know? I wanted to know what the people in the villages knew. I wanted to hear the words of the rainman. Who lived here? I wanted to hear the voices of people who lived here. What did the environment mean to them?

There were other things, too. I thought of the dead man killed in these forests. I thought of old man Jema's high-pitched voice and all the things that I had heard, all the things long gone, and the things happening now. I thought of Lipun, now an old man living in Itanagar, and I thought of Umsi being back and how I had seen Lutor hunched over his typewriter punching out the Party manifesto, struggling to win a battle in a political environment fraught with duplicity and greed. Transition had happened. Where had we reached?

I knew Lutor had invited his uncle many times to stay with him in Itanagar but the rainman had always said, what will I do there? I am okay here, and Lutor had not insisted because the rainman was linked to that spot of land and anyone who needed his help could go straight to his shack by the river. Now I heard the sound of the river like a faint murmur in my head as I drove past the Riba canteen heading straight on towards the DC's bungalow and Paglek where the Siang fanned out into a wide, glistening plain. The road was busy with motorists and young college kids riding to the bazaar or some meeting place, everyone going somewhere.

Once, long ago, the only words I had actively sought were the words of the rainman. It was a time when I was leaving Pasighat. If anyone had asked me who was the rainman I would be at a loss to describe him. Perhaps in every generation there is a rainman, or someone like him. I thought his name was appropriate because the rains always brought on a sharp, passionate awareness of life. It brought a sense of sorrow, but without blame, and a wondering tenderness at the delicate tracery of thought that seemed to cocoon the world when the skies wept, as if the world shared in the cleansing like a deep sigh, breathing in patience, such an old, undisturbed patience, overcoming all error and human frailty. It was true, what Umsi had said. People like the rainman made our journeys possible because deep in our hearts we knew that through him we could find our way back to rejoin the tribe. As a friend and mentor, the rainman was the one who was always there to remind, console, and give counsel. When all of us moved in different directions thinking our destiny lay elsewhere, the rainman stayed where he was, never venturing out beyond the circle of the hills. 'I look at the clouds outside my window,' he had said, 'and I can travel. The world floats on green oceans contoured by ocean currents. We travel wider and wider in our quest to draw closer and closer to the centre.'

They called him the rainman because he had once brought rain to a thirsty land, but he could do other magic, people said, and turn into a tiger shadowing his enemies until they succumbed to the power of his spells. But to me he was the sound of rivers, rain, fire—that touch of gold from the first sun. The rainman was the one who had said, 'I can look through the sun's face, and peep through the light of the moon.'

When I reached the familiar spot by the river I found it quiet and deserted. Lutor's uncle was not in and since there was no one around to give me information about his whereabouts I drove along the river barricade and turned into the narrow lane popularly known as Ladoo-Moori-line that led to the market. I spun the car around the familiar statue of the Mahatma and headed towards Gagil's house. Here too it was quiet, but the old lady was in, there around the back, a young maid told me. Pasighat houses have this aura of quiet with no sign of life in the front rooms. All the activity is at the back, in the Adi kitchen with a fireplace and traditional smoking rack above it, and sure enough I went in to find Gagil in deep conversation with a crowd of women sitting around an open fire.

'Hai!' they exclaimed all together. I realised they were all from Balek and Rasam villages who had dropped by for a chat in the evening, just like in the old days. Gagil signalled for me to come and join them. 'They're inside,' she said, when I told her I was looking for Lutor's uncle. Tanmut had been complaining of aches and pains and the rainman was, in fact, sitting with him. Tanmut was resting on a long chair in the veranda with a white rug pulled up to his chin. Rudar and Lutor's uncle were sitting on low stools and both of them were drinking rum and laughing.

The rainman smiled when I appeared before them.

'You're back,' he said, sounding pleased.

'Oh, my dear girl,' cried Tanmut, throwing off the rug and sitting up. 'Here, here, have a seat.' He patted a stool.

'I thought you were not feeling well,' I said.

'Ach! I'm just feeling lazy. Would you like some rum too?' He pulled out a half bottle from his pocket.

'No, no,' I turned to Lutor's uncle. 'I went to see you and found your place empty so I came here.'

'Oh ho,' Tanmut said. 'Tanik has been looking for him too so Rudar has hijacked him here. I know that man has something on his mind and you know how persistent he is. I think he wants to enlist Uncle's help for the elections.'

'Why would he do that?

'These days things are not what they seem,' said Rudar. 'Tanik may be scared.'

'Scared of what?'

'Well, all this insurgency stuff, maybe he took the help of the armed militants to return to power, and now maybe he's lost control. Who knows? A man has to pay up sometime or the other.'

'What's Uncle's role?'

'Oh, no role,' the rainman replied. 'Tanik, like all our

politicians, likes to perform rituals and that's what he would want now. Rituals. It has an impact on his followers, you know. It makes him feel good and it frightens his opponents because we are all still superstitious believers.'

'What are you doing now?' he asked me.

I told him about the new project.

'The idea is to set up a biodiversity office,' I said. 'First I have to submit a proposal, but it's difficult to collect data. I have to travel a lot to find out about one little thing.'

The rainman considered this. 'Well, it's something new you are starting,' he said.

'People say Arunachal is a green paradise and there is a lot you can do. But you have to be patient. The land is a being, just like us, and to know the land you have to live here. When you are closely linked to the land, it speaks to you in little whispers and nudges. That is a feeling of happiness.' He looked at me and I held my breath. The cold air was filling my nostrils and it made me feel a bit giddy as though I was inhaling big gulps of the past. I might have forgotten many things but I had never forgotten the stories about the rainman and his powers to reach the truth of human relationships.

'Our world has changed,' the rainman continued. 'But when all is said and done, we can honour the spirits of our forefathers only through our love for the land. Love regenerates. The world grows. The breeze lifts the canopy of the trees. Light filters down. Things arrange themselves. Between sleep and death, fruit and flowers are born. Even in sorrow and desert aridity something is born—a shoot, a blade of grass; a creeping vine, or a thorn bush.'

A young girl carried in a cup of tea and I almost burnt my tongue sipping it. The rainman shook out some biscuits on a plate and said, 'You have to be patient and sit with people to hear their stories. It's not so easy getting people to remember, and people who know things cannot put their knowledge into words. As you can see, these days no one is talking. But you can try!'

I thought this was a reference to the veil of secrecy that shrouded political campaigns. I was already facing a setback because my mind was diverted by the exhilaration of being back in my hometown and being involved, in some way, in the political developments of the state.

'I am sure you will do well,' said Rudar.

I heard Tanmut saying, 'I don't fish anymore. I have left those things. And things don't come into my hands either. These days the fish can't be caught. Ha ha! But you know what, your aunt, the old woman is suddenly very patient. She, who used to be bossy and talkative is now saying "Never mind. Take it easy. You should rest now." Ah, Maying, my girl, what is rest when a man's heart wants to wander up and down river banks and catch fish, eh?'

'You can fish in the river all day but that won't be enough to feed you,' the rainman said. 'You have to work the land.'

'You should tell Lutor that,' said Rudar, taking a swig of rum, teasing the old man. Rudar's house was close by in this old part of town called Mirmir, so named after the susurating sound of the wind that blew in from the river and shook the leaves of jackfruit trees. The old trees gave the place an air of permanence and Rudar was as plain and solid as the fields and forests that he owned. For Lutor it was different. His life as a politician had taken him away from Sirum village, the solid base of his electoral success, and he returned only on tumultuous visits when everyone would flock to feast and honour him. It was Rudar and

Tanmut, the Gagil family and the rainman who held things together and protected him against the complaints of a periodically disgruntled public who cried, 'We want more. We want more.'

'After all this is over Lutor should come back and look after his land, go fishing, keep us company,' said Tanmut. 'How is the campaign going?'

'We are getting there,' said Rudar.

Tanmut lowered his voice. 'I heard a black snake has been attacking the chickens in Tanik's house. The snake was in the hen house but its shadow was reflected on the wall of a woman's room. She couldn't believe her eyes.'

'I know, said the rainman. 'He has consulted a limay—shaman.'

The limay keeps twenty to thirty selected stones with him. He throws these stones on the ground like dice and working on a set of calculations he places them in groups or withdraws them. One plus five, six minus eight, withdraw two, place nine here, four in rows, five in pairs, one extra—a dark spot. Who is that dark spot? The old man with his stones had only said there was a difficulty. He could not foretell more than that. But it had made Tanik think, a difficulty! I have been besieged by difficulties all my life! The black snake had been killed with a shot of a catapult but it had left a feeling of fear. Tanik wanted to hear a prediction and he wanted to reinforce his powers. This he could do only through mysterious rituals for the bewilderment of his enemies.

'We have known Tanik since he was a child,' said Tanmut. 'You know, his mother used to bring him here. Ah! Who would have thought life would turn out like this?'

The wind was starting up, the famous wind of Pasighat,

stealthily rustling through the trees. The evening was fading into a murmur of soft, indistinct sounds. I waited, sitting quite still.

'Ah ha…who indeed?' The rainman seemed lost in thought. He was old now and under his knitted woollen cap I knew his hair was steely grey. 'It was in the time of the great storm,' he said, 'when we prayed for the dead.'

In our language there is no word for Time. Time is a river, a road, a moving landscape; an unknown, irrecoverable place of origin when the world was liquid before a big wind blew away the film of mist and fog and dry land appeared with the piercing eye of the sun. Everything that happens in a person's life, from birth to death, is measured by a calendar of reference to the seasons, or to the rising slope and bend of the sun for the hours in a day. Time is a song, a journey, a narrative strung like beads in a necklace worn by the wearer whose destiny it is to be garlanded at birth with such a talisman.

The 'great storm' that the men were remembering was a time reference to extraordinary events associated with the time of Tanik's birth.

'What about this great storm?' I asked. I was curious and treading carefully, as if on a secret errand to uncover connections that might finally lead to the unravelling of a mysterious legend, or the origin of a rumour about Lutor's political opponent. I had heard some of the stories about Tanik, but I knew how stories grow around public figures and great heroes—stories of magic, strange visitations, spirit wives; the thin veil between the living and the dead. The past was a jumble of images and it seemed to me that in one way or another all the images were linked to the rainman. This time I had come prepared to stay and listen to everything he had to say.

The story of Tanik the mythmaker

Tanik was a dealer in false hope. The day he was born his mother cried out with joy. Even through her confinement and pain she had wept and laughed at the same time because she could feel her heart beating again with unstoppable hope. A son! This was what she had been praying for. A son! A son would be the unbreakable tie that would now keep her husband with her forever.

The tall, taciturn man who was the father of the boy had received this gift with a thin, wordless smile and did not display any other visible sign of happiness. Everyone said he was a strange one, never showing his emotions, but they predicted that once the baby began to gurgle and clutch at him with his tiny baby fingers his heart would melt and he might even secretly weep for joy. What man would not? A baby was a miracle! But all these happy thoughts and predictions were dashed when the father left the family house one grey afternoon and never came back.

Tanik was born in the small village of Sirkung in the Ketak hills far north of Pasighat. Lutor's uncle who knew the region said it was a lonely land of deep gorges and crystal-clear lakes. A few villages clung to narrow spurs and the only cultivable land was along the valley of two icy rivers flowing through a cleft in the mountains. To the east, in a wide semicircle, rose the mountain peaks of the Abroka range that marked the border with the land of the Idu people, where Lutor had gone on his first journey with Lipun and the man called Singa. Most of the old settlements like Sirkung had been abandoned, and its population dispersed following a series of bitter wars with neighbouring villages, while many had died in sudden outbreaks of fire and epidemics.

A long time ago a man of the Daji clan of Sirkung was out hunting. He was setting traps for birds and small game in a dark and unknown forest, living off dry rice and the black, gummy mushrooms that grew on decayed wood. Late one evening he had returned to his small bamboo shelter bone-tired and shaking with fever. The hot, steaming forest seemed to have robbed him of his senses. Day after day as he set his traps deeper and deeper into the unknown heart of that green and tangled land, he felt that the land he knew had turned into a monster he had to do battle with, fighting with his feet, limbs, hands, everything. His breath, body and mind seemed to be surrendering to this invisible force that he felt was bent on breaking his spirit and enslaving him forever. He was on the verge of collapse. He barely managed to drag himself to the mat on the floor where he threw himself face down and fell into a deep slumber.

The summer night was hot and still. In his sleep, perhaps during the middle of the night or perhaps it was towards dawn, the man thought he could hear rustling footsteps. Maybe it was a breeze building up for a storm. Was he awake? Was he dreaming? He lay as if dead but a smile was turning up the corners of his mouth. Softly, slowly, the breeze seemed to touch his house, shaking the thatch gently. What a beautiful sound, the man thought, turning over to yield to the delicious sensation. He threw out his arms and moaned with a sad ache that crept up his tired, heavy limbs. A soft hand was caressing his arms. His bruised and hungry body was being stroked carefully and lovingly and he tried to open his eyes to see what was happening but his lids were so heavy he could not lift them. He sighed. A woman's breath sighed softly beside him. Now she was stroking his face, touching his cheek, breathing against his mouth and calling out quietly, but he could not turn to see her nor answer. He was being unclothed and he lay there unable to move, aching with longing. A cloud of mist wrapped around him in a cool, delicious sensation and he cried out when he felt the pleasure of making love in a slow, tantalising agony that mounted as he felt a woman's body, soft and tender, wrapped around him. The woman murmured unintelligible words as he cried out in his terrible desire and she cried out with him when he felt heaven and earth slip away, receding into a deep and twisting tunnel that seemed to stretch and suck him into an endless universe.

When he awoke he saw a fire had been lit. There was rice on the pot and his ramshackle hut was swept clean and the water vessel was gleaming as if someone had spent time polishing it all night. Food. Fire. Clean water. He rose slowly, still feeling a latent fire in his limbs. His mind struggled with confused images and feelings. What had happened? Had he taken a woman? Where was she? Who had lit the fire...Who? Who?

He rose swiftly and rushed outside. The night and dawn were mingled on the crest of the hill and a pale glow from the light of the sun was spreading over this patch of forest that he had cleared with such labour. The sun! A thought flashed through his head. The woman had run away with the light of the sun. Then, could it be? Was she a ghost woman? A spirit woman? He had heard stories of such women who came to visit men and stole their senses, and loved them, if they were lucky. Such things had happened before. There were spirit husbands too. Young women had been carried away by them. Sometimes they became demented with lust and on full moon nights ran around wildly opening their naked bodies to the night sky. Many women conceived and invariably gave birth in the dead of night howling like dogs. But for a man it was different. A spirit wife was a boon. If a visitation was honoured a man could amass great wealth and become very famous and powerful. All these thoughts crossed the man's mind as he gazed at the strengthening light of the sun. He felt rejuvenated. He remembered the shape of the woman. She was like a fish—smooth and firm, spread over him like a slow burning fire. Was it real? Had anything happened, or was he hallucinating? Maybe he was going mad with all the days spent alone in the jungle. Maybe he was already mad and no one in his village would recognise him now?

He would soon find out, he thought. He left the hut taking his fishing traps and net and spent all day by the river thinking about what he had experienced. The afternoon sun waned. He met no one. Very few villagers came here at this time of year when the river was red and swollen with the silt pouring in from the tributaries upstream. He did not think of returning to his village or to his young wife whom he had married a year ago. She was a simple girl who had cried out in fear when he had approached her on that first night of love. He remembered her to be sweet and innocent but she had never inflamed his desire and since his departure from the village he had never thought of her once in all these months. His relatives argued with him and said he had no right to leave a young wife and go away into the forest. It was his duty to raise a family and live in the place where he had been born. But something was driving him. He said he wanted to carve out a new patch of land for his family, but he knew this was a lie. He did not want anyone with him. In any case his father had enough land and fields and as a son he would inherit everything. He left the village and then returned and left again. His wife stood aside with tear-filled eyes. His uncles avoided him and he in turn became wilful and taciturn. The forest was calling him and urging him on as if on the verge of revealing something and he knew already that this revelation would be made only if he was alone.

Now he returned to the hut and shut the door fast. He sat down on the mat in a state of self-hypnosis and sat unmoving like this for a long time, waiting for whatever would happen next. He did not think of cooking. He did not light a fire. There was no moon and everything was in darkness. The familiar hum of the jungle seemed to reach him from a great distance. Maybe he dozed, but suddenly he was jerked awake by the sound of a slow, lifting wind approaching the hut. The door creaked and the hut itself seemed to lift and sway. The door swung open as the lashing of twine that fastened it to a bamboo post fell in a soft coil on the earth.

Oh! Mercy! I am being visited again! He had to act quickly. He jumped up and shouted at the top of his voice, 'Before you enter tell me who you are!' He thought he heard soft, tinkling laughter. There was no time. 'Wait!' he shouted again. 'Let me speak first. I will honour you but you must come in peace. Give me your blessings and I will honour you!'

Again that sound of tinkling laughter. His eyes were closing and he felt a rush of air in his ears as he stepped back and fell into a crouch. The hand that touched him was full of tenderness. His body shuddered. He sat back and felt the soft heaviness enveloping him. He had never felt like this before. He grunted and grappled with the unseen woman as she moaned and scratched his back with her nails. She was taking him, possessing him, and he was joined in a delirious burning embrace that made his body thrash wildly on the hard floor. But this time he was grasping the woman's wrist firmly in his hand. He had sworn that he would not let her escape this time. In a dream he thought he heard her whispering instructions: 'Before the next dawn my brothers will come to honour you. They will be here in the evening bearing gifts.' If he was good and did everything as she instructed him he would live and become rich and renowned.

'No,' he said. He wanted to live with her.

'Do not attempt to follow me,' she said. 'We pass this way but once. It is a brief moment but it will last all your life. My brothers will take me away but they will pay you with gifts. You will be a wealthy man. Don't forget to honour them. Your life and the life of future generations will depend on it.'

When he awoke the sun was high in the sky. He lay in a daze and his senses cried out for rest. He thought he would fall asleep again.

'Hey! Is this your hunting and fishing?' His friend Kakir was peering in through the door and grinning from ear to ear. 'You must be fishing in your dreams, eh? Caught anything?' Then he screwed up his face as he stepped in and inhaled deeply. 'What a peculiar scent. What is it?' Kakir looked at him and then around as if expecting to see leaves or flowers he had never seen before. 'Shall I sit down? What have you been cooking?' He lifted the lid of the pot and peered in. 'Ha! Rice! What a wonderful smell it is. Ah…did you cook it then fall asleep again? Are you sick?'

The man shook himself and sat up. He was feeling unwell. He was startled by his friend's sudden appearance and the thought crossed his mind that Kakir might decide to spend the night and that would be the end of everything. 'I am alright,' he said, coughing to give himself time to think. 'I am just tired. I was walking all day yesterday and I got nothing. I was planning to cut some bamboo today.'

'I'll help you,' Kakir offered happily. 'But come on, first let's eat this wonderful rice. It smells delicious!'

Now the man lifted a handful of rice to his mouth. He was transported as if in a dream. He was eating and the grain rolled like cream on his tongue. It was wild scented with a texture that made a man feel happy and strong.

'This is wonderful! It is like cream on my tongue,' Kakir exclaimed.

The two men ate without saying another word as if they were suddenly assailed by secret thoughts and longings that they did not want the other to know.

'Well, that was something,' said Kakir at last, leaning back and looking at his friend with half closed, glittering eyes. Then he said, 'You know you will be a father soon.'

'Yes.' The man remembered his wife and the child she was carrying. He should be back in the village awaiting the birth of his child. Was this not what every man wanted? But he felt no joy. He felt the ties of family like a terrible bondage. To break the spell and will his friend to go away he pulled himself up and went over to the old bag that hung on the corner post. He fished out a bottle of rum that he had bought from a store in town. He had forgotten all about it until now. 'Here's something to celebrate your arrival!' he said.

Kakir looked at him keenly then dropped his eyes and nodded. The two men drank silently for the rest of the time as if waiting for something to happen. At five o'clock the man started and remembered the words of the woman. Her brothers' visit! Who were her brothers? 'Your life depends on it. Honour my brothers!' she had said.

He looked at Kakir. Kakir looked back at him. Then he said, 'You don't look so well. Why don't you lie down? I can keep watch.'

'No!' He was startled by the unexpected force of his voice. Kakir also reared back and stared at him.

'No!' he heard himself repeating. Then suddenly he was saying he had something to tell his friend but that it would be possible only later. Now, he said, he wanted him to leave and tell everyone in the village that he would be returning soon, maybe even tomorrow. But Kakir should leave now, immediately, otherwise he would not reach before nightfall and tomorrow it would be of no use to tell his family to prepare for his return as he would probably arrive before the message was conveyed to them. 'Do this for me. Please leave me now. Go back to the village!' he cried desperately.

His friend listened to him and said nothing. Instead, he seemed to be contemplating something deeply. 'What is this thing you want to tell me, eh?' he finally said.

'Not now! Not now!' The man was almost shouting now. He could feel the world turning dark as if the sky was sucking away all the light from the land as the sun began to dip behind the great mountains. 'What should I do?' He thought of many things. He thought of running out and crawling into the undergrowth. He thought of telling Kakir everything—maybe he would know about such things and offer help and advice. He saw Kakir lolling there with his head bent and unmoving and the thought flashed through his mind that he could hit him with a rock and knock him out or even kill him and drag his body into the jungle and hurl it into a ravine. As if sensing his thoughts his friend began to rise slowly and turning to face the man who was almost on the point of hitting him, said, 'I think I'll move off then. I'll tell your wife to prepare food. Be sure to return tomorrow.'

The man saw his friend to the door. He pointed to the clump of wild cane and said that he would clear them before Kakir came to visit him again. 'Yes, tell them I'll be back tomorrow,' he said, even patting his friend on the shoulder. Now that he knew Kakir was leaving he was friendly in a clear, deliberate manner. He looked around. The world seemed to have darkened. What sort of time was this, he wondered. He could feel his heart beating so hard he laid his hand over it hoping his friend would not hear or delay his departure. A dark cloud was looming over the treetops. It was rearing up in broad, sweeping spirals and the man felt his blood turning to ice.

'Run! Go now!' he shouted. Kakir swung around and as they stared at one another he saw realisation and terror flare up in the eyes of his friend. He pushed him now with a great deal of force. Kakir stumbled forward then began running without another word towards the narrow path barely visible in between the trees. He did not look back as he disappeared into the swaying, rustling forest that was being bent by the force of the wind, but the man had a feeling that Kakir's eyes were still pinned on him, as if he was running backwards and still trying to see what was happening to him.

A great force swept him off his feet and hurled him into the hut where he fell in a crumpled heap, unable to move or see anything. All he heard was a high, keening wail that rushed around him whooshing and churning in an endless stream of air spiralling and spinning faster and faster until he thought his head would explode and his body would be shredded into pieces by this appalling current.

'Honour them!' He heard the words tearing into his ears through the current that swirled around him and he struggled to remember and obey. 'I cannot move,' he thought, 'but I can think.' He willed his mind to be still and clear. Obscene shrieks pierced his ears but now he could hear the thud of his heart. It was growing louder, like the sound of a drum. He saw himself—a child again, laughing with his mother by a stream. The water was tingling cold. He splashed his feet and felt all the happiness of the world seeping into his body from the bright sunshine and the lapping water.

I am a boy again! What joy! Ah…he sighed. If I live I will repay life for this wonderful moment with all the obligations due to a man who is so blessed. I will repay! He repeated this to himself over and over again. He saw the waving pattern of signals travelling in bright flashes inside his head. He was nothing but a conduit of signals, waves, energy, and zigzag currents of light. A great peace descended on him and he wanted to weep, overcome with a peculiar emotion of relief and tenderness. He was running by the river again. He saw the water rolling back and standing up as it swept him under, right into its deepest depths. It was cold and fresh, and looking upwards he could see a stream of light rising all the way up to the sky like a long, shimmering ladder. Perhaps I am dead, he thought, and it did not bother him at all. He was spinning slowly and lazily like a leaf floating upwards in this circle of light. He heard the sound of crashing trees and boulders slipping and rubbing against one another as they sank past his feet onto the river bed below that stretched so clearly before him like a brand new landscape. He saw his poor hut, smoke blackened and derelict, lifted in a gust of wind and obscured from view as grey mist settled over it. The last thing he heard was distant cries, echoes, and metallic sounds. Then he fell asleep. Or his soul flew away and perched on a tree. He saw it hanging there, glowing like a tiny pinpoint of light and he thought he would never return. He was dead and his soul would rest here forever.

When he opened his eyes again the world was calm and silent. His bamboo door was shut fast and he was all alone in the hut lying face down on the floor. He dared not turn around, not yet, and he lay crouched for a while staring straight in front of him at his old bag that he had touched, so many hours or days ago, to pour his friend Kakir a drink. Now he was unaware of the time, or day. What had happened to him? Was he really alive again? Sunlight filtered in through the cracks in the bamboo and he calculated that it must be close to midday. There was no rice. No fire. No sign of entry or movement or anything at all. 'It must be the silence—this jungle, these dreams that torment me. I must return to the village…'

He rubbed the back of his neck and turned around slowly. His gaze moved around the floor and up the flimsy bamboo sides of the hut—up towards the corner loft that was the place where he kept his spear, firewood, a bag of rice and some items of daily use. Now the man's eyes bulged out in surprise. What! There, piled high on his old homespun blanket was a mound of beads! He leapt up on the loft and peered closely at the shining strands of tadok necklaces coiled in an enormous heap like a colourful snake. There were the precious blue and white beads for men, the yellow beads for women, green beads, red beads, cowry shells and metal discs, and as his gaze travelled he saw huge brass plates and urns and marriage ornaments and bells and vessels of all shapes and sizes strewn across the length and breadth of the dark, secret loft.

'Hai! What is this?' His breath was escaping from him in long, slow gasps. He knew the precious tadoks were a man's highest symbol of wealth. Among his people every one believed that each bead has a story and there were shamans who could touch a bead and tell you the journey of that single bead like the story of a man's life. He was filled with wonder and fear. There was no sign of anything else. The afternoon continued to hum and blaze. He felt the hut swaying in a pool of light.

'The gods! The spirits! Why have they visited me? Why? Why? What shall I do now! How shall I answer! How shall I live the rest of my days?'

This was how a man became rich, once upon a time, a long time ago. For the rest of his days he offered sacrifice of cattle, mithun, fowl, and pigs. He offered them unfailingly to honour the gods, the spirit brothers, and the unseen woman who had loved him better than any woman on earth.

These periodic propitiation rites became a regular feature of the Daji household, and as the news spread far and wide, more stories of spirit wives and rich gifts bestowed on other families began to emerge until wealthy families of every clan began to offer sacrifice and fix dates for all sorts of rituals recalled from a distant past. But the Daji man continued his prayers and sacrifice because on dark, lonely nights he saw again the fallen trees and the torn clumps of wild palm and fern strewn all the way to his abandoned hut. It was a vast clearing now, fertile with the fire and ash of fallen trees but sometimes, when he walked through this land he saw the face of his friend Kakir with his head almost twisted off his neck as though he had been lifted by the roots of his hair and thrown against the broken tree. His eyes were staring and his mouth was open in a wide scream.

'It was the storm,' the villagers said. 'It was a storm like we have never known before and pray will never happen again,' they murmured, as they carried Kakir's body back to the village for burial.

Kakir was well known as a brave hunter. How could he die so suddenly? There were questions but the Daji man said he didn't know anything. He had stayed in his hut during the storm. When he came out he had found his friend lying dead on the path. He had come back to the village, running like a mad man to bring them news of Kakir's death. Everyone wondered about the storm that had whirled up out of nowhere. It is the work of spirits, they whispered. Only powerful spirits could bring wild clouds and that rushing wind as if…could it be…that the spirits had been looking for someone? What had happened in the forest, in the hut of the Daji man? The villagers took refuge in silence. No good came of talking too much. There was work too be done and funeral rites to be performed for Kakir.

The Daji man sat with the widow and the young son of the dead man all night. A frightening thought was nagging at him. Perhaps his friend had been taken as the token of honour for the brothers of the ghost woman. Why did the spirits take him, he wondered. Did they want him for something? It was because of Kakir that his loft had been filled with riches. He owed his life to him. If his friend had not turned up when he did—what would have been the outcome? It was impossible to live with these questions. Oh! If only his friend had left earlier, just before the strange cloud appeared over the hill, just a few minutes before the appointment made by the woman for her brothers!

For the rest of his life he would regard women with fear and awe. But for now, yes, it was the storm, he kept repeating, it was the storm, the terrible storm, and he was almost convinced of this until he felt the eyes of Kakir's son watching him. He was not the rainman then, just a village boy who had lost his father, but it was at that moment that the ceremonies and spells of hundreds of years were taking birth in his heart, as if his dead father had begun planting seeds in him to atone for his sad, mysterious death.

Tanik was four years old when his father left one grey afternoon never to return. The Daji household was a prominent and influential family in Sirkung and Tanik was surrounded by uncles and the old parents of his father. He did not pine for his father. It was his grandfather, the old man, who cursed his son and not a day passed when he did not utter Tanik's father's name with rage to anyone who came to the house. Then, after many years he had begun to mutter to himself and the young Tanik heard the words—'exchange' and 'beads' and 'the storm.'

These words imprinted themselves in his mind. He was a quiet, peaceful child who might have stayed that way like his friends in the village if his mother had not decided to strike out on her own, in search of a better life for her son.

She remembered the man who was her husband and father of Tanik, but it was more than a decade that she had seen him. In all this time he had not sent a single word and she could barely recall the tone of his voice. Perhaps he had died somewhere far away. No one spoke about him and she did not seek news of him from anyone.

It was a godsend when an outbreak of cholera and strange fevers that rotted away a person's teeth and left the skin raw and blistered crept up the hills and struck their village. It was time to leave.

It was during this time that Gagil had first met Tanik's mother when she arrived one hot afternoon, her face flushed with exertion and her hair soaked with sweat. It was a year before the China war and Gagil herself was a young mother who had moved into the first concrete house of her husband's family in Pasighat.

'This is the child,' she had said. Gagil saw a charming, fresh-faced young boy stepping forward and it had struck her even then that the boy seemed to possess a clairvoyant air. His mother had brought him here to introduce him, she said, to families who had travelled to their remote villages as Dinu, the legendary Lomey and Tanmut had done. Gagil had immediately risen to go into the kitchen to ask the young girls to prepare something for Tanik and his mother who was now speaking in an angry, shaking voice. Everyone knew the boy's father, and everyone knew that he had deserted mother and child. What no one could figure out was why. The man had withstood all the pleas of family and friends and had simply fled as if he could not bear to answer their questions. He was living in a faraway place where, they said, people were cutting trees and selling them. Other stories reaching them said he had become a soldier and had gone away to live in one of the towns in the plains. No one knew for certain, and as there was no word from the man his relatives ceased trying to find out anything more about him. For all purposes he was dead to them since he was so adamantly resisting all their efforts to reach him and spurning all their cries of love.

Now he lived solely in Tanik's heart. Tanik never asked his mother anything about him but he kept his ears open and did not miss anything. He heard his mother weeping softly sometimes, but when she looked at him her eyes were bright with a fierce light that halted all the questions churning in his heart. After the visit to the Gagil house Tanik noticed that his mother seemed to take heart. In fact, she became determined that he should study in the town. To achieve this she resorted to an old, forgotten gift that she had. She wove cloth and said that she would sell them to the aying traders.

'What will we do with this, hah?' The first trader they went to asked his mother.

'Put it up there,' his mother pointed to a corner, and added, 'then you will see what happens.'

The aying stared at her and for a long moment seemed to be trapped in her dark, bitter eyes. Then he laughed and said, 'Ok. But I will give you twenty rupees for it, not fifty.'

The woman took the notes of money without another word and mother and son left the market. They lived in a shack like a cowshed that Tanik's mother had occupied with the help of a relative. His name was Tasong, but he was an uncle, his mother told him, and Tanik should call him

Tasong-Paji. Tasong had left the village a few years before them and just like Tanik's father he had never returned to Sirkung village. The man squeezed Tanik's shoulder and promised his mother that he would try to help her earn some money. Now Tanik wondered if the cloth had been sold. When his mother asked him to run down to buy a box of matches he leaped at the chance. A small kiosk nearby sold matches and bidis and thread, but he sped right past this down to the main market unable to resist the desire to see if his mother's cloth had been sold. He was startled when he saw the corner empty. It had been sold! Someone had bought it! He ran back and almost choked when his mother said, 'Is it sold?'

'Yes! It's gone.'

He saw her smiling and his heart filled with joy. His mother was smiling! Later he worried that the cloth might not have been sold after all, but that it had simply been moved to another corner or even put away out of sight, but his doubts were laid to rest when his mother began weaving another piece immediately because the shopkeeper said he wanted more. At this time the NEFA government was setting up craft centres in the bigger towns and weaving units were being opened to employ local women to produce cloth for sale to visitors and outsiders who were beginning to show an interest in the region. This was how Tanik's mother got herself a job as a weaver in the long weaving shed where the first treadle fly-shuttle looms along with drums of thread were placed in rows for weaving instructors. The clacking sounds of these looms became the rhythm of their days and nights like the rhythm of the years passing. His mother, however, had no love for these new looms. She worked on them because the weaving centre offered food and shelter, but at night she wove on her back-strap loom by lamplight.

The colours of yarn were the bright red of the temen creeper, green from a small rhizome called gamba, and indigo dye. Each piece of cloth was unique. From his place near the fire Tanik would watch his mother stooped over the bright pattern. He saw her fingers stretch and curl over a strand of thread as she pulled it through and looped it round again making the dots and small squares that became the 'grasshopper's tooth' design. He listened to the soft thump of the batten, the sumpa, as his mother pressed the thread down, and he saw the woven strip expanding inch by inch as the light flickered and the woman still continued with her labour, weaving attentively and lovingly with her legs stretched straight in front of her and the cane belt around her waist holding her up together with the wonderful band of colour.

The years passed. His mother acquired a plot of land and opened a small shop of bamboo and thatch with the help of Tasong. Their lives were untroubled and soon Tanik met Kijji Ongo who looked at him and said, 'Timber! Timber is the new wealth.' Whatever Kijji touched turned to gold. They went into the timber business and Tanik followed Kijji through hot, dusty towns and watched as the man stood before timber merchants and stopped in mid-sentence, rolled his eyes and then craned his neck forward to whisper something into their ears. When NEFA became a Union Territory, Tanik's career took a turn when he plunged into politics and became a member of the first Provisional Legislative Assembly in 1975. Since then he had not looked back. His political acumen and stature had grown as one with the growth of the state, rising from humble legislator to the man at the helm of affairs and becoming the chief minister of the state. He had enough to support his mother and make her live like a queen but the woman never gave up her weaving. Tanik did not know it then but in all his life, in all these years of political ambition and struggle he would never again experience that sense of rest and comfort that filled his heart every night just before he closed his eyes to sleep. His mother spun cotton on a wooden spindle and she was spinning his life, spinning colour and texture, spinning dreams and desire. Each movement of her hand over the shimmering band of cloth, smoothing it, pressing it down, pulling it taut, each thread she lifted, each strand she wove, each beat of the sumpa and each time she leaned back a little and began again was a magical expression of a mother's blessings for her son.

Book Three

INSURGENCY

Interpretations

Dear friend, the letter began. *Do you see the row of hills upright, there, as if waiting for something to happen? Yes! If you look carefully you will understand that they are waiting for someone to set them alight. Everyone is saying a conflagration is needed. We need fire. Smoke. War cries. Why is the land so quiet? Why is the sunlight standing still? There should be tongues of fire!*

Dear friend! Last night I had a dream. I was climbing a high hill. Maybe it was even one of those hills, there, that tall one sticking up with a flat top like an old volcano. It is familiar and recognisable. Yes, I was panting and clawing my way up and I was choking on dust and heat. No one else could climb this mountain. I thought my legs were breaking. I thought, why am I climbing like this? But friend, I kept pulling myself up higher and higher because I felt I would find something when I reached the top. And there it was! I saw the figure of Lord Jesus standing on the top like a figure of pure light. I shut my eyes but my soul burst open and I cried out and started sobbing like a child. 'You are my soldier,' the lord told me. I collapsed and hugged the ground where I had fallen down at the feet of the lord. It was as if a fever had knocked me out and I was delirious. When I opened my eyes again I saw there was no one, only fires burning everywhere, all around me in all the hills and right down along the mountainside on which I was standing. But I felt no fear. The fires were beautiful and when I awoke my heart was consoled because now I knew what I had to do.

What on earth is this?

Kampo and I were in Orin's place that functioned as his press room and newspaper office from where he churned out his weekly newsletter, *The Eastern Chronicle.*

'It's a letter circulating in Tirap district,' said Orin. 'These letters are being received by everyone but no one knows who is distributing them. It was in the letterbox. The letter was captioned *Truth Will Prevail. Our motto is to attain UT for better life in future generation. We want peace talk.*'

'Are you going to print it?'

'No, of course not,' said Orin. 'In the first place it's dramatics, and then I may also be in deep trouble if we do. The peace talk is with the NSCN but some people here want to hold their own *peace talks* with militants operating in Tirap.'

'What's wrong with reporting it?' said Kampo.

'Well, it's just a theory I have that we sometimes give undue credence to something that should be ignored. It will spread by word of mouth. They have their leaders. They should speak up, but you see they don't.'

'But the public, what about opposition from the villagers?' I asked.

'There is no public.'

Kampo stared at me before turning to Orin. 'What do you mean there is no public?'

'Well, let's say there is no public opinion,' said Orin. 'Everyone sways with the wind. Look, all these reports,' he swept his hands towards the bundles of newspapers, 'they hardly make a difference, I am sorry to say.'

The small room was crammed with books and papers lined up on rickety shelves. Facing the town's Indira Gandhi Park it had once had a good view of the only green space left in the heart of the capital, but within a year the small hillock with graceful trees across the road was flattened and a big squat building came up. This was promptly occupied by the State Bank of India, and now all one could see was a constant flow of cars and people going in and out of the bank. Orin had put up a green mesh to maintain privacy and retreated into a long rectangular room at the end of the building. He had divided this into two rooms with a bookshelf as a partition to make a computer room, while the front of the building became the rather unwelcoming printing room crammed with rolls of paper and smelling of glue and ink. The back room with the computer looked out on the other side of the building where a small trickle of water ran between the office and the next slope that was still covered with grass growing wild beside the state museum on top of the slope. The view was not much, just a small patch of hill, but at least this was not crowded out yet and above the museum hill stood the gompa surrounded by tall prayer flags.

'What's happening here? What are you talking about?' Kamin had stepped in quietly and was standing by the door and looking in at us.

'Oh, come in,' said Orin, shifting his chair and making way for Kamin. 'Politics, terrorism, conflict. Take a look at this,' and he handed Kamin the letter. 'What is your feeling about this?'

I could tell that Kamin had already seen the letter. He was a politician, after all.

'Yes, I have seen it,' Kamin said, as if guessing my

suspicions. 'It is all over the place. The timber wealth in the last decade has ruined the place. And the rivalry among the Tirap politicians has turned out to be the perfect backdrop for the entry of militant organisations. You might say we have lost these districts.'

'It has been going on for a long time,' said Orin. 'If you remember, the Tuensang Hills, before it was ceded to Nagaland, there was trouble brewing.'

'What kind of trouble?'

'Well, just look at the reports of the old officers. New Delhi had posted people there too, you know.'

'What people?' I asked. Orin's way of scattering clues was a mystery to me. It was as if he was digging up unknown nuggets of information to draw me away from my original aim of focussing on environment issues. Who, after all, could remain unmoved after reading letters like the one Kamin now held in his hand?

'Well, Kellan's father started as a school teacher in an outpost there. He was a language officer, and even then there had been talk of armed men collecting money for the Naga Nationalist Council. Kellan knows the stories and the reports. The NNC broke up after that into the NSCN, and then the NSCN split into two factions. It's history.'

'Oh yes, but that's Naga political history, and it's different from ours,' said Kamin. At that time there was never any question of any territory being part of greater Nagaland, or Nagalim as it has become now. Tell me, in those days who knew about lines and boundaries?'

Orin didn't reply to this but I could sense the drift of his thinking. Since then no more had been heard about the presence of armed men in erstwhile NEFA. The state seemed to be on course moving forward as an island of peace until the early 80's brought the first reports of an ambush of an Assam Rifle team and then more and more reports of extortion and killings in the two eastern districts had begun to surface. And today all we were hearing were news of militant organisations and separatist demands.

'Of course there's a war going on,' said Kamin, 'and yet all you people talk about is the NEFA days, environment this, culture that—you and your environment! Who says it is a beautiful land? It is a hard and craggy land and we live like animals, only half a step away from cave-dwellers. We fight using our forefathers' swords and kill our enemies with impunity. There is no law except tribal law and tribal law is arbitrary and brutish. Is this what you are trying to romanticise? The jungle is a jungle. The river is a river. What is fabulous about the river, can you tell me? It is a river of sorrow. Every summer it slurps up land and drowns people. It washes away our fields and throws sand on our faces. We string up a black chicken and tie a dead dog on a pole to appease the spirits and observe a long taboo for everlasting protection. Pathetic! It's time that we grew up, don't you think? Fifty years! Sixty years! At this rate even after a hundred thousand years nothing will happen. No lights. No power. No roads, industry, nothing! We might as well just roll over and die! So what should we do now? We should be harder, fiercer, and we should act!'

Kamin stopped and looked at Orin, waiting. Orin stared at the computer screen and began to hum a tune.

This made Kamin laugh. 'It's not so bad,' he said, shaking his head at me. 'It's just an opinion. What do you think?'

The small room was airless and cramped and Kamin's presence made me uncomfortable. I didn't feel like saying anything. Orin intervened, saying more or less what I was thinking. 'It's not about us. It's them—our leaders—you politicians, we're not sure about. Are we in safe hands?'

'Ah, the government. Well, how will we know unless we are prepared to find out?'

Nothing against roads and electricity, I was thinking, but what about the people, what did they want? I thought of my friends and how we talked about corruption and dirty politics in our home states. As if reading my thoughts, Kamin said again most of the time the people didn't know what they wanted. How can they, when they don't know the issue and what choices they have?

'Well, that's what we try to do,' Orin said. 'What do you think I do this for?' He made punching movements of his fingers over the keyboard. 'At least we try to tell the reader what is going on so that they can make an informed choice.'

'But ninety-nine percent don't read the papers!' exclaimed Kamin. 'And the one percent who do, do you think they will go back to the village and tell the villagers about their choices, will they?'

'That's a drawback. But never mind. It's my job. The rest is up to you,' said Orin blithely.

'Hah! Now you see how we are down to zero again,' said Kamin. 'And you see why local leaders are so important. Everything depends on them.'

'That's why they are so powerful. They can pocket a few thousand voters easily,' said Orin.

Kamin stayed silent. Then he said, 'Well, everybody wants development, and everybody wants peace, but this new Bill that Lutor's friend Aohun is so keen on, it's a tricky thing and it's going to create a lot of trouble.'

'Here,' Orin pulled out a sheaf of papers from a drawer and handed them to me. 'This is what's making news at the moment. Take a look.'

It was the draft for an Anti-terrorist Bill that Kamin was talking about—pages and pages of it, along with copies of police reports. Orin told me that it was 'under consideration,' but Kamin was saying that Lutor's friend, Aohun, was pushing for the Bill to become an Act and that Aohun was caught in a bitter Congress versus Congress battle between Tanik's coterie and politicians, like Aohun himself, who opposed him. Yet Tanik had included Aohun in his current cabinet. 'It's complicated, huh,' Kamin was bending over my shoulder and trying to turn the pages for me. 'Aohun is being used by Tanik to push this controversial Bill through, and Aohun thinks he can beat Tanik at his own game, but to do that he needs our ANP party's help. Look here…here…' he rustled the papers; 'look at the reports here—village headman shot dead, Assam Rifle jawans ambushed, businessman kidnapped, bank looted…it's all murder and bloodshed and loss of civilian lives. Here in this place, that village—the acts of violence are growing all the time.'

'Then maybe this Act will be a deterrent?' asked Orin.

'Oh haw, don't be stupid,' said Kamin. 'You know politicians. Now that there is imminent enquiry about Tanik receiving finance from militants to return to power he has come back with this Ordinance to fool the public. It's his way of getting rid of us through public agitation. Everyone is going to be against this Act, mark my words. Then he will withdraw the legislation saying he never wanted it in the first place, that he will never compromise an inch of our territory. He's looking for a scapegoat and Lutor will be the fall guy. Maybe Aohun will be axed too, but we don't care about that.' He took the papers out of my hand and slapped them down on the desk. 'That's more or less the long and short of it.'

'I think Lutor is against the Bill,' said Orin, 'but he has nine legislators with him and Aohun needs him.'

'Yes, there's that,' said Kamin. 'But why talk about politics all the time? What about other issues? Look at your office. Look at the road outside. Everything is crumbling away—roads, bridges, territory, people, youth, schools and colleges! Can you see any development? What about the drug menace, inter-state boundary disputes, huh? The Centre keeps repeating no roads for strategic reasons. Ha! It's always one factor or the other for us—the China factor, the Naga factor, security issue; this is the picture. Pathetic! You should write about these things.'

There was silence. 'This kind of thing is returning after all these years,' said Orin finally. 'Now we claim it as our history but it's still a piecemeal understanding. The last word has not been said on this.'

'The subject will come up in this assembly session,' said Kamin, standing up to leave. 'Let's see what happens then.' He looked at me and said that he might join Lutor when he visited my place sometime. Would that be alright?

Of course, I replied. Umsi was staying with me, and I knew Lutor would be visiting, but Kamin giving me the news was unexpected.

'He looks a bit like Johnny Depp, doesn't he?' Kampo said the moment Kamin was gone.

'Johnny who?'

'He's a pirate,' Kampo said. '*Take what you can. Give nothing back!*'

'Everyone looks like someone else,' said Orin.

'It's a way to exercise the imagination. Otherwise what will we do in this place?' Kampo snapped back. 'Look at us,' she said. 'What's wrong with us?

'Nothing. What's wrong with us?' said Orin.

'Exactly!' Kampo nodded her head, as if to irritate Orin some more. 'I don't know if something's wrong with me?' She twisted her face and grinned at me, and pointing in the direction of the Gompa and Dariya hill said, 'nothing's wrong with us. That's what I mean. Nothing! It's just that we don't have enough space. One road. One town. One clock tower with the hand permanently stuck at half five. Can you imagine?' Kampo glared at Orin when she said this. 'What will happen to us, the *inmates* of this town?

'Nothing will happen. What would happen?'

'That's just it. Kamin is right in his grumpy way. Nothing happens!' Kampo mimed a silent scream.

This seemed to irk Orin. 'Well, you can always be somewhere else, wherever whatever happens,' he said, not once looking up from the keyboard.

Kampo burst into laughter. She had nice white teeth and her short, straight hair shook and shimmered when she bent her head and laughed.

'You *are* funny,' she gasped.

'We are all funny people,' said Orin, a fine smile lighting up his face too.

Once he had nurtured hopes of becoming a painter. He would stay up all night and by the light of a kerosene lamp paint the most extraordinary pictures on plain chart paper. I had seen many of them tacked up on the walls of his room in Pasighat. One day he had thrown everything into an old leather suitcase and shut them away. 'Time to do something else,' he had said. Ongat and Tibul had showed no interest in his talent, it was a wretched hobby, and Orin had decided to settle in the capital and start a newspaper. Ongat opposed his moving away from home. 'Who will look after us?' she had cried. But aunt Tibul had come to Orin's rescue and even raised some money for him from Gagil and Lutor. No one remembered Orin's talent for painting any more but when Orin was in the mood to show some of the old pictures everyone exclaimed in wonder at the remarkable line drawings of mythical women in green robes and life-like dogs sitting bolt upright among the throng of children circled around a dancing shaman.

The office was quiet. Kampo was swinging her legs lazily and reading the letter with one finger placed over each line. 'If I were you I would never have come back,' she said, looking up at me. 'People always say you must return to your hometown as if it's the law. Why should anyone want to return to this place? To do what?'

Orin looked at me but didn't say anything. During the years that I had been away Orin had been the one person who had sent me letters regularly reminding me of life in the hills. I had travelled a bit, not half as much as Umsi, but enough to provoke Kampo's interest. Europe! She had cried. I would love to go to Europe! But I had found Europe flat and dull. Of course there were some splendid sights and beautiful architecture, but the overall impression was monochrome with images of browns and greys, cold, hardship, and discipline. In the hills everything was different. It was tumultuous, green and humming with expectation as if a tiger would cross the road or a thundershower would wake you in the middle of the night to see a herd of wild elephants sheltering silently right outside the window.

Now I wondered what I had learned, if anything. 'You've learnt so many things,' said Orin. 'You're okay. Be patient.'

'Nothing to be but that!'

Orin laughed and pulled up his chair close to the

computer. I looked at him. Words, more words. Do they change anything?

'Well, look at this letter,' Orin replied. 'It's compelling enough, isn't it?' He squinted and bent closer to the computer screen, 'It's like travelling, this journey of words,' he said. 'The things I once wrote about have no more relevance, like my paintings. This is how things pass from us. Once it was all that mattered—the colour, the story, the words, the meaning. So maybe writing is life, and a part of that life is now changed, just like the chapters of our lives. But I'm just a hack, okay.' He held up his hands. 'We don't know what destiny is until it finds us.'

'Phone, your phone,' said Kampo. My phone was ringing. It was Umsi saying she was back in the house from my great uncle Lipun's place. She was ringing to remind us. I had almost forgotten my promise to help with a dinner hosted by Lutor at his old mentor's place. There were issues to discuss and he needed Lipun's opinion. Umsi had done the shopping and cooking but she was making her escape before the arrival of guests, saying, 'I'll leave it to you now. It's a political meeting!'

'Come on,' I said, turning to Kampo and grabbing my bag. It was already quite late.

Orin stood up. 'Good luck,' he said. 'You've got your work cut out.'

Centre-state

Lipun stood by the gate and stared down the road. A low, swirling mist hid the houses and curled around the lamp posts lighting the street in a sad, fading glow. A car swept up but did not stop. He leaned a little on his stick and craned his neck. Another light was approaching, no, it took the turn into the market.

So much for Lutor and his group, I thought. Kampo and I were watching from the kitchen and wanted Lipun to come inside but he continued to stand there facing oncoming traffic. He was the same silent, eagle-faced man who had climbed mountains and marched into unknown valleys to open up the land, and I felt a little ache watching him, thinking how he might be feeling like an outsider now. Lipun was in his seventy-ninth year. A few years ago any car would have stopped, windows would have been hurriedly rolled down or the door flung open for a friend to clamber out with a jovial greeting. Not now. Times had changed. The road sloped right down to the highway linking the market and the fire station to the centre of the town, and there was plenty of traffic but they drove past without slowing down to look at an old man standing by the road.

Another flash of light beamed up the road. I saw Lipun shade his eyes against the light and step back. It was them.

He began walking back towards the house swinging his stick.

'Hello there!' I heard Lutor's voice.

'Go ahead,' Lipun waved them on and walked back again to shut the gate.

They were all there, alighting in the porch. A black dog had appeared silently and was getting in the way wagging its tail and jumping up on Lutor and Rudar.

'Welcome, welcome!' Lipun cried, hurrying forward to usher them in. 'Hey, Dilip, where are you?'

Dilip emerged with a wide smile. 'Ar-ey, migom, ar-ey!' was all he could say. He was Lipun's helper from the time Lipun and Nefa had moved to Itanagar, and he had stayed on and never returned to his birthplace in Assam. His wife and children lived in the compound and helped with the housework and the maintenance of the house.

'Hut, hato,' Dilip was now pushing the dog away and bending to lift the bags of rice and oranges that Lutor had brought for Lipun from Pasighat. 'Ah hah, how cold it is,' he said. 'What will you eat?'

'Let them get in first, Dilip, will you?' said Lipun.

In the kitchen, Dilip's wife was beaming with happiness. She was too shy to go out. I looked around and saw the familiar tins and pots and pans still in use. The wall over the stove was dark with cooking stains and the kettle was already spitting steam, making the gas flame hiss and turn blue.

I heard another car pull up. A man got out and the car drove round the back, Dilip showing him where to park.

'It must be Aohun,' said Lutor.

'Is he the party president?' Kampo whispered.

'Yes, he is.'

'Gosh! Isn't it exciting?' Kampo began to walk on tiptoe in the kitchen. A broad, thick-set man wearing a long coat came in hurriedly, blowing onto his hands and rubbing his cheeks.

'Hello, is everybody here?' he said.

'Yes, come in, come in.' A fire was going in the sitting room and Lipun was already settled in his old chair.

'The people are baying for my blood. They are calling me Hitler now,' said Aohun without preamble. His flat, good-natured face was screwed up in disgust. The government was threatening to break up. More than this, he had become the target of Tanik's wrath and his days were numbered.

'This is because of the Bill?'

'Yes. A-P-COCO, COCA. Someone's put Tanik up to it. I must say I think it would be good if we can push this through, but now it's called the Black Act and I get the blame. You know we are poised for a fall. They are comparing us to Stalin and Hitler and Saddam Hussein!'

Rudar was pulling papers out of a briefcase and Lipun bent close to look at them wearing his thick reading glasses. *'The Arunachal Pradesh Control of Organised Crime Ordinance (APCOCO)...'* He read, *'to fight nefarious, anti-social and anti-national activities of terrorist outfits and organised crime syndicates or gangs operating in the state.'*

'That's a big thing, "Organised Crime Syndicates,"' he said.

'That's the worst thing,' said Aohun. 'Underground organisations are sprouting like mushrooms. Our youth are being lured by established terrorist outfits. Look at the list. Arunachal Dragon Force, Tiger Force, People's Volunteer Force—there are so many of them, United Socialist Council of Arunachal Pradesh, the United Liberation Movement for

Arunachal (ULMA)—so many revolutionary organisations!'

'You knew this was happening all along,' said Lutor.

'Yes, but you know Tanik. It's his response to the imminent enquiry about receiving finance from militants to return to power. The Ordinance is an eye-wash, to fool the public. But you know what? I have a plan, if only we can play straight. How about beating him at his own game and throwing out the ultra elements in our state at the same time?'

Lutor was remembering what Kellan had told him about how things were getting out of hand and how the government needed to take strong action or else it will be too late. How is it, he now wondered, that suddenly all the talk was about militant organisations and separatist demands. Only now? If only the state police could gear up and take action. If only someone could have realised the growing alienation that was going to affect public peace. Look at the widening gap between the people and the leaders. Look at the politicians, so affluent and heedless of the signs! On the other hand, the way things were now, how could the government remain a silent spectator? The state needed strong action, yes, but he was afraid of misuse of an Act like APCOCA.

'It's worth a try. It's worth a try. I tell you it will have a psychological impact,' Aohun insisted. 'We need special provisions. As an Act APCOCA is more suitable to our needs than the Prevention of Terrorism Act since what we're dealing with here is not listed in the schedule of POTA. The Act will be a deterrent. We are talking about *prevention.* We're talking about the ground rules of the ongoing peace talks.'

He was rubbing his hands and holding them up to

show how many letters had been sent to the PMO and the Home Ministry and the Defence Ministry appealing for help to *prevent*, Aohun stressed the word again, militant activity, but there had been no response—only one-liners acknowledging receipt, he said, or a line to say the matter is being looked into. 'What can I do, huh? I am in a no-win situation. If I push for legislation of this Bill the Tirap legislators will be up in arms. Why? Because the militants will tell them to do so! If I don't, I will be seen as weak and wavering and the place will be overrun.'

It was a point to consider. Everyone sitting in the room knew that the troubles were not confined to a few districts. All along the border with Assam politicians were paying various organisations not to threaten their business operations. In the worst-hit districts groups of militants armed with sophisticated weapons roamed the villages and rounded up men and children at gunpoint. People were taken captive in broad daylight, never to be seen again. In another case a villager had been marched off in the middle of the afternoon by a group of armed men. He returned to his village after three days but said he could not identify his abductors since his eyes were bandaged.

'How much can one man do?' Nabam Tunar had come in after Aohun. He looked like a studious schoolboy with his diminutive build and round glasses, but when he spoke no one could doubt his ringing sincerity. 'In our hearts we know that now everything is changed. The taste of money has changed everything. Rivalry and ego, and blood feuds—it was there before too, of course, but now the rivalry is in the political arena and that affects us all. It's worse because the stakes are higher. Easy money has ruined us. We have lost our value system.'

'What about Army operations in Tirap. Is there something planned?' asked Lutor.

There was a silence. Aohun took a deep breath and lowered his voice. Yes, something was under consideration…there had been meetings with the military and the joint secretary in-charge of North-East…Aohun fidgeted and coughed and then said, 'I think we have the go-ahead for Operation Flashpoint, to flush out militants, yes. I know there will be flak. But the Centre is pushing us into a scenario so familiar in the North-East. Wait, wait, negotiate, until everything goes haywire and they have to send in the armed forces. They're saying it's a sinking ship and everyone wants to abandon ship. At the moment we are waiting for additional paramilitary and then we can launch Flashpoint—maybe, huh, I'm saying *maybe*.' Aohun was rubbing his face with his hands and stretching his cheeks back, looking at Lutor.

No one said a word.

'I cannot understand the Centre's attitude,' said Aohun at last. 'How many meetings have we attended? How many civil-military liaison and security co-ordination meetings with secretary this, and secretary that, government of India. What comes of these meetings? It's all tokenism. We are ushered in and ushered out! Aargh!' Aohun leaned back and began rubbing his forehead hard again with angry, impatient movements.

It was true, what Aohun was saying. Everyone rushed to Delhi at the drop of a hat, it had become that easy, but in the end one was left with a feeling of not having communicated with each other. Lutor had experienced many such meetings. The region seemed to merit attention because of conflict in the area. It was the China factor, the Myanmarese border,

Nagaland, Manipur, Assam. Yet there must be something more, he thought. A worm of doubt was gnawing inside his head. Surely we have something to offer to New Delhi. We have given something in the past; something of the land, a piece of history to add to a wider map.

'They think Arunachal is the soft target they can bargain away in the interests of peace in the region,' he said at last.

'Who knows what they are negotiating. Everything is decided based on an assumption of what will be good for us. It is non-inclusive; it's a security issue,' said Aohun.

There it was. Aohun had said it. A security issue. It was a question that had always bothered Lutor. He remembered the recent incident that had almost resulted in friendly fire casualties between security forces hunting terrorists just because it was a security issue so wrapped up in secrecy that the right hand didn't know what the left was doing. In a group, sitting together like this, it was easy to talk about the terror of villagers and say that the best way to deal with this was to go all out and take the place by storm. But the public of Tirap were protesting. Was it a protest of the people? The bitter rivalry that everyone spoke about between Tirap politicians seemed a lie when all the elected representatives functioned collectively. Everything they said came in long letters signed by hundreds of names behind them, but they were faceless, voiceless signatures. Not a single individual had come forward to say anything about influence of insurgent groups in the state's political affairs. Was there no personal opinion? Only Kellan had come to Pasighat and told him that Rasa, their parliamentary candidate in Tirap, wanted to meet him. Maybe Rasa wanted to say something. But so far it was all 'public opinion,' a collection of opinions. Who influences this? Who shapes public opinion?

'Now it is down to us,' Aohun was saying. 'Tell me, what can we do? How can we clear this up? My opinion is that we must achieve a decisive victory with one push. Only after that will people resist militant activity.' Aohun leaned back, still rubbing his head hard. 'Perhaps we won't need Operation Flashpoint if the Act works as a deterrent. It would be easier to act in a group, sharing information so that we don't feel helpless and isolated, but how, in this climate of fear?'

The territories of thought

I overheard bits of the conversation and saw Lipun gazing intently at the fire with compressed lips. He was listening to the men but not saying anything. How far they had moved away from the frontier days!

He knew questioning history was a complex thing. History offered random answers. The people who know are silent. The ones in the forefront are the politicians. They are not truly representative, but they rule the roost. A new administrative set-up was in place and gone were the days of district postings and long tours. Now everything was concentrated in the state capital. The present was a rush of feeling, an unpredictable momentum of time flying by with a random gathering of events and actions, teetering between the vehemence of the past and the longing for the future.

His right hand clutched his walking stick at a slant and he leaned on it slightly as if he was awaiting the arrival of someone—an apparition or a beloved ghost to emerge out of the quiet evening.

It was in this house that he and Nefa had lived together, settling into the growing town. Lipun was a regular officegoer and Nefa stayed at home planting trees and starting a kitchen garden with cabbages, beans and lemons along with begonias and clumps of anthurium and jungle ferns. When villagers appeared at Lipun's doorstep he shouted with joy. 'Migom! Yes, Jai Hind! Jai Hind!' These were the people he had welcomed most. They brought gifts of roosters trapped in tight bamboo baskets and sat in the veranda wearing cane hats and carrying spears and daos. People stared. What was going on in Lipun's house? Some thought he was going way beyond the call of duty letting villagers take over his official residence like that. In reply, Lutor and his friends had constructed an outhouse, just like a village longhouse complete with a central fireplace and drying rack for Lipun's village guests. I had seen the villagers when my mother had taken me to visit the place. 'She's my great-niece. She's going to school,' Lipun had said with pride. And they had clapped their hands and smiled at me. Lutor was a constant presence and in those days I had thought that he lived in the same house. He lives in Pasighat, my mother told me. She also said that Lipun's wife, Nefa, would have been the first woman graduate of the state if old Dinu had not fallen off that bridge and if Lipun had not set eyes on her then, when she was recalled to help look after her father.

My recollection of Nefa was of a pale, solitary woman with expressive eyes languishing in the hot summer afternoons saying the town was dull. Perhaps she had not been happy. Something was lacking, but what I recalled now was my mother's resentment at Nefa's sudden outbursts that became more frequent as the years passed. She scoffed at official dinners and stayed away, sending Lipun alone. Sometimes Lipun might have wondered if he had not forced the old couple Dinu and his wife to give their daughter's hand in marriage too early. Everything had happened so fast. He thought Nefa was sensitive about their age difference and he would return hurriedly, smiling and ready to relate anecdotes but Nefa would be lackadaisical and he soon stopped going to these parties. He buried himself in work and brought home enough files to line the narrow passage at the side of their bedroom. Visitors stopped coming and Lipun's relations with his beloved villagers became strained. Nefa did not mingle easily and the kind of people Lipun loved to talk with seemed to be in awe of her. 'Everyone is only after making money,' Nefa used to say. 'The place is filling up with strangers and half breeds. You are somebody only if you have money.' And my mother had never understood if this was said in derision for the settlers who were turning into shrewd business-minded people, or if Nefa wanted Lipun to become more acquisitive. Lipun could not change. He was twenty years older than Nefa and I heard my mother tell relatives that her heart winced when Nefa served dinner silently and Lipun said, looking around with a tentative smile, that eating good food in one's home was indeed a blessing. The house became a silent, uncomfortable place. Lipun huddled quietly in his old seat and read books, afraid all the time that Nefa was bored, but unable to do anything about it.

It was only when I announced that I was going to study in Delhi that Lipun bestirred himself and said No! He told my mother I should study in Shillong. It was good enough and there was no need for me to aim for Delhi. Suddenly Nefa had intervened.

'Let her go,' she said to her husband. 'Umsi is there.'

'Umsi eloped!' Lipun shouted back.

Nefa was startled at Lipun's outburst. 'Umsi is a good, responsible woman. She is married and leading a respectable life. What is wrong with you?'

'Nothing is wrong with me. How can Maying go to Delhi?'

'You travelled all over the state dragging us with you. Why can't she travel to Delhi?'

'She's a girl!'

Nefa had burst into a peal of laughter. That was what was bothering her. Lipun was afraid! It gave her a certain pleasure now to see that he was having more trouble than her in coping with change. If women wanted education, well and good! He would never say no to education, but he would say where and how they got it. He quoted his own lines repeated so many times to so many tribes: *the hills are safe for us,* but Nefa knew nowhere was completely safe. She had chosen to marry this strange, reclusive man and she had stayed, there was nothing for her beyond the house, and at this moment she saw through Lipun's defence and even felt a little pity for him for demonstrating his concern in this churlish manner.

She spoke to Lutor, 'Say you will escort Maying,' she pleaded. 'Lipun trusts you. See if you can convince him.'

Lutor had winced. He was afraid of the city, but he was afraid because Umsi lived there. What if they met again, he had asked himself many times, but he could not refuse Nefa. That was how Lutor became my guardian who escorted me through the streets of the city with the heat of the desert burning down on our heads as we moved through the University campus.

Lutor did not see Umsi, he did not know where she lived; and at the time I had no sense of how he might have suffered on that trip as he watched me filling in forms and doing everything in what, I hoped, looked like I had been planning this all my life. He must have secretly hoped to bump into Umsi and been cursing her for being giddy, selfish, ignorant, when he failed to meet her. We had one lunch outing together when he ordered a lot of food saying, 'Come eat, eat,' while he tucked into a full thali saying how hot the weather was and that he would never visit Delhi again.

When Nefa died, Lipun, who had always been a taciturn man, clammed up completely. He went away on long tours and returned without a word to say about the places he had been to. By and by my mother and even Lutor ceased to share that tenuous relationship that could be identified as filial or fatherly, and I had seen him barely more than a dozen times in the intervening years since Nefa's death.

And now here I was, looking again at everything with new eyes. I could hear Aohun talking and Lutor's deep voice saying something in reply. Kampo was lying still as a log watching TV in the old bedroom. I saw the rug, the small stool, the mantelpiece with its flaking plaster covered with old newspapers. Things, objects, trees and shrubs were moved around sometimes but some people, some things, never changed nor moved away. A small patio grimy with moss and sprouting grass opened out from the room onto a slope full of fruit trees. I stepped out and paced up and down. A new emotion was stealing over me. A lean, spare feeling like a road stretching straight and level into the distance with an old tree standing here and there, sturdy and self-contained. Everything recedes, I thought. Childhood, adolescence—whatever shaped us, killed us or shielded us has become unimportant. It does not matter. Now is as it is, perfect and complete like this to simply be in the moment with the night wind on my face, and small-town sounds all around me—the lumbering echo of a lorry, a dog's bark, gecko murmuring sounds.

Kampo turned briefly, saying, 'What are the honourables going on about?' and answered her own question with, 'The same old thing, I guess.'

'What are you two up to?' It was Rudar peeping in. 'Maybe uh, if dinner is ready?' He beamed a smile at me.

'Of course!' Kampo jumped up. 'We were waiting for you gentlemen,' she said.

'Whoa,' said Rudar, rubbing his hands in anticipation. 'Dilip! Dilip! What have you made?' The kitchen was choc-a-bloc with pots and pans.

'All boil,' said Dilip. 'Siang fish, beans, mixed vegetable boil.'

'Aaah…' said Rudar, eyeing the steaming rice being scooped out of a big pot. There was a big bowl of fruit—papaya and melon sprinkled with red cherries, and a full plate of golden crumbed fish cutlets was already laid out. 'This must be Umsi's preparation,' said Rudar, pinching a cutlet in half to taste, and smiling at me with one eye shut. Rudar's positive manner was making me feel quite happy too. I think we both wished for something to happen between Lutor and Umsi again. Rudar was Lutor's closest friend, and as for me, maybe it was just my addiction to love stories and happy endings.

'Come on, folks, we are ready to eat!' Kampo called out like a bird laughing at Rudar's presence in the kitchen.

In the sitting room the men raised themselves as if from a stupor. The house was filled with the fumes of wood smoke and Lipun's rolled cigarettes. It was so warm and cosy sitting by the fire that Lutor wished the food could be fed to him in mouthfuls while he lolled in his seat. 'Now I know it's true,' he said, 'about those emperors eating bunches of grapes from reclining positions. I always thought it was only for effect!'

'Come on!' Aohun said, carrying his glass of whisky to the table. 'In today's world no one will feed you like that.'

Lipun stood back for a moment and looked at them.

After Nefa's death he had pondered his fate deeply and wished he could have died, but look, he was still alive. My mother and Gagil had rallied to be with him, filling the house with their presence. But it was his work, they said, his habit of seeing a project through that had kept him afloat. He had struggled on and attended every official meeting in different parts of the country. He had been feted as a senior local officer who knew the pulse of the people but Lipun, while submitting carefully prepared notes, remained withdrawn. He nodded as if he was tired of talking. The nature of administration had changed since the old frontier service had been replaced by a new administrative cadre. Lipun was not one to stand in the way of change. As a government officer he had preached change and development all his life. But here was the thing; without love for the people, he said, the administration was meaningless.

Times had changed, but what now? The town was in the grip of election fever and it seemed everyone in the house tonight was eager to support Lutor. It was a wonderful camaraderie. Perhaps he was looking at the last batch of authentic politicians from different parts of the state who were working together. But there was one worrying factor that he could sense. He could feel an undercurrent of divisive force that was breaking up the state slowly but surely into different factions. It had to do with change and aspiration. 'We want change for a better future,' people might clamour, but Lipun knew that change, when it came, came on its own terms. It was a mighty force, unpredictable as a rushing current ushering in dignity and awareness in a society, or a whirlpool leading to discontent and strife. Did Lutor know this, he wondered. Lutor had one foot in the past and he could not quite break away from the time when men like Dinu and Tanmut had worked with painstaking slowness to build a small bridge, a school, install a new tap, a few lights into some homes so that children could study. Read and write! Now it was about catching up. The hard-won foundations for pan-Arunachal unity and development were tossed aside and everything was about quick solutions.

He lit another rolled cigarette and inhaled deeply. What now?

'Hey, no more smoking. You must eat,' said Lutor.

Lipun nodded and came in. Aohun rushed to hand him a plate. Lipun was not a sentimental man. In the past it was an unnecessary luxury. Even now it was unnecessary, but now he smiled at us so happily that we almost broke into applause for his very presence. Dilip fetched more food. Kampo served. Everyone talked politics and governance and I stood by, looking on. If Lutor had walked with him, I was the one holding Lipun's notebooks and I had followed that slanting hand as if I too were living in a specialised or imagined version of a land that we had moved far away from.

There was Rudar and Lutor, and Aohun. And there was Tunar and others like them all across the state from Tawang to Tirap, Anini, Subansiri, Lohit, Itanagar, Pasighat. Lipun had known them all. He knew their relatives and he knew their hometowns. And he knew Lutor, like a beloved son to him. Lutor, the hawk-faced boy who had climbed mountains with him. Brave boy! There he was, sitting there, waiting for him, and I knew that even now, as if it were yesterday, with all his heart, he wished the boy success.

Something about cake

In April, the days are lustrous with light. Itanagar is a city of mixed and variable temperatures and vegetation with hot, steamy summers suddenly turning to cold, chilly weather the moment it rains. Pine trees thrive alongside bamboo and cane, and many sector link roads remain covered with wild creepers. Through the window Umsi caught a glimpse of something. A white butterfly was flying very high, lifted by the wind right up to where the tall branches of the trees were bending and swooning in the delicious breeze. The whole of life passes before us like this, she thought, without anyone knowing what we are feeling. It is no big deal, yet the desire to live exerts itself. To live! To love!

There were other murmurs she heard mingled with the twittering of birds and a delivery van making a racket in the neighbourhood. Itanagar was new to her. When she had left, it was but a rainy town with a bare, scarecrow appearance of half-finished buildings, pot-holed roads and a slushy market oozing drainwater and garbage. Now a whole generation of people she had grown up with lived in the capital. They complained that there was never enough time to meet friends, no time for quiet dinners like in the old days, it was continuous urban stress, but all the same they stayed on, just like Lutor and his politician friends stayed on, because Itanagar was the capital and the power centre of the state. Thank god we were never a political family, she mused. No burra khannas, no politicians to kowtow to and no favours to ask of anybody. When she had left there had been nothing else except the desire to go on a journey as if moving out was as natural and desirable as breath. One image—coastlines, contours, life. Before her was spread the 'bright colours of the atlas,' and that was it.

She said she had forgotten Lutor but it was not true. He had always been there somewhere at the back of her mind like a roaming ghost. 'Don't go away, stay near me!' She had never forgotten those words. When you make someone unhappy it stays with you forever. No matter how late, how remote the memory or with what gestures you try to erase it, with what gauze you bind it, suddenly, after many years and even up to the end of life it will come before you again—that unforgettable voice, the frightened smile, the unanswerable question: 'Why did you leave me?' Maybe Lutor had thought a car would stop by his house. Maybe he had waited, imagining her stepping out of a taxi, calling for help with her luggage. Was she really gone? Why? Why! How could anyone dare to shake the universe, inflict such injury, disappear? And for such a person what would the punishment be?

A wave of sadness seized her. Dwindling images with voice and expression so long hidden were appearing again, fresh and dazzling, when least expected. Once, only once, had she picked up the phone to answer his call.

'At last!' he said immediately in his loud, booming voice. 'What's wrong with your phone?'

She compressed her lips. 'I didn't hear it ring.'

'Throw it away,' he laughed. It was a sign of nervousness

but she was annoyed. Why could he never show some sense and tenderness, be a little more suave, romantic? 'I was wondering if I could visit you one day if it's alright with you?' he said. She laughed uncomfortably and he thought she was being snobbish. She is happy with someone else, he thought, with a sinking heart. He waited.

'I think we should give each other a break. We can always meet later,' she said.

'Later, when?' He sounded hurt but he was bluffing his way. 'OK then,' he had said gruffly. That was the last time she had spoken to him, hiding in her heart the words of a woman who had looked at her hand and made a prediction.

What is it? Umsi had asked.

You will travel a lot, said the woman.

Really?

Yes. You will be gone for a long time.

How long?

I don't know. But it will be many years.

Seventeen years. She had been away seventeen years!

That evening, Lutor drove slowly through the town, taking in everything as if he was seeing it all for the first time. Aohun's words were still there, ringing faintly in his head reminding him that time was passing, but right now it was something he wanted to push out of his mind as he steered his car carefully towards the centre of town.

He was on his way to meet Umsi. There was a rush of traffic and in his happiness he was elated to discover that Itanagar had changed so much. He saw cyber cafes and new bakeries with shining glass fronts that he had never seen before. The town had grown without his noticing anything. His house was still set apart from the town centre beyond the police headquarters, but the vicinity of the college meant new shops, restaurants, a cluster of tailors and paan shops and big hoardings advertising Student Homes and Digital World. The narrow, broken highway had turned into a lively, vivid street with motorcycles zig-zagging their way through the stream of cars. As usual he was stuck in traffic by the hotel PYBSS and the BB Plaza. The number of automobiles in the capital seemed to multiply in a matter of months but today this gave him more time to calm his nerves as he slowly inched his way towards the other end of town.

The place was a small brick cottage set in a square plot of land surrounded by trees. The tin roof was painted green and the building was not visible from the road because of a bamboo fence overgrown with flowering creepers that had never been trimmed back. Lutor drove in and around, past the bed of anthurium and giant ferns and turned into the small porch that faced the western hills. A young girl opened the door even before he had pressed the bell and urged him to come in, saying one of the 'madams' was in. Lutor wanted to turn around and flee. He wished that he had not come alone. It would have been much better if Rudar or Kamin had been with him. He was aghast that he had been so careless and in such a hurry to get here that he had quite forgotten all about being circumspect. It was too late. He was seated on a blue sofa and left to gaze distractedly at the collection of small ornamental boxes grouped together on the glass table. He heard the clink of cutlery, tap water, someone's footsteps, a breath of wind, and suddenly Umsi was there looking at him with an indescribable smile.

'Hello, you made it,' she said.

Lutor jumped up. He knocked against the table and reminded himself to be careful here. It would take all his self control and presence of mind to survive this meeting and come out of it with dignity, and who knew, new esteem for him in her eyes.

How are you, he replied. He quickly saw that she was looking pale, as if she had dusted herself with translucent powder, but he knew this was a trick of her complexion. Like magnolia, he remembered. She was wearing a light pink woollen scarf wound around her neck and a long printed skirt dotted with brown and pink flowers. The whole effect was quiet and simple and Lutor was torn between excitement and despair when he looked at her. After so many years here she was again, older, sweeter, and dearer to him now, he felt, than she had ever been!

'Should we have some tea?'

'Yes. Why not?' He wished he had not said the last two words. It sounded cavalier and flippant. I must tread carefully, he reminded himself again, and studied his hands, so useless, so awkward, hanging there unable to do anything except clutch his knees. The young girl chose to come in at this moment with a tray of tea things, two cups, and a plate of cake. Umsi swept aside the ornamental boxes and placed the tray on the table. She leaned forward and asked him if he wanted sugar, milk.

Yes, yes, he nodded obediently.

An image rose before him again. Umsi, his beautiful, laughing, madcap Umsi, and now this fragile, grown-up woman who still filled him with such tenderness and astonishment that he thought he would die if she even let him talk to her again.

'What is the matter?' she said.

'What!' The cup clattered in his hand. 'Oh, nothing, nothing! I was just thinking…'

'Oh,' she said, calm as ever. 'I thought you were looking uncomfortable.'

'No, no!' His heart was thumping. Lutor was not one to be easily made uncomfortable and he coughed.

'The tea is too hot,' he said uselessly. In the old days she might have snapped a reply: then let it cool down! But now she ignored his remark. He frowned and told himself not to act stupid when she bent closer with the plate of cake.

'Wow, did you make this?' The words were finding their own way. He lifted a piece and yelped when it crumbled in his hand and a big piece fell to the floor. Umsi put the plate down. 'I'll get a napkin,' she said.

'No, no, here, let me…' Lutor struggled to help but the young girl had appeared again like a flashing pixie with a big smile on her face. There! Lutor was trying to bend down but he was holding the cup of tea and his other hand still held the remnant of cake so he sat rigid while the girl dusted the crumbs off and, still smiling, ran off into the kitchen. He popped the piece into his mouth hoping he didn't look stupid while eating. He crunched on a piece of walnut. It was delicious! Slowly the thought stole into his head that maybe Umsi had made this cake in honour of his visit. Ah! She remembered he loved sweets, not the dry, sugary barfis but the syrupy gulab jamuns and jalebis. So, she remembered! And though he had turned his nose up at cake and fancy western confectionary Umsi had thrilled him one day with a chocolate walnut cake and he had eaten half of it in one gulp. This was it! Maybe it was walnut crumble cake! He felt rejuvenated and leaned back a bit now feeling more relaxed and ready to be plain and honest.

At last he said the words, 'I was very disappointed when you left.' She was silent. 'Why did you leave?'

'Leave this place, or leave you?' she asked.

'You know what I mean, Umsi.' He had uttered her name and it was like a sweet pain, as if he had crossed over into something that had been forbidden him forever.

'I don't know,' she said. 'It happened.' Long silence… 'Would you like some more cake?'

'No, yes, okay.' How could he eat with thousands of words struggling to get out? He sipped his tea. Ah, it really was hot and burned his tongue. He felt hurt when he saw Umsi watching him with her hand against her mouth, palm outward, laughing. Laughing! Look at her, sitting there and playing the hostess. Did she have no memory of anything?

'You never tried to find me,' she said suddenly.

He stared at her. 'But I did. Even until yesterday I was trying to find you.'

'Would you have recognised me? In a crowd, I mean, on the streets, somewhere?'

He considered this. 'Maybe not in a crowd, but close-up, yes. I would recognise your eyes.'

She tilted her head back in a pensive manner.

'Come closer,' he said.

She rose obediently and sat by him. He took her hand and she let him. Time stopped, or flowed very gently and Lutor was unaware of everything around him. He was oblivious to the house, the voice of the girl calling to someone, the room they were in, the green shrubs shining outside in the golden light. Ah, the last light of summer always reminds me of you! How many times had he repeated this to himself until he thought he was going mad! Now they were sitting together and facing one another as if seeing each other for the first time.

He said the first thing that came to his head. 'You should come back and live here.'

She made a face. There was a long silence. 'I am back,' she said at last. She spread the fingers of her other hand on her lap. He clasped both her hands and held them up to his face pressing his head into her palms. She did not move away. She moved closer and opened her hands to touch his cheek. He pulled her arms up around him and embraced her. They were silent like two figures in a painting. How many years had they struggled to reach this moment! For Lutor nothing mattered now. The lost years, the years of pain and waste rolled away as though they had never been. Perhaps we will never catch up, we will never find that lost time again but what does it matter now, he thought. Everything had been moving towards this one moment, and when Umsi nestled her head against his heart, his heart said how many years, how many years! Who cared? One moment equals a lifetime.

Lutor learned that Umsi had moved into a separate apartment in Delhi more than a year ago. He had heard rumours about this, that Umsi and her husband were living apart, but who could tell about these things? Now he heard her saying, 'Oh we are friends. He visits and we are in touch, but we have our separate lives.' They had a teenaged daughter in college in Delhi.

It gave Lutor a strange feeling to imagine Umsi as mother of a college-going daughter. 'Does she look like you?'

'I don't know. You can see for yourself, next time you are in Delhi,' she said. This frightened Lutor. To meet Umsi's daughter! He remembered his lost son and his estranged wife. His son would have been about the same age, if he had lived. He remembered his wife shouting at him, 'Get away from me. You don't know the meaning of love!' He had remained silent then. Maybe he was unfit for love. Everything he loved had been taken away from him. Yet at the time he remembered thinking that he knew more about love than anyone else could. Now he realised that everyone felt exactly this way. How strange it was! Such intricacies, such strands interwoven and braided together as if every life and every story was connected by some loss, some similar sorrow, some complex point and turn of events that was always generated by a search for love.

Umsi said that she wanted to spend more time in Arunachal. The family home in Pasighat was still there, and some small property of her late mother was being looked after by relatives. 'There are so many loose ends,' she said simply. 'I need to tidy things up a bit and help Kellan because he is stuck in his Tirap posting and my sister-in-law is busy with politics.' In fact, she said, she was taking Kellan's son with her to Delhi where he could join the same school where her daughter had studied. 'We can start like this,' she said. 'Families should know each other and it will be good for both of them. Maybe I can also look after some ariks—agricultural fields,' she finished, laughing.

Lutor was wonderstruck. His beautiful Umsi was speaking to him like a family member and telling him all these things. His heart responded immediately to this Umsi, a new, simple, comfortable Umsi.

The evening waned and he lost all sense of time. If there were periods of silence in between he did not try to prevent them. If you had not gone away we would have been together like this, he wanted to say, but he was comfortable and assured.

It was in this mood of silent reverie that Kampo and I found them when we returned, looking more like the settled houseowners than I felt I could ever be. The young girl rushed out to grab the shopping bags. Kampo said, 'Oh hi there!' without stopping on her way to the kitchen and I was quick to announce that I would need Umsi's help to set up house properly now that I could be sure of more visitors.

Lutor looked up now and said, 'Yes, um…if it's okay with you we could meet here sometimes for discussions. Aohun mentioned this, you know…Going to Lipun's house is conspicuous. It's also not fair to the old man. It puts him on the spot. Too many spies around.'

'What! You want a safe house! But here too, it's not safe,' said Umsi, turning to me. 'Everyone has their own work to do. Who wants a bunch of politicians hanging around in the house?'

'Oh no, I don't mind. There's nothing to hide,' I was quick to reply, still in that mood where I wanted to be part of something. 'But I'll have to get some more stuff, like pots and pans and what not.'

'We'll work it out,' Lutor said.

Umsi stayed a week and then announced that she had to go back to Delhi. Lutor sent his car around with Orin and we all drove down to Naharlagun to see Umsi off at the helipad for the flight to Guwahati. The day was bright and I felt happy looking at the green hills. I saw Umsi's face turned towards the light and I felt sure she would be returning. Who could resist such beauty, such pristine surroundings? In the back seat I tried to talk to Kellan's son who was going to Delhi with Umsi. He clutched a big book and was reciting *Arunachal Pradesh is eight-three-seven four-zero-three square kilometres in area. The capital is called I-ta-na-gar…*

'How big?'

'What?'

'The area,' I said.

'I already said that,' the boy answered, squinting at me with his small, pointed face with the crew cut hair and the new white T-shirt.

'Wait till you see the helicopter,' said Orin, but the little boy was not talking anymore. Instead, he was running his small hand up and down on the glass pane. Maybe he is angry that he is leaving his parents, I thought. Kellan had told him that he would be coming but had been unable to get away at the last moment. 'Take good care. I will see you soon,' was all he had said on the phone. The boy's mother had left everything to Umsi. 'I know you will look after him. We'll all come to Delhi soon, don't worry.' Umsi had laughed because she knew how Mentiri was a political animal at heart and that she loved the bustle and chaos of electioneering. 'I am campaigning for Lutor. I am working for Kellan to get him a new posting,' she cried. 'Why is he absent all the time?'

The trees

In Khonsa, Tirap district, Kellan walked down the main street every day and saw the tattered banners hanging over the tri-junction in the centre of town. At the height of the mass movement for a separate Union Territory for the two districts, banners and posters with slogans had been plastered on every tree and shop front by NSCN activists. The police had torn them down but scraps of cloth still clung to the high electric posts and he knew the words by heart.

Lot of water has gone down for last 20 years...Our motto is to attain UT for better life in future generation. We want peace talk. All misleading words, he thought. What peace? What peace talks, and between whom? Nothing had come of it except a deadly silence and apostolic letters still circulating in the town like a hideous joke. He stopped at the paan gumti to light a cigarette, buy matches, hail some passerby. It was a way for watching any suspicious movement, maybe someone was following him, but so far he could not detect anything to cause him alarm. He reached his office and slowly climbed the front steps wondering at the growth of shrubs that threatened to cover the place. The Forest office was an old building, half concrete, half mud and wattle plastered with white paint, and a tin roof that had turned brown with the constant rain. The old peons grouped together and boiled tea in an old saucepan. They served him black tea in a small glass. Sipping tea was a way of passing time. The departmental heads came and went, once in a year maybe, a ministerial visit made everyone sit up and feel important, but that was the sum total of government work. For the rest of the time everyone was away on tour or medical leave except for the old woman who shuffled around and sometimes carried in thin files, pretending to be busy. Everyday Kellan saw her knitting and sunning herself in the hilly slope at the back. Perhaps, like him, she had nowhere to go. It rained a lot here. Shops downed their shutters early and the rain was like a screen that drenched the town and kept people indoors. There was little traffic except for motorbikes that roared up and down the muddy streets bumping over stones and chipped cement. They were the in-thing now, these gleaming black machines carrying riders bent low over the metal body as if to escape the wind or maybe it was just a way of hiding their faces.

Kellan peered out of the window holding his glass of tea. A gust of cold air blew in and he caught a glimpse of a tall man striding down the road dressed in a monk's yellow robes. Who was that? Suddenly there were so many strangers in town. He got up to push the other half of the window open—here every window was protected by iron bars, but by the time he could fling open the cracked panes there was nothing to see except the rutted road puddled with rain.

He thought about his recent meeting with Lutor. It had been a great meeting, going to Pasighat and seeing his friend Lutor of the old days—shouting by the river and challenging his gang to watch him dive in into that small pool in that small town. How long ago that was! From that time on he had known all of Lutor's dreams, his politics and yes, his pain when his sister Umsi had left them all suddenly and disappeared into the city.

They had parted when he had taken the job interview for its guarantee of security. His father had been a great one for a government job. Come to think of it all the old timers had had an unswerving respect for government jobs 'Nothing like it,' his old man had said. 'Take it, and you can do other things too.' At the time there was nothing else on offer and Kellan had no option but to go for it. What now? What now, he wondered. He had put off marriage for a long time but when he married Mentiri the urgency for security had grown stronger. It was a time when everyone was growing rich and his wife had said she would look after the home if his job took him elsewhere. Money was pouring into the state for countless schemes and everyone was learning the art of acquiring wealth.

'Go, go,' she had urged him even though she herself refused to accompany him and move out of the old hometown. 'Go, there's money in Tirap. Look at their timber.'

She was a practical, forthright woman with political views and she might have aided his posting to this place by her carefully planned dinner parties for key politicians, but Kellan realised that after the euphoria of his appointment he was unable to do anything that pleased his wife. He simply did not know how to make money and he did not want to have any part in the booming timber trade. Timber merchants had arrived from all over the country and they were going deep into the forest and felling trees like demented forest dwellers. They camped in makeshift huts and fell ill with malaria and cholera. Hard liquor and worms ate their guts but they did not give up. Young men left everything and went deep into the forest to look at trees. The old awe of spirits and sacred trees was quashed as they slavered, looking at these giant trees that meant Money! Money! Money! The Forest Department issued 'permits' recommended by the minister and those lucky enough to obtain a permit 'on compassionate ground' was allowed to claim five trees. But who would chop them down and haul them through miles of jungle? The easy way was to sell the permits to middle-men who were in the timber business with ministers and politicians who owned saw mills and plywood and veneer mills. Five or ten trees—who cared? There was no one around to count. The timber barons despatched a labour force armed with mallets to mark their trees. They marked hundreds of trees and devoured them with men and elephants clinking with metal chains. Their eyes turned red with fever and greed. What would they get out of all this labour? Perhaps a motorcycle, a wad of money, a new car. The heavy, inert logs tried their patience and their strength and they dragged them out crudely through the undergrowth crushing plants, leaves, roots, insects and orchids in a mangled and rotting green trail of death.

Kellan had arrived at the height of this boom. He was aghast but soon found that he was alone in his protest against the wanton destruction. He had shot at a man once for poaching and people were afraid of him, but this timber trade was unstoppable. He seized illegal timber at the railhead in Tinsukia but the timber lobby was so strong, the department so weak and in league with the big operators, he knew he was alone and fighting a losing battle. 'Take the timber, but take it properly,' he said at last. He was horrified at the stealth and greed of these men. The logs were carried away to plywood mills and more logs were choking the waterways of every small town as more and more people looked at the shining trees as a source of quick money. The forest was being scooped away. In a few years there would be nothing left except ugly stumps.

'It's employment,' said Sombang, a Tirap politician. He was a short, moustachioed man who, many people suspected, entertained militants in his house. He looked like a martial arts expert and was a close aide of political heavyweight Temat, who was known for his outspoken ways and for his bitter rivalry with Mankong of the same clan of hereditary chiefs. 'Our youth want employment. At least they are getting something now.' But even this was a lie. Kellan knew from department records that less than one percent of those employed in the timber mills were local youth. It was a business of outsiders in cahoots with a chosen few. But the big owners said, 'We want development. What are we going to do with this jungle?'

In another time Kellan might have said, 'Feel it, caress it.' He was, after all, the romantic son of an old-fashioned educationist, but now he said, 'There are better ways of doing it. You are getting less than you know. You can get more if you organise it better, and make your wealth last longer if you keep the environment.' If he could not appeal to their intellect he could appeal to their greed.

'Ha, ha! Ha!' Sambong laughed. 'We are concerned with the present.'

Twelve years had gone by like this. Kellan could not believe he had been stuck in this post for so long, in the land of timber and money. Half his life was over and he had not started anything yet. Instead, he had suffered two severe bouts of malaria. A doctor in Dibrugarh had prescribed new drugs and he took them regularly until he thought he was going deaf; but the malaria had left him and he had continued to stay on in this town because it was a job, and also because he had grown attached to the place. His tour duties had taken him deep into these pristine forests and he had encountered the beauty and splendour of its sky-touching trees.

'These are the Hollong trees,' said his friend and assistant Ramwa Hosai. The Hollong, *Dipterocarpus macrocarpus* were exclusive to the south bank districts along the Patkoi mountain range, their spread to other parts of the state on the opposite bank confined by the wide Brahmaputra River. Hosai worked for the State Forest Research Institute. He was a reticent, hardworking trainee from Murem, a big, progressive village with more than a thousand households, and he was the only person Kellan had met here who showed a love and interest for the beautiful evergreen forest. They stood under one such tree in the Namdapha biosphere reserve straining their eyes skywards. No one who had stood under such a tree would fail to be astonished by the wonder of such a thing. The bole was pearly grey and some nine metres in girth. It rose straight up into a spreading oval canopy crowned with enormous bean pods. The pods opened out and seeds equipped with 'wings' spiralled down to earth for regeneration. It was magnificent! The tree was a sanctuary in itself. 'The Namdapha flying squirrel lives in this tree and the Hoolock gibbon also likes this tree because of its high protective cover,' said Hosai.

Kellan felt as if the forest had become a protective niche for him too. He went on long tours visiting all the villages. Here people were simple and friendly, but now a silence seemed to have descended on the homes he visited.

For a decade the timber boom had kept everyone happy until the dream was shattered when the Supreme Court suddenly clamped a Ban Order on timber operations in the state. A shudder of rage hit the timber barons. People gasped in shock. The ban was a response to an investigation report prepared by an environmental organisation, complete with satellite photos of vast clearings in the middle of Forest Reserves and Protected Areas attached as evidence. When the whole world was concerned about global warming, environment and climate change, the state of Arunachal Pradesh was burning and destroying thousands of hectares of virgin forest. In frenzied reaction, the state's political parties, youth organisations, merchants and local industrialists, everyone, rushed to New Delhi to shout, plead, curse, threaten and chant slogans in the capital against the ban. 'Pay us for keeping our forests,' they cried.

'Well, why not,' thought Kellan, feeling relieved and secretly pleased about the Ban Order. Give them money to keep their forests. The people had tasted money and nothing else would appease them now. Stuff their mouths with bundles of money! But Hosai had said, 'This is going to cause trouble.' And he was dead right.

Murem village

It started in Murem village. One January day a group of forty men approached the village and asked for shelter. The surprised villagers didn't know what to say. The men said they were hungry. They entered their homes and Hosai saw that they were all armed. The villagers mobilised themselves to slaughter pigs and fowl and cooked rice for them. How else can we help you, they asked.

'Oh, nothing. We are travellers passing by. Thank you for your hospitality. By god's grace we will meet again.'

Four months later a second group of young men came to visit the village. This time they carried a letter. 'It is a letter from our commander to proceed to X village,' one of them said. He was a lean, dark-skinned young man who spoke with the village elders in pidgin Assamese. He sat by the fire and looked around at the waiting circle of faces. 'Five of you have been named to go.' He read out the names. 'You will come with us tomorrow.'

The villagers huddled together and tried to decide what to do. But the watchful presence of the young men made any heart-to-heart discussion difficult, and hoping that what was left unsaid would be understood by their kinsmen, the five men left the village at mid-afternoon of the next day. One of the listed names was of a nephew of Rasa, Lutor's political ally. He was a well-known athlete in the village and before leaving he had whispered to Hosai, 'Don't show fear. Better not to inform anyone until we return. Then we will know what all this is about.'

Three days later another group of men appeared. 'Our brothers have told us about you,' they said. 'Your kinsmen are well. They will be returning soon. We will await their return here with you.'

The strangers stayed in the village for three weeks and slowly, as the days passed, they drifted into all the homes and disclosed that they were there on a mission. The villagers heard the word 'saadin', the fight for Independence, spoken like a gospel message and an icy fear crept into Hosai's heart one night when he noticed that the young men were preparing to leave in the dead of night. Where were his brothers? He thought the men had said the villagers would be returning soon. Where were they? Who were these men and what were they doing here, carrying firearms and enjoying their rice and salt?

'We want to know where our brothers from this village are,' he said, standing before a big-built man with a broad, inscrutable face and close-cropped hair that stood up in spikes. He had heard the men address him as 'Major.' The major looked at him hard and then turned to his companions. 'He wants to know,' he whispered, lifting his eyebrows and making a face. Then he told Hosai, 'We were sent to test your village and now we are leaving. We are not responsible for your brothers but I am sure they will be with you again soon. Goodbye.'

They trooped away from the village and no one dared say a word. It was a cursed time of fear and ill fortune. The villagers stayed in their homes and wondered what to do. Should they inform the police? But the police would arrest the villagers instead. Should they tell the authorities about it? But it might jeopardise the lives of their brothers. Those men were carrying AK-47s and they looked tough. It was very frightening. A couple of days passed in restless, anxious waiting. Then one bright morning a tall, elderly man appeared in their midst and told them that he was a special emissary and that he knew all about the fate of their brothers. They were being kept at headquarters for questioning and would be back soon.

'What headquarters? Questioning for what?'

'Oh, you don't know? Your village is the chosen one. We need good, strong people like you to fight against the corrupt government and win freedom for your people. However, your village also has a reputation for being rebellious. You have too many thinkers, ha! ha! If you are not careful you will be exterminated. Do you know what that means?'

The man said his name was Guma, and he wore the loose-fitting robes of a monk, projecting himself as a spiritual healer, but Hosai had heard about him as a man of unknown antecedents who moved from place to place saying he had the power of healing. 'I was born with this gift and I have cured many people and driven out Satan from the hearts of men.' He glared at Hosai and Hosai, looking at the dark, narrow eyes, felt himself shudder. The man was not young, maybe in his sixties, but he was big and florid with life, and his hard, shaven head shone like a polished stone. The villagers discovered that he had married a young local girl whom he had cured of a mysterious illness by sleeping with her in her sickbed. He lived in a border town near Assam and he told the villagers, 'If you want to see your brothers again you will have to pay me five lakh rupees. This is the demand of the commander and he knows what he is asking of you. He is a very capable man, mind you.'

'But we have already paid the visitors who came here the second time. What about that amount?'

'Rubbish! That is for the protection your village is receiving. Otherwise you would all be shot dead, do you know that? Your village is targeted for destruction if you are not careful.' He glared at the silent men, challenging them with his taunting eyes. 'This amount is different. It is because I am taking the trouble of negotiating on your behalf. What do you think I am here for? These people, they all know me and they listen to me. If I speak on your behalf your brothers might be home tomorrow. Who knows? Take it or leave it.'

He sat hunched before the villagers' fire, a tall, gaunt man shamelessly eating and drinking, tapping his fingers together and shaking his knees in rapid, impatient movements.

There was no help for it. The village was captive and the village elders decided to pay the amount. They wanted their men back and they wanted to live in peace.

'We should inform the police,' Hosai had insisted. Kellan, too, had met some of the villagers and tried to find out what was happening but they were too frightened to talk to him. The behaviour of the villagers who had put aside everything once to sit and chat with him was changed. They looked away and the way they spoke now, hesitantly and in a guarded manner as if skirting around the issue and trying to guide the conversation so that they could hear his opinion first before giving theirs, was something that filled him with foreboding.

'The government is the government. It will never

change,' said the village chief. 'If we tell them about this they will punish us instead. They will turn our village into a battlefield. The army will move in. And if they don't, and if the men with guns come again they will kill us all. We have wives and mothers and daughters. Our young men are not armed. Tell me, what would you do? We will continue as before in our time-tested manner to overcome hard times. We will wait.'

But Kellan knew that the anxiety had been too much even for the brave, patient village chief and after a long wait he had undertaken an arduous trek of nine days into no-man's land deep into Burmese territory to reach NSCN (K) headquarters carrying a petition for the chairman. He was accompanied by five villagers and though they did not meet the great leader, the villagers had received a letter signed by the chairman himself saying that his outfit was not in any way connected with the incidents in their village. He hoped their brothers would soon return to the village safely.

During all this time Kellan kept in touch with Rasa Lowang whose late father was a powerful chieftain when Kellan's father had served here as a schoolmaster in the NEFA days. Rasa was a big, silent man who kept to himself but he opened up with Kellan because of his friendship with Lutor.

'Rasa is an upright man,' Lutor had told him, and Kellan began to see this as they met more and more frequently and Rasa talked to him. 'It would be hard for anyone to understand what is happening here,' he said. 'You see, in the old days people from Myanmar would visit my father and present hornbill feathers as a mark of respect. We intermarried and we still have cultural affinities. There were no boundaries. The whole area was marked

Naga Tribal Areas, subsequently renamed as Tirap and Tuensang Frontier Division, NEFA, and we, the Nocte, Wancho and Tangsa people were identified as Nagas. Now this nomenclature has become a bone of contention and has raised claims of Tirap being part of the Greater Naga territory. That is the larger picture. What is happening now is a power struggle between leaders like Mankong and Temat that is making it easy for outsiders to claim our territory. It has to do with family, with titles, with ownership, with big money, and ego. First it was the timber wealth and private armies working with the backing of one militant faction. Now another faction has arrived and they are a force totally alien to us.'

Kellan knew the Tirap leaders Rasa was talking about. Temat was urbane and soft spoken. No one would think him a dangerous man but that's just how it usually is, said Rasa. 'His image blows in the wind and in his heart lurks the assassin's knife.' Mankong, on the other hand, was a stocky, bull-headed man known for his sudden fits of rage. Kellan had seen Mankong only once, at a public meeting where Mankong had stared at the crowd with a set, aggressive face. He was accompanied by Sambong, who was small fry, Rasa told him, but he was a wily man who lived by his wits. Once he had told Kellan, 'The top leaders of the NSCN are very clever people. They are intelligent men and they don't mince words.' He shut one eye and made a gun with thumb and forefinger.

Yes, but where were they, these leaders? Kellan wondered. All that was visible were cadres fighting each other who seemed to have no connection with their leaders who were engaged in peace talks with the Government of India while the ground burned and everyone paid money for a semblance of peace. And he had been found out too. Maybe it was because of his association with Rasa, or his visits to Murem village in the company of Hosai, that he had received that threatening phone call and Rasa had received an envelope with a bullet. Well, if that is what it is we have to stand up now, he thought. But he had to admit his own feeling of shock when he had answered the phone and heard that low, empty voice telling him to pay up. The thought of someone knowing his house and watching his movements was frightening. No man could pretend to be unaffected. On the other hand, it also provoked a feeling of deep anger. He hated that he should feel terrorised in his own state and he hated that breathless, choking feeling with his heart thumping every time he walked the street or entered his own house. He was a forest officer and he had no interest in political matters. In another year he would be up for retirement anyway, he thought, but he did not want to run away and he could not stop wondering why everyone obeyed in silence, as if ready to surrender their land and their lives without a word.

'You don't have to live here,' said Rasa. 'Imagine a night in a village. No lights. No phones. Just a small clearing in the forest. Suddenly a group of men come into your house and they're all carrying guns. Are you going to run out to call the police? No. You will ask them what they want, you will try to be pleasant so that they will be satisfied and go away quickly without hurting you or your family. This is the part that no one understands. That is the part that holds us back. Imagine a father with young daughters? Can you imagine the fear for their sons and daughters? You can't imagine the intimidation. My god, if you know there's one armed man running amuck in your neighbourhood would you not hurry to shut your doors and windows? You can call the police or ring up a friend, but here? Where will the villagers go? If anyone speaks up militants will pounce on him. You know they can do anything. They are everywhere. If someone volunteers information the Army will take him away for interrogation. For any villager the Indian army is a terrifying prospect. If you say "army" or "sepoy" people don't even want to look on their faces! But now, what can we do now? We have seen so many wars and troubles in our history. Something always happens. But we are still here today. In the end what the villagers are trying to do is right. We will watch and wait. It is the way we have survived. No need to say big words.'

This is also a way, Kellan thought. Watch and wait. Maybe it was a bad dream. Maybe it would go away. But recurring dreams portend something and shadows continued to flit across the landscape.

One summer morning when the whole world seemed to be resting peacefully and the town was just waking up as the sun struggled over the mountains and tried to pierce through the tall trees, Kellan thought the sound of rapid knocking on the door was part of a dream. He heard someone calling him.

'It's me, Hosai!'

He was fully awake then.

He opened the door and Hosai said, 'They have found a body.'

Kellan waited for him to come inside the house before saying anything. He followed Hosai in. 'Whose body?'

'It's Rasa's nephew. That's what they are saying. The dead body was found by the police on the side of the steel bridge on the way to Nokphen village.'

Hosai was splashing water on his face and talking as if he were narrating a very simple story. 'You see, the police have already buried the dead body. It was decomposed, they say. But they did not give out any information. Only today a copy of the circular from the Deputy Commissioner about this death has reached us. Now they have gone to claim the body.'

'How do you know it is Rasa's nephew?'

'We know,' said Hosai, slowly rubbing his face with a hand towel. 'They found a watch and Rasa has identified it.'

In Itanagar the news was a small item, under 'Report from the Districts.' *The villagers of X are being harassed by unknown gunmen.*

Harassed! They've found a dead body! And four people are still missing! Harassed? Kellan wanted to run out and shout at the officers, the district magistrates and police and politicians but he was a lone forest officer whose words would have no weight with anyone.

It was on that day that Kellan had decided to resume his association with Lutor. He could not believe no one was saying anything. He was suffocating in this empty, silent place. He had heard about the dead man found in Pasighat and wondered if it was linked to the Murem village case. He tried to talk to Rasa, but the man was withdrawn and would not disclose anything more about the disappearance of the villagers. 'When you meet Lutor tell him I also hope to see him soon,' was all he had said.

Namtok

Kellan pulled out his suitcase and sat down on the bed. He stared at the old case. Since that last visit he had agreed to let his son go to Delhi with Umsi but he wanted to see the boy again. Maybe he should go to Delhi, give his son a treat and see how his sister was doing. We should all get together again, he thought. There was a niece too, Umsi's daughter whom he had seen only as a baby. What sort of person was he, he asked himself now, waiting here in this godforsaken place, blind to everything else except the trees and the shadow of gunmen lurking in the forest? It was time to think of something else and move on. He peered out and saw the low hills glowing in the surreal light of the sun shining through a smoky blue haze. He had heard about a love story associated with these hills, and how the name *Pat-koi* was a combined word to denote a place where chickens were sacrificed. Perhaps it was through these hills that eloping lovers had found safe passage for which they had performed thanksgiving ceremonies. How sad it is, he thought, that present-day reality was a far cry from such loveliness. Every day the streets were growing dimmer and the villagers more secretive and silent than they had ever been, as if awaiting something terrible. Maybe I am imagining things, he told himself. Time will tell—ah,

Time! Some day all this will be past. Some day there will be new leaders, a new generation growing up in a field of light, with a future to live for. If only the villagers can wait it out. If only!

The high whine of a welding machine working down the street across his house was drumming in his head when he heard a car drive up to his house. It was Rasa's white Scorpio splattered with mud. Rasa was alone. He looked rumpled and tired.

'Good day,' he said.

'Hello, what's up,' Kellan said cautiously.

'There's been a killing,' Rasa replied loudly, too loudly, as if he hoped there would be eavesdroppers all around them. When Kellan looked around out of habit to see if there was danger of being overheard, Rasa laughed loudly and announced, 'A circle officer of Namtok has been shot dead. He was resisting extortion, I believe, so they shot him in his newly constructed office.'

Kellan wondered if Rasa was drunk, the way he was throwing his arms about and talking so loudly in an angry, contemptuous manner as if he were talking to an enemy and challenging someone to shoot him dead on the spot.

'Come in,' said Kellan, running down the steps and shepherding him into the house. 'Come in. Who? Where?'

Inside the house Rasa went straight to the bathroom. He did not emerge for a long time and when he did Kellan noticed the puffy rings around his friend's eyes and realised how tired he must be. Namtok was a small town in the foothills on the border with Assam. Recently it had been turned into circle headquarters and a young non-tribal man had been sent there to take charge. He had a wife and a two-year-old son.

'Why was he killed?'

'Who knows? Because he was resisting, because he didn't pay up, because he was foolish—who knows?' said Rasa. 'The finger is pointing at the NSCN (I-M) but why shoot someone dead in broad daylight for thirty thousand rupees? They can get that from any shopkeeper. Why kill an unarmed civilian? This is a signal by one group to their rivals that they are here. Who has enlisted their help, I wonder.'

Kellan sensed this was a turning point. The militants were taking their own course of action. They were here to stay, and from now on the districts would be under their diktat. Rasa was rubbing his brows and swearing. 'It's too much. How can we live like this? Look at the land,' he said, waving his hands. 'See how the sun has left us. We are living in shadow and the assassin's gun is pointing directly at us.'

The news of the killing shook the capital. The town of Namtok had no phones and a ministerial team from Itanagar was rushing to the place. 'Now you see what's happening,' said Aohun. 'Tanik will make some statements but his act is all atmospherics. We have to push the anti-terrorist law. Think about it. Give us your hand, will you? Give us your hand!' he told Lutor.

Tanik announced an ex-gratia payment of two lakh for the bereaved family and said the cold-blooded murder would not deter the government's resolve to fight terrorism. His cabinet colleagues said no stone would be left unturned to book the culprits but nothing happened except that in another border town near the famous Namdapha biosphere reserve two young tribal men were picked up by the police and held for questioning.

'They are not locals, I mean they are from Manipur, oh, no—Dimapur, and they acted suspicious,' said the officer on duty.

'What do you mean, suspicious? Were they carrying arms, bombs?' The local MLA appeared upset and irate when the news reached him.

'No sir, they were carrying a bag…'

'A bag! What, an empty bag?'

'No sir, it was full of clothes.'

'Well, what's wrong with that?'

'New clothes, sir. Jeans and T-shirts, and some books.'

'Books! Jeans! Are they doing business?'

'I don't know sir.'

'For god's sake, find out!'

The police lock-up was a sad, dim building with no fans. People crowded in all the time and the policeman felt the weight of dirty walls and human stench pressing in on him. What to do now? The magistrate was out of town. There was no one to consult, and the two men who had been picked up were glum and silent. One of them appeared to be a studious type and kept his eyes glued to a book that he held in his lap. They said they were doing business. They were visiting a friend. Did the policeman know so and so? The officer heard the name of a minister and felt tiredness seep into his bones. That was the way it always happened. Some big shot would be down soon shouting at him for a fool and an idiot. 'These are my boys!' he would say. 'Why are they here?' Money on the table. Release them! It made a man feel small to be treated in this way, but better to be small and safe than to stand up and get shot. Forget about peace. Who said peace is not the absence of conflict but the presence of trust? Two hoots to that! Who could trust the leaders?

The heartache that is politics

The police force received a boost only in the capital. 'It is impossible to cover all the districts,' said Aohun. But he had tried his best in Itanagar. A flying squad of three new police vehicles wailing with sirens was deployed to circle the town. Itanagar was divided into patrolling sectors with each sector consisting of five halting points. A police control room was set up to monitor the deployment of patrol vehicles and a fresh batch of letters were despatched to the Home Ministry appealing for help to modernise the state police force. 'Who would have thought things would turn out like this,' said Aohun, shaking his head. 'We are seriously handicapped by manpower shortage. There are only two battalions of armed police, one CRPF, and the 150 AK-47s are used mainly for VIP security, wasting about 300 police personnel.'

Orin dropped by regularly, bringing the papers. Sometimes he was accompanied by Peter who said, 'Nothing about us. No Namtok. No predawn raid and killings, no extortion. But the Indian Government is saying they will fight terrorism globally. All terrorists must be immobilised.'

Orin shook the batch of national dailies. 'Look, look at this. Is this the news? It's all Bollywood starlets in states of undress. Superfluous! When the national papers write about us it's only hurried reports of a shoot-out or something exotic and weird,' he said.

'So, what of it? Who wants to know about us? People write as they see us. What's wrong with that? If you don't like it file a counter report,' said Kamin, angrily thumping the papers down on the table.

In the run-up to the elections, Aohun and his dissident group had made a secret plan to topple Tanik. Every day they counted names and made lists. In a sixty-member house Aohun almost had the numbers to win but he needed Lutor to throw in his lot with him. Lutor had nine plus three Independent legislators, dubbed the ANP's dirty dozen. The rest were in-between people, fence sitters, who might be wooed.

'We need a couple more names,' said Aohun, 'and then we can oust Tanik in a no-confidence motion on the floor of the house. But not a word about our plans before we strike.'

Lutor disagreed. He told Aohun, 'If we fight, we fight openly. I do not believe in secrecy, and I don't trust these men. If they are against Tanik let them say so openly and be counted.'

'We will, we will, in time. But Tanik is too clever. He'll buy everyone back if we are not careful. It has to be a surprise attack otherwise we will fail. Everyone is scared of him.'

Kamin agreed with Lutor and scoffed at Aohun and his apolitical allies saying there were other things to do than to be afraid. But the men were not assured. Tanik was unpredictable. He was a master politican imbued with great powers. Soon after the Namtok incident the government had announced a twenty-five crore development package for the two districts under a separate Department of Tirap and Changlang (DoTC).

'The UNC is playing economics,' said Kamin. 'If people are prosperous they will not want to jeopardise peace.'

'But economics can be manipulated! What is money without structural change and working plans?' shouted Lutor. He was fed up of this money talk. 'It is nothing but bribery. Go ask the people! They will tell you, if they are allowed to speak, "We don't want the packages. Who will benefit? It will go straight to the underground." It's peace they are crying for. It is the only thing they have scribbled on pieces of paper: *Give us peace.*'

Somewhere around this time it dawned on me that Kamin was beginning to pull away from the Lutor camp. I could not quite place a finger on it but I could feel Kamin's dissatisfaction about the way the campaign was going, and his impatience with Lutor and Aohun and men of their generation who were now caught between the slow, painstaking habits of the past and the urgent, insistent demands of the present. Change! Change! There was so little time and so many changes to worry about. Everything was happening all at once, everything was a priority and everything had to be taken care of at such speed that there was no time to say, look, this is how it is. This is how we feel. This is what the people feel. Can you hear us? Why don't you listen?

There was simply no time.

Lutor came by my place often, with Aohun, sometimes with Tunar and Kamin. Kampo and I stayed out of the way while they consulted at length, cooped up in the small sitting room.

'People are fed up with this insurgency issue,' said Kamin. 'We should ask the government of India why they cannot come out openly and say, nothing doing, we will not negotiate with terrorists.'

'That's what we are saying. You know the implications. But Aohun is not one to give up. He has a vision and he's working on it.'

'If you mean the anti-terrorism Act, this APCOCA is going to blow up in his face.'

'I don't know. The politicians are in league with the underground, that's why they are opposing APCOCA. All this protest is being done at their instigation.'

Kamin stared at him. 'You are going to support the black Act?

'All I'm saying is Aohun thinks it might be a solution. It's his definition of peace—when you think you have a solution.'

'Peace with arms! Arrest everyone for the sake of peace? What kind of method is that?'

'It's the method the underground has been using. Are you listening to me? The militants are riding in ministerial cars to carry out their criminal activities. There is a complete meltdown of law and order. The PMO is aware of this, and the MHA and the Defence Ministry—everyone knows! But nothing is happening. It's like an iron net that we beat our heads against. Law and order? It's a state subject, they say, so we have to try it our way then.'

'I thought you said more laws breed more criminals. I thought you subscribed to that!' cried Kamin.

'I'm concerned about the provisions of the Bill, if we can check that it will not be misused.'

'Ha! Now it gets complicated with legal issues.'

'Aohun thinks it can be a psychological deterrent, a chink in the armour. That's all I'm saying,' retorted Lutor.

A new presence in the house was Orin's brother Kasi, who was spending more and more time in the capital. I was wary of him—it was his manner, or the smiling look in his eyes that seemed to hide something, but Kamin had taken him under his wing and he accompanied Kamin everywhere. He was eager in an edgy, jumpy manner and he walked as if he was swaying to music. Music made him happy, he said, shuffling around in khaki cargo pants while constantly plugged in to his headphones.

Where is he staying?

'He's got some friends in Ganga market and he's got a room in one of the hotels there,' Orin said.

In the past there had been controversy regarding the status of children of mixed marriages as bonafide Arunachal tribal. In Kasi's case of course everyone knew his father was an aying. Maybe this had hurt Kasi, I wondered. Perhaps he was hiding psychological scars and bitterness against a society that questioned his antecedents. But Kasi gave no indication of this. His mother Ongat had converted to Christianity and was active with church service and prayer meetings. Sometimes Kasi said he was going to church, but Kamin told me Kasi was doing most of the leg work for the party, he was such a big, burly chap. He drove Kamin's car and breezed in and out of the house, smiling at us and humming to himself. Recently he had shaved his head bald.

One day Kamin said, 'Why you don't join the party?' He had a way of tilting his head back and narrowing his eyes every time he spoke to me and I found conversation with him difficult. He was stealthy and inscrutable and his stance was such that it seemed he was always preparing to reject anything I said.

'Why are you asking that, any particular reason?' Kampo suddenly spoke up, staring at him.

'Well,' said Kamin, hesitating for a second, smiling and turning to Kampo, 'no reason. I just think there is great scope for women in politics these days. Why not?'

'*You're* giving us *scope*—that's insulting,' said Kampo.

'Why? Look at you, for one, you are educated,' he said this in a slightly patronising tone, 'you can take part in decision making. And you have no liabilities. You don't have to look after a baby or a husband. You are free.' Now he was taunting her and she flared up at this.

'No one is hankering for a party post,' she said. 'We are not in a contest with men to flaunt our female selves and we,' she waved her arms to include me, 'we have been taking decisions without any help from anyone, thank you.'

Kamin laughed softly. 'Why are you so serious?' he said, trying to placate her. Kampo didn't bother to answer. She moved away and sat down on the kitchen stool. 'Well, let's hear your opinion anyway,' he said, turning to me. 'Tell me one thing. Why do women who are qualified desist,' he said this with a taunting emphasis, '*desist* from politics? Good people don't get into politics, huh?'

'When the time comes I'll let you know,' I said.

'Time comes for what? Is there a marriage plan I don't know about?'

Kampo sniggered. 'Time to join your political rat race,' she said.

'Everyone wants to engage in politics. It's the greatest game.'

'I want to do something else,' I said. 'We can't all be politicians.'

'No, of course not,' replied Kamin. 'Already we are a state full of unemployed politicians.'

Book Four

THE FALL

The cicada's song

The long month of August was gloomy with thundershowers and road blocks. People were trapped in their districts, unable to ferry across swollen rivers or tackle roads torn apart by mudslides. Half the town of Pasighat and Namsai, and the Dibang valley were submerged underwater and in Tezu more than a thousand Chakma villagers and twenty policemen were stranded in flood waters as the countryboats used for evacuation had all been washed away. The Air Force was grounded due to bad weather. Six districts were totally cut off from the rest of the world and in Itanagar electricity and piped water supply collapsed.

'What a dump!' said Kampo. 'Now we are really stuck.' At night the howling of dogs echoed around the town and the sound of cars, doors opening or closing, a muted cough, someone whispering something, became part of the routine for everyone involved in the great political game. Every day the clouds piled up behind the mountains and crashed down with heavy, straight rain as if they wanted to wash away the town and tear into the centre of the earth.

At the height of this flood fury the government launched Operation Flashpoint in Tirap district to flush out militants. Orin came by with the news and said there was widespread protest against Tanik and Aohun. The letterbox of the

Eastern Chronicle was crammed with press releases and handwritten protest letters. A young AINA union minister came to tour Tirap district at this time and in a public rally accused the UNC of cancelling panchayat elections in Tirap as a travesty of democratic practice. The government is now sending in the army to harass innocent villagers of Tirap in an attempt to divert attention from their failure, he shouted.

Aohun was tight-lipped and grim. In a press statement he said that panchayat polls had been cancelled by the Election Commission based on intelligence reports that insurgents were waiting to capture money flowing into Panchayati Raj institutions and preparing the ground for a similar exercise during elections to the state assembly. Candidates who filed their nominations on party basis had been coerced to withdraw. Further, a security Coordination Group constituted by the Home Ministry had given its mandate to conduct operations against insurgents with all available resources. 'And that's what we are doing,' he said.

The thing uppermost in Aohun's mind now was APCOCA. The atmosphere was tense. In a predawn raid in a Tirap village seven people were abducted by NSCN militants. They were looking for rival cadres hiding there, Rasa told Lutor on the phone. Militants snatched away the weapons of the security officers accompanying government officials who came to investigate, and no one could do a thing. 'Look at our state. It's a joke!' he had said, laughing mirthlessly.

Peter told us that villagers had been brainwashed to believe that with APCOCA everyone would be arrested because they gave food and shelter to terrorists. In some cases villagers were made to sign public petitions at the point of a gun to protest the anti-terrorism Bill and court arrest, saying: 'The government will need twenty football fields to build a jail for us just like Hitler and the Nazi camps!' But the truth, he said, was that they were all well and truly trapped in a deadly political rivalry. 'Actually our politicians have started a civil war. It is the worst crime that they have committed.' Peter was very succinct. 'And now everyone is fed up with Tirap and Changlang. Who knows,' he said, looking at us, 'you people might soon want to dump me too. Let them go, the district is a nuisance! Some people are saying this,' Peter laughed.

Orin shook his hand. 'I'm not saying this.'

Ah! If only the political leaders could break out of this vicious entrapment, I thought, looking at Peter's face and his eyes blinking rapidly as he spoke. It seemed somewhere along the way a point of no return had already been crossed. But Lutor was adamant. 'Don't worry,' he said. 'I will never condone the idea of a fragmented Arunachal.'

Sometimes it seemed to me that it was Lutor's will holding us together. There were times when I felt that I could hear words in his mind echoing back to me. It was about a narrative I had heard so many times that passed before his eyes again like the brilliant flash of a hot summer day. The sun stared down on a small jungle clearing as if contemplating how much its inhabitants could bear the pressing heat. Lutor remembered his illness and his mother's face bending over him. He could see the sky and a burning light rippling down in waves. The rainman was an illuminated silhouette in this cone of light. He was chanting and dancing, up and down, up and down, and Lutor held his breath when he saw a grey wisp of cloud starting to creep up into the sky. He saw the cloud roll into a big, fluffy ball and start spinning—faster and faster, gathering momentum as the rainman chanted louder and louder and the cloud started crackling and shooting sparks of light. 'Look, I bring you rain and spears of lightning! Is my voice not great and fearsome?'

Lutor recalled people saying they had never seen such a dark, thundery day. The image stayed with him and his years with Lipun nurtured it. It was an image of silhouettes that nothing could wipe away, they were so imprinted in his mind. They came to him as the outline of mountains and the shapes of trees and there—on the furthest peak, he imagined the rainman and other ancient medicants racing across the tops of the hills, chanting in ecstasy. Where did this feeling of ecstasy come from? It came from loving the land, from looking at the light lifting the hills and burnishing it for the gods. It came from living in contentment with the river and trees and fighting and losing and struggling and realising, one day, how closely all life and land is tied together. This was the wonder!

He knew this image was about Time and the transition of an unknown land into a modern state. This was due to men like Lipun and all those frontier men who had done the patient groundwork. He knew this image trapped him in the past, but he willed for it to be the constant picture in his mind through which he would be able to draw the outline of new beginnings. It was always there, somewhere, stirring in his heart, the hope and desire for the images to fuse and settle so that past and present would evolve into a new picture of the future.

Now he shunted between Itanagar and Pasighat, campaigning hard for his friend Nabam Tunar for the prestigious Itanagar Assembly constituency. The capital needed someone who could tackle the myriad issues of a growing city with influx of people from all the different communities of the state and other parts of the country, and there was no one better than Tunar to do this. Tunar was small, bespectacled, always smiling, and he was the only person Lutor knew who could negotiate bandh calls and political rallies and communicate with youth leaders and student organisations in a spontaneous and genuine manner. The Itanagar Assembly seat was also the cause célebrè of the UNC and AINA parties. Tanik was pumping in money to support the re-election of his party crony, a slow, sickly, middle-aged man with corrupt ways and the AINA had come up with a young firebrand who spoke about indigenous faith and compared it with ancient Vedic forms of worship.

One day I overheard Lutor on the phone, shouting, 'Yes! It's bad. No, not like the Maoists…what? Naxalites? No, no, not like…hey! It affects our lives. Why do you compare? How DARE you compare?' and he slammed the phone down. 'Media,' he said to me. 'They want a statement in five minutes, and then they ask funny questions.' If Lutor was away in Pasighat people still dropped by asking when he would be back. Kamin stayed around and took charge of the situation whenever Lutor was absent. Orin came by daily and together with Kamin met visitors who carried briefcases that I suspected were full of money.

'I hope we are not noticed,' Kampo said.

'There's no harm. It's party funds. Election time is always like this,' said Orin. 'This is payback time. The public will be all over their candidates now and give them no rest.'

On one occasion Kamin pulled out a wad of money and held it out to us saying, 'Here, take this…Budget, for all the food and stuff…' His voice trailed away seeing the look on my face. 'Okay, I'll get some mugs…' He stopped again. 'All your cups are chipped.'

'Yes, you can get some decent linen and blankets and how about a maidservant?' retorted Kampo. 'What do you think this place is, open house?'

Kamin looked at her and said, 'I like your style.'

'He's against everything,' Kampo hissed when he had gone.

'It's okay, he's a bit rough, that's all,' said Orin.

I will get some blankets, I thought grumpily, feeling unsettled by all the talk. In between the visitors and the excitement of being involved in some way in the history of the state, I despaired of ever returning to my chosen task. Through the clouds I could see a patch of sunlight spreading, catching the house and garden in a bowl of light that was intensifying minute by minute. This made the cicada shrill its heart out. I could see one on the grimy kitchen window, see its tight body pressed against the glass pane as if it were resting, so plain and brown, but it was engaged in a mysterious ritual as if life and being alive depended on this fantastic rapture of vibration. So many days were lost in uncertainties, confusion and movement, without getting anywhere. Field work! How would I ever get down to field work?

'What hurry is there for you?' Orin tried to console me. 'Let the election be over.'

What about the images and feelings that are always knocking against time, I wanted to say, and what about those moments, the anticipation of moments, the best moments waiting, for which I am always in a hurry running towards them, across this river, beyond those hills, somewhere, somewhere? The risk was that the moment would pass and I might forget.

A few days ago, Lutor and Aohun had come into the house. There was no one about and Lutor had said that they would be there just for a short while. 'If anyone calls, we are not in,' he said. Then he was on the phone talking to Rasa Lowang in Tirap. 'Okay, let him come with you.' He was talking about Kellan. It was hard not to overhear his loud voice.

More visitors, I thought. There was another occasion coming up, the men were talking about a football tournament. It was a big annual event in the capital. The inter-district football tourneys were over and the final play-off was between the Tirap Tigers and the Champion Eagles of Papum Pare. Aohun was betting that the Tigers would win.

'Ha,' said Lutor, 'I'll bet for Tunar's team!' Their voices sank to a whisper again but I could still hear Lutor. 'Rasa thinks the evidence is there. He'll tell us when he gets here.'

I worried if Lutor and Aohun's car could be spotted from the road. A feeling of apprehension was nagging at me and I wished this election was over and done with. I had abandoned my books and had not looked at a plant since I had teamed up with Kampo and Orin, following the election trail, except to check if the glinting bodies of parked cars were well screened by the rampant growth outside my cottage from the jealous eyes of Lutor's opponents.

Gohpur Road

I felt better after a shopping excursion in the Akash Deep complex. I bought a quilt and headed towards Orin's office. The conversations with Kamin irked me and I was glad to be out of the house. The roads were surprisingly bare of traffic and I wondered if something had happened, was it another bandh day? Usually the joke in Itanagar was that there were more cars than roads, and recently, more cars than people. I saw the big banner of the football tournament fluttering above the bank building. 'Ah, that was probably it. Everyone must have headed down to the Rajiv Gandhi Stadium.' Orin and Peter were carrying camera equipment and getting ready to go out.

'Aren't you coming to see the match?' said Orin.

I thought about it. 'I'll come a bit later. I'll drop this and pick up Kampo.'

Orin was putting up his keys on a hook and saying, 'We're taking Peter's van. My car is here, and the office keys, in case you want to hang around,' when we heard a motorcycle splutter to a stop outside. Someone was humming and I knew it was Kasi.

'Hello there!' he said, 'where's everyone going?'

'We're going to the stadium for the match,' said Orin. 'Aren't you coming?'

'Nah! You've seen one you've seen them all.' Kasi was still humming and looking around the office as if prepared to stand there all day. He slung a big bag on the chair.

'I hear Mr. Rasa is coming to Itanagar?' he said suddenly.

The way he said *Mr.* Rasa gave me a start. Kasi was looking at me with a big smile on his face.

'I know,' he said. 'Why, is it supposed to be a secret, or what?'

I pretended not to hear him. As far as I could tell Lutor and Aohun had acted as if they did not want anyone else to know about this visit. But Rasa was their man, I thought. He was a politician who could come and go as he pleased and maybe he had spoken to other people, it was no concern of mine. Maybe it was Orin who knew his programme and had mentioned it to Kasi. I waited, but Orin was standing still with his back to us and not saying a word. I thought the best way to reply and get rid of Kasi was to leave out Rasa's name and mention Kellan who was accompanying him.

The response I got from Kasi for this piece of news was totally unexpected. 'No, he can't do that!' he exclaimed.

'Why not? Kellan is coming here to meet Lutor.'

'But Kellan is an officer. Why should he travel with a politician and get mixed up in political matters?

'Well, he's not. He's coming for official work and he's taking a lift with Rasa.'

'But he can't!'

Kasi was breathing hard. What was wrong with him? I felt a premonition and now I was beginning to breathe hard. Orin had turned around and was staring at Kasi. His voice was very quiet. 'Why can't he?' he said. 'Why?'

'Oh, forget it,' said Kasi, compressing his mouth as if he was grinding his teeth.

'No, tell me! You know something.'

'Forget it. I was worried about the road, that's all.'

'What road?'

'The Gohpur road.'

Orin looked at me. I knew in a flash then that Orin had no idea of Rasa's impending visit. But now he guessed I knew about this road journey that was meant to be a secret. His journalist's instinct told him something was afoot. He put the keys back in his pocket, went into the next room and told Peter to go on ahead. He would follow later.

'How do you know he's coming by road?'

'I don't!' Kasi glared at Orin. 'Will you stop questioning me like that? How am I supposed to know about these things?'

'But you know Rasa is coming to Itanagar by that road,' Orin insisted. 'Who told you?'

Kasi jumped up. 'Where is Kamin?'

'I told you everyone is at the stadium,' responded Orin. 'Now do you want to come with us or not?' He was taking charge.

Kasi turned his head aside to avoid looking at Orin and asked if I had had any communication with Kellan. I told him I had not. Were they coming by the ferry, perhaps?

'There is a Dhemaji district bandh in Assam, don't you know?'

Kasi looked at his watch. 'Then it's the Gohpur road… Hey, it's almost one!' He cried. 'I think I'll go and meet them. I'll meet them at the check gate.' He jumped up again.

'Why? Why?' I was right at his side. Now I didn't want to let him out of my sight.

'Well, it gets dark early and you know that road…' he left the sentence hanging and I felt as if I had stopped breathing.

'It's alright. We'll go together,' said Orin.

He walked out with the car keys jingling in his hands. 'I'll come too,' I cried, still holding my bundle and hurrying after them.

'No way!' Kasi turned on me. He kept his voice low and his eyes were furious. But his fat face, his gait and manner incensed me. 'Shut up,' I hissed at him. 'It's Orin's car. You tell me what's going on or I'll kill you!'

Kasi's breath was hot on my face. 'Are you mad?' He exclaimed. But he got in quietly when Orin nudged him into the car. Orin turned the key and handed me the office keys, saying, 'We'll be back soon.'

Orin drove straight past Ganga market towards Chandranagar. Near the trijunction that led to the lake and the zoo, Kasi swivelled around in his seat, almost opening the door, making Orin brake sharply.

'What! What are you doing?'

'Oh, nothing,' Kasi answered irritably. He thought he had seen someone he knew, but he couldn't be sure.

The Gohpur road was devoid of traffic. The mountain wall reared up on the left and to the right the winding road fell away in a sheer drop to the thin stream below. It was a breathtaking patch of forest so convoluted and secretive, and so fragile, as if the ravine and the river would dissolve at any moment. A naturalist's paradise, that's what Orin had once written in a feature article about this twenty-nine kilometre stretch with the road connecting the capital with the police check gate at Hollongi on the Assam border. Now a highway project had scraped away the mountainside and bulldozed tons of mud over the stream in a bid to widen the road. The new alignment was a four-lane highway but here and there the sandy mountains still stood, almost stuck together except for the dark, thin gashes running in between. Ancient tree ferns stood out of these dark, unexplored clefts. Everything looked ghostly. Patches of wild plantain covered the lower slopes and their powdered fronds swayed and bent like a warning of portentous evil. The car rattled across one of the last remaining Bailey bridges that resounded to their passage with a great clanking of metal. Kasi winced. 'It's enough to wake the dead,' he said.

They didn't speak after that. Orin was turning the steering hard left and then twirling it back fully to the right, taking the sharp bends in the road. By the time they had covered ten kilometres the light was already fading. Soon the sun would dip behind the mountains and Orin knew it would be dark as night in this godforsaken strip of forest where not a single firefly beamed even in summer.

Approaching them from the other end Rasa and Kellan had stopped at the railway crossing eight miles into the Gohpur road before the checkpost at Hollongi. The barrier was down. In a few seconds they heard the rumble of an approaching goods train that disappeared as swiftly as it had come. This was a line that went all the way to Jonai station near Pasighat. Kellan suddenly remembered the face of his son when he had taken him from Pasighat to Rangiya station and on to Kolkata on this very line. His son had been so excited, sliding into his seat and smiling at him with a shy look in his eyes. His pants were rolled up and he wore striped nylon socks. I should have talked to him! I should have talked to him! Kellan thought, recalling that tight, eager face of his son and how the boy had pretended to start reading when he had opened a newspaper and settled down for the long journey. I should have talked to him! I should have hugged him! It was a single, measly holiday he had given his son.

'Why don't you get in front,' he said, turning around to Rasa who was sitting stiffly at the back. It was an arrangement for Rasa's protection, so that he wouldn't be seen. Now Kellan felt they could relax a bit. They were in Rasa's white Scorpio car and the driver had done record time driving without a break since early morning.

'I am fine here,' said Rasa, but Kellan insisted and opened his door. I'll drive, he offered. He wanted to talk and he wanted to remember his son. He stepped out and stretched. The small Nepali driver also hopped out and examined the wheels. He opened a small packet and popped a paan quickly into his mouth before climbing into the back.

The barrier was open and Kellan got in behind the wheel with Rasa in the front seat beside him. An orange-coloured pick-up van parked on the other side of the barrier was moving ahead of them. The metal grill around the sides of the van was laced with rope over a dirty piece of tarpaulin partially covering a pile of bricks.

'Look at that,' said Rasa. 'Everyone is in the building business.'

When they overtook the van at Hollongi checkpost, Kellan caught of glimpse of a young man wearing a peaked cap driving, looking straight ahead. The policeman on duty at the gate peered at their car and seeing Rasa and Kellan he raised the barrier quickly. Kellan waved and they shot past. The rice fields were left behind and very abruptly they were climbing into the mountains. Kellan felt his heart lift. It was his patch of haunted forest. A big chunk of the capital complex was still classified as a game park but of course no one paid any attention. People had to live, and desperate rural migrants had built their homes wherever they could grab land. But here it was still comparatively untouched even though Kellan could see the hand of man reaching out and scratching at the steep hills. Someone had tried to burn the forest in small patches and shacks had been erected here and there perched precariously on stilts over these burnt clearings. He had had some say in retaining this as a green space and now he felt the old desire to fight again for this beautiful land. The red, sandy hill rose up straight on his right and he drove slowly, trying to see the river through the green foliage on the edge of the road. If one didn't know better the dense tufts of grass and shrubs could easily fool someone into thinking it was a patch of earth and veer off the road into the dark ravine below. He had driven on this road often in the middle of the night and now he wondered what kind of life existed in that inky darkness that could swallow up the moon and stars.

They had driven some eight kilometres past the checkpost when the orange van appeared behind them and began hooting insistently.

'Let him pass, if he's in such a hurry,' said Rasa.

Kellan slowed down. He signalled for the man to wait before he could pull up to the side where the Border Roads people had cut into the hillside to expand the road. The van swept past. There were neat beds of gravel to his right, boulders, cement pipes, tin drums, blue plastic sheeting and barrels of pitch all along the way. Now the rainy season had put all work on hold, Kellan thought, suddenly noticing the emptiness of the road.

Rasa looked at his watch and said, 'We'll be in time, just like we said we would.'

At a wide turn in the road they came upon two boys on a motorcycle dragging two pieces of bamboo lashed to the side of the bike swinging up and down, making Kellan brake sharply. It was one of those hunky black bikes that seemed to be popular everywhere. One rider wore a helmet and his friend had a kerchief wound around his head and partially covering his face. Kellan followed slowly. It would be pointless to try and overtake the bikers and he felt content to negotiate the turns in the road slowly. Another turn—there was no sign of the motorcyclists. Kellan looked around. They were barely ten kilometres away from Itanagar. He pulled the vehicle up slowly over a steep incline and crawled around a wide loop that seemed to embrace the mountain. Here they came upon a level stretch dotted with clumps of reed glass wedged in between two towering peaks, and Kellan saw the orange van ahead. It was parked to one side and its doors were wide open. Kellan was seized with a sudden premonition.

'Hey!' he said, when out of the corner of his eye he saw that the motorcycle was also pushed up against the mountain. There were three men standing on the road as if waiting for something.

Without another word Kellan was steering wildly and trying to turn the vehicle around in that small space but everything stopped when the windscreen shattered and a hail of glass blasted into the car. He saw a car approaching out of the explosion of light. He was surprised to see Orin's face, screaming something. And there was Kasi…What on earth! He seemed to be shouting something too. Go back! GO B-A-C-K! Now he heard Rasa shouting and pulling at him. Get out, GET OUT! Kellan tried to move his body but his feet were clamped on the brakes and he felt stuck to the mountain on his right. There was a sharp cracking sound and Kellan felt his breath was leaving him. With a burst of strength he pushed Rasa away from him.

'Come on!' Rasa was yelling at him, straining with all his might to scramble clear of the car. There was a scuffling sound behind him and the door fell open as Rasa rolled out, still tugging at Kellan who had bent his head forward with his elbows on the steering wheel. In a brief flash just before he rolled off the road Rasa saw the other car with two staring faces suddenly shoot forward towards them and then plunge straight over the edge.

It was a long, slow fall. Orin felt the vehicle turning once, turning twice, then three, four times and his hands were clutching at the steering wheel or Kasi was clutching at him, he didn't know which. All his concentration was focussed on trying to break the momentum of the car. He saw a jutting tuft of broom grass right before his eyes. It was so close it was brushing his face. He grabbed at it and at this point Orin parted with the vehicle as he felt himself thrown out, clinging only to that swaying tuft of grass. It gave under his weight and he was falling, rolling and tumbling down as everything—thought, feeling, fear, horror, all vanished into a rushing wind that filled his ears and made his eyes turn blind.

When he opened his eyes again it was still daylight. It must be a new day, thought Orin. Is that sunlight? He saw Lutor and tried to call him, but the image faded and he struggled to focus. He saw a small bundle rolling towards him. The bundle passed by very close and his heart almost stopped. He saw a small man covered in blood crawling painfully over the stones. It was the driver who had survived the fall when Rasa's vehicle had crashed into the rocks. Hey! HEY! He shouted but no sound came from his mouth. Orin was wedged against a smooth, brown boulder that partially hid him from view. A police rescue team had rushed to the spot but the steep slope offered no foothold. Everything above and below was slippery with landslip gravel and tangled fern strewn with stones falling down to the stream bed below. It was Kamin who had made the descent. Hey! HEY! There was a babble of voices and someone was shouting his name. There he is! The voice was shouting again.

'O-r-in! O-R-I-N!' It was Lutor's voice!

'Give me your hand.' Kamin was tied to a thick rope, bending over a rocky ledge and stretching out his hand. Lutor was holding one end and more people were pulling on it from the roadside. Orin tried to crawl his way out by pressing against the rock but the exertion almost made him faint. His left leg was red with blood. Inch by inch he nudged his body into a slanting position with his fingers clawing at the mountain like talons. Again, a tuft of grass brushed his face. He strained his right hand upward to clutch at the grass and found the twisted brown root of a ramang cane. It was sturdy like a warm, living hand. Sometimes these roots are so strong they split open the smallest, hairline cracks in hard rock and eat into their surface. Lutor and Kamin were overhead, bending over him.

'Give me your hand!'

Orin tugged at the stem. It swayed slightly but held. He was still trying to shout and wondering if it was the wind lifting him. Kamin was by his side. One two three—panting and choking, his right hand met Lutor's. Other hands caught his arms, his body, and gripping him with superhuman strength they slowly heaved him up.

The news of the accident spread like wild fire. The hospital was teeming with people and the compound had to be cleared by force, with Lutor standing outside right on the road with a group of policemen. When Kamin arrived, Lutor left him in charge of the crowd now clamouring with questions, and went in to be with Orin and the driver who was under sedation in the next ward. He was out of danger—the brave little man. Orin was in a hospital bed with bright lights shining all around. His face was bruised and swollen like a pumpkin, he had cracked his jaw and suffered multiple fractures and dislocated his left ankle but miraculously he had survived. He was coherent and said that Kasi knew the killers.

'Shh…Don't talk now…' Lutor whispered, bending over Orin's cracked and broken mouth. It had been five hours of terror before Orin had been pulled up and the rescue operation had been called off.

It was Rasa Lutor was worried about. Rasa had suffered severe concussion and he had lost a lot of blood. A bullet had hit his inner right thigh and mangled a big artery. A bullet wound! Lutor was waiting to donate blood. All his workers were with him and a helicopter had arrived to evacuate Rasa and Kasi to Guwahati. Everyone had offered to donate blood and go with them. Kasi had been hit by the car when he had tried to jump clear of it. His inert body had been lying on the side of the road and the doctor feared that an injury to the spine might leave him paralysed. Both were airlifted to the neurological centre in Guwahati accompanied by Peter and Rasa's relatives. In the melee Lutor was silent as a rock. He felt his heart was a heavy, deep tunnel of unbearable stillness. The young boys milling around the hospital awaited his instructions, but they fell silent and moved away when they saw him approaching. Something had happened. Kellan was dead! A burst of gunfire had shattered the windscreen and Kellan was covered in blood and shards of glass. He had reached across and yanked the passenger door open to push Rasa out. In that same instant the frightened driver had toppled forward too and after that Kellan had nosed the car into the mountain and buried his head in his arms as if to hide the bright red stain that had spread over his heart.

Lutor felt like throwing up. He still clutched the walkie-talkie that felt like a stone in his hand. It had crackled and hummed and the news of the ambush had reached him like a spitting, evil flame that grew bigger and bigger as he and Kamin had rushed to the site. He wanted to kill somebody. The old rage that used to burn in him flared up, he could taste blood and steel again like the knife blade of his dreams and he wondered how he had grown so old and careless to allow such a thing to happen.

The police were helpless. Whom shall we question, they asked. Lutor was aware that Kasi knew something, but for now that was irrelevant. Kellan's death was the knife that was stabbing him and Lutor was prepared to investigate anyone and everyone—friend, foe, brother, wife, relative, the leaders, students, the whole damn state if it came to that.

Aohun was the first person to rush to meet him at the hospital. Two ministerial colleagues were with him and Aohun did not stay long. He knew, and Lutor knew what was happening but there was no point exposing their weakness here in the hospital grounds. All Aohun could do was to okay the helicopter flight and make sure that every medical facility in Guwahati would be available to Lutor's friends.

'We'll meet,' he said, and departed. He had offered to resign on moral grounds but the cabinet had refused to accept his resignation, so now he could bargain.

'No arrests,' he told Lutor. 'Only encounters.'

When Tanik appeared at the hospital Lutor looked at him as at an enemy. Oh god, what horror! Who has done this thing, Tanik exclaimed.

Lutor did not answer. He was sick of this man's face, his small glinting eyes and the phoney air of concern and sympathy that he came with, saying, 'We will leave no stone unturned to nab the culprits,' more for the benefit of the press than out of any conviction. There were a lot of press people around and Tanik's lackeys shuffled around eagerly though they were careful to give Lutor a wide berth. One of them proffered his hand in a gesture of condolence but Lutor ignored it and the man swept forward to join Tanik who was conversing with the medical attendants and pointing upwards, saying, 'Almighty God will punish the culprits.'

Lutor had already radioed the checkgate and the orange van had been impounded. The driver was a young Assamese boy who said, yes, he had been there when the shooting started but he had run away because he was afraid. He didn't know anything. He was only carrying bricks to Itanagar. He wore a striped T-shirt and a leather wristband, and his sleepy looking eyes avoided Lutor's gaze.

Why was his van parked at the centre of the road facing the wrong side if he was coming to Itanagar?

Another car had come up from the opposite direction and bumped into his van, he said.

'Bumped it so hard to turn it right round with its heavy load of bricks?'

'I don't know. Ask the driver of the other car,' he said hotly.

Lutor wished someone would beat this young thug to death. Orin's car was lying in pieces at the bottom of the ravine and evidence would be inconclusive. Of the two motorcyclists and their machine there was not a sign. Two long bamboo poles had been found crushed under the van. Why was he carrying bricks? There was an order for it from a building contractor. Who was this contractor? The boy gave the name of a man who was a friend of a former legislator. 'Oh yes, I ordered bricks but I ordered a truckload.' He had been dealing with a steel fabrication unit in Assam. 'I don't know anything about this man,' the contractor said. Lutor knew the case would drag on. At every turn more complications would crop up and in the absence of forensic experts and laboratory facilities the case would meet the same fate as all other investigations in the past. A dead end. No clues. Everyone goes home on bail. A cold case.

This is what it has come to, Lutor thought, walking up and down the hospital corridor and nodding silently to the frightened nurses. Peter had handed him a small notebook before he had left for Guwahati on the chopper telling him that he had found it in Kasi's bag hanging on his office chair. A brief glance had shown him that it was a personal diary full of notes, songs, and a list of names that appeared to be coded with references to an 'uncle,' and 'grandfather'. In one of the pages Lutor saw a copy of the letter with the caption: *Truth Will Prevail* that had been circulating in the town. How had Kasi come by this?

'I think he's had it since we found that guy in Pasighat, remember?' Peter had said.

Lutor cursed himself again. So many signs along the way and he had missed everything! Murders, deaths, kidnappings—so many random acts of violence, but they were supposed to be happening elsewhere. Not here, not in this town, not in Itanagar, not in this state!

So Kamin was right, after all, he thought. Time was running out. It had already run out. His friend was dead and there was the other pressing thing weighing on him. What would he say to Umsi now?

The women

In another room Ongat looked at a girl sitting up on the hospital bed and felt bitterness rising up to her throat. Yet when she spoke her voice was calm and her eyes betrayed nothing, only concern.

'Tell me what happened.'

Everything, every shred of evidence pointed to the girl being the key to unlock the terrible mystery that had thrown her son Kasi on the road so badly crushed by the weight of the car that the attackers had left him for dead. Now he lay on a hospital bed fighting for his life while she—this girl—was sitting here with a clear face and sad, shadowed eyes.

'Tell me…'

'I can't remember. I heard them shouting and then they came and looked at him.'

'Who came?'

'Two men…I think. I don't know who they were.'

'What did they say? Did they say anything?'

'They said, come out! We are going to kill you.'

Ongat held her breath. 'Come out from where?' Oh, how hard this was going to be. But she had to know the truth. 'Were you inside the car?'

'No. I was outside. I was waiting…'

'Waiting, where?'

'I was with a friend. I was alone…' Everything she said was garbled and contradictory. 'I saw them at the Gohpur crossing.'

Ongat knew she had been on a two-wheeler that had almost crashed into the police van speeding towards the accident site. She had clutched at a passing auto-driver and told him to turn around and drive away, shouting, 'There's been an accident! Take me to the hospital, quick!' That was how the police and Lutor had met her on the road. It was much later that she had been placed in hospital because of an injury to her head and it was then that the police had been told, by her, that she had seen the car flying over the edge of the road when some men started firing.

Who were these men? She would not say. She said she did not know anything. She wept. She said she wanted to die. God was punishing her. All she prayed for was for everyone to live.

Liar! You lying whore, Ongat thought. Look at your tear-stained face. False. Your hair, your body. Witch. Where were you coming from? Why did you follow my son on that road? The questions raced through her head. So many questions. But the only one she needed an answer to was: why were you there?

Ah! It had been a rough life. It was not over yet but the years were running out and her heart was tired, tired like a drowning bird. She had kept still, holding the past away from her and she had succeeded. Where was that man who was the father of this boy? She did not know and she did not care. But she wanted her son. She wanted him alive. That was the only thing she wanted now. How dare the government talk about security and wretched policies when her son was dying and no one could tell her why?

It was a strange case. Maybe the presence of the woman was secondary. The audacity of the attack suggested professional killers. The presence of the pick-up van, the missing bikers and the useless bamboo poles they were dragging, probably as a decoy not to be overtaken, suggested a careful and well-timed plan. But professionals operate as hired killers. The question was who had hired them? The police said they were on the case but already they appeared to be flagging. There was no forensics report forthcoming even though the scene of the crime had already been examined by the whole town.

The image of Kellan's face kept coming back to haunt Lutor and one question turned over and over in his head. Who gains from such an incident? Who would create such a situation, force such circumstances?

When Lutor saw Kellan's body hanging out of the broken car the first thing that came to his mind was a story he had heard as a young boy about a pre-dawn raid when a band of warriors were nearing their target village. His father had looked up and seen a woman perched on a tree. She had let out a great shriek as she shot an arrow at him. In reflex he had pointed his rifle and pulled the trigger. Like a wounded animal the woman had fallen straight down with a thud. Dinu and his friends had run back towards him. They stood in a circle around the fallen woman who lay prone on her back with a red flower spreading over her half-naked torso. Her neck was covered with beads and that was all that hid her bosom, but now her necklaces had swung aside and were being swallowed by the pool of blood rising up out her body, just there, underneath the beads. She was still breathing and looking directly at him. Lomey, the great warrior had felt his heart cringe in fear. He crouched down but she had turned her eyes away as if she did not want to die with the image of his face bending over her. At the same instant Dinu had pulled him back. Don't touch her. She is a woman of the village. See how wild they are! We have to harden our hearts.

His heart! Lomey's heart was beating in rhythm with the laboured, rasping breath of the woman. If it had not been for his gun he would have been dead! They left the woman where she lay, staring at the treetops. Perhaps she would turn into a spirit, he thought wildly, as they moved forward into forest cover. A woman! What a frightening sight that had been. Who was she? Step by step his breath returned to him but he could feel a new presence that was to stay with him forever afterwards, as if the woman and her beads had displaced his heart and turned it into a stone. And just like it was for his father, Lutor had clasped Kellan and felt a new presence—as if sorrow for the death of his lifelong friend would kill his heart.

They were a band of women rising above the dip in the road approaching silently like ferocious lionesses. There was Gagil, Tibul, and Ongat and their compatriots. Their faces were devoid of expression. They wore their work-day clothes, simple ga-le and blouse, and their eyes showed no awareness of the bright sunlight and the stirring day full of bird calls and the soft, fluttering breeze. Lutor saw them approaching and prepared himself.

They entered quietly and he barely greeted them, so compressed was his heart at this terrible time. 'We are going to meet Tanik,' Gagil said at last.

Yes. Now he stole a glance at the group seated in his Itanagar home. Ongat was sitting before him staring at nothing, her empty gaze fixed right there, just beside his left arm. He saw that her face was puffy and strained and his heart quailed at the sight. He was grateful when Tibul said, 'It is time that we spoke to Tanik. We all know he is linked somehow with this case.'

'We want a report. We want answers,' said Ongat.

Yes. Lutor was thinking of Orin lying in hospital with his face and body all battered and bruised. Rasa was critical. Kasi was coming round but it was still touch and go. He wondered if Ongat knew about the diary in her son's bag.

'My poor boys,' Ongat was saying. 'What have Orin and Kasi got to do with all this? They were just there, driving to meet Kellan and look what happened. No law and order. No security. How can we live like this?'

We'll find them! We'll get the killers! Lutor wanted to fall on his knees. Forgive me! What shall I say to you? I have failed and now we have to bury the dead.

'No law and order,' Ongat repeated. 'Tell Aohun, tell Tanik that! Tell them to wipe this blood from that road. See if he can remove the bloodstains!' She buried her face in her hands. The women waited. Lutor waited, staring at nothing, feeling the silence killing him.

'We will go back to Pasighat tomorrow,' Gagil said at last. 'Mentiri, she didn't want to come. She's been badly frightened.' Gagil did most of the talking until she stood up and said it was time to call on Tanik. 'We don't know politics. We don't know about money and guns,' she said, 'but we know life. See what our lives have come to! Why like this?'

It shamed and hurt Lutor to think of how he had persisted in his investigations and brought Kellan into the picture. He should have kept him out of it. In a way Kellan's association with him had cost him his life and brought about the terrible accident that had hurt so many people. Rasa was fighting for his life because he had had something to say, and he and Aohun had called him to Itanagar.

When Tibul touched him on the shoulder and told him to be careful it made him cringe. They needed him and they were determined to look after him too. Was he forgiven then? He felt crushed and timid. Their willingness to forgive him hit him like a hammer blow. Ah! How great a thing is forgiveness! Am I forgiven? He wanted to ask again and again but the women were leaving. Lutor walked with them to the gate, all these women, not so young anymore, suffering such grief. It was a matter of family, and Gagil was leading them like an aging lioness determined to do battle, just like in the old days, for hearth and home and for the lives of their sons and daughters. Oh! That bloody road! One could wipe the rocks clean of blood, scrub them till there was not a sign left of what had happened, but who would remove the bloodstains now smeared in their lives?

The immune state

Tanik's reaction to the visit of the women was to call a press conference. Kamin received the information and said the press was sure to play it up. Five boys of the Arunachal Pradesh Revolutionary Force (ADF) were going to surrender. The outfit, formed in the early nineties, had begun as the United Peoples Volunteers of Arunachal Pradesh (UPVA) and regrouped a few years later under its new name.

Everyone was seated in the big conference hall. The curtains were drawn but a breeze made them balloon out and the wide windows threw in plenty of light. Tanik was seated on the dais flanked by Aohun and his cabinet colleagues, the chief secretary and the Inspector General of Police along with the Home secretary and a young police superintendent. The press sat in a row to one side and cameramen and electronic media covered the front space, pulling equipment and wires while harassed officials waved at them to move aside. Peter was there. He had returned from Guwahati for the meeting. Rasa was stable but would need constant monitoring and medical attention for some more time. Kasi was bedridden and the doctors said he was suffering delirious fits.

'Today is a very important day! It will go down in the

annals of history. Today is the first surrender of militants in our state and we are very happy that our boys have decided to surrender with arms. They have come back to the right path.' Tanik turned to the IG who was staring vacantly but who now sat up and began to nod vigorously in agreement. 'So we can begin?' Tanik said.

Yes!

A name was called. All eyes turned to the door as a young man marched in. He was the chairman of the outfit and he had spent all his life in jungle camps operating in the eastern part of the state, and in the riverine tracts close to Pasighat. They managed arms and ammunition with the help of one or the other faction of the NSCN and had recently established links with militants in Assam. Sixteen criminal cases were registered against them. They were in the age group of thirty-two to nineteen years, and the youngest looked like an unkempt schoolboy dressed in camouflage jacket, baggy pants and canvas shoes. What had they done? What did they want?

'We want development. We realise we must work and help the government to achieve our desired goals. We have surrendered of our own will,' said the leader of the outfit.

The surrendered weapons were displayed on a long table and Lutor went up to have a closer look. There was a 12 bore SBBL gun with cartridges, three revolvers of Chinese and American make, an M20 pistol, 59 rounds of ammunition and two AK series rifles, five improvised (crude) bombs and detonators, and twenty kilos of explosive powder. Lutor picked up the rifle. It was shiny and heavy. It was hard to imagine anyone carrying it all the time up and down hills in rain and hot weather wondering when they would hit camp and eat something. Now and then they would be engaged in a skirmish, get some money and feel good, thinking that they were doing something. And then? They would escape to the jungle again. They would hide, plan, grow old, and suddenly one day they would be dead—killed in crossfire, or they would surrender arms, wanting to belong to the other side. Who had so many chances to 'belong', and at such cost to other people's lives? Where were the camps? Who commanded them? As far as he could understand there was no high command. The outfit was a small group hoping the older, bigger outfits would take them in.

'The government is the parent. The mai-baap,' Tanik was saying. 'We welcome our boys back and we will do everything to give them jobs and live a meaningful life.'

Lutor watched Tanik smiling and shaking his head pleasantly at the silent boys. The organisation had also surrendered their letter, seal and stamp pad. A policeman was escorting them out. Tanik had not said anything about the rehabilitation package. What would become of these young men? They would join the political bandwagon and receive money to run errands for politicians. Mai-baap! Tanik stopped at nothing to wring sympathy and appear magnanimous, but rumours were rife that young boys had undergone training with insurgent groups with the approval of their political masters in order to build up a force to drive out illegal settlers and refugees from the state and intimidate political rivals. Over the years they had splintered into the different revolutionary outfits of the state. True, or false? Who could say in this secretive atmosphere heavy with allegations and counter claims?

The boys filed out and Tanik said: 'I condemn the terrible attack on innocent people on the Gohpur road. We have lost one of our best officers and people who are my own kith and kin. My own brother from Tirap is also seriously injured. We will spare no attempt to nab the culprits. Our police are already on the job.' He stopped and looked around with unblinking eyes. Then he said: 'But I tell you, this was a plot to assassinate me!'

Lutor knew it was coming, yet when it did, the words shocked him. He felt the afternoon stretching back a hundred years and saw hillocks and streams where boys had raced in the light opening their torn shirts to the sun. It was a flashing image of another time, when he and Tanik were village boys, before the hillocks disappeared and the boys grew into men in concrete buildings surrounded by advisors and sycophants. He saw Aohun sitting rigid and upright in his seat. What was Tanik saying now? Yes, he was the target. The attack was instigated by political opponents who were afraid that he was going to crack down on militancy in the state and expose links between certain politicians and the ultras. They wanted to topple his government and seize power for themselves. 'But I tell you,' Tanik was shouting now, 'politically these people cannot do anything against me. They can't kill me! I will always be protected! There is the one above, almighty god of our fathers who sees right and wrong. If someone wants to grow taller than me let them. I do not envy anyone, and no one should envy me. But I tell you nothing is going to happen. I will survive. My colleagues will survive.'

In another country, in another time, Tanik might have been a fearless despot, a dictator, a man-eating empire builder, but here, today, he was simply an interesting politician who made visitors laugh with his charming naivete. There was something youthful about him, debonair, and one could not resist his gifts and immense hospitality.

This contains a wonder drug, he would say, pointing to plants and fruit. The world does not know anything about this but our people have used it for years. We have these secrets. If you have a proposal we are ready to provide land for a medical centre, for tourism, for culture, for development of the state…

Nothing came of these offers except secret understandings with shadowy businessmen and the growth of new companies and property developers who would close shop after a few years. The general trend of the bureaucracy skirmishing with politicians did not exist here. Tanik and his political cronies had succeeded in rearing the deadly virus of immunity where the civil and the political combined to join forces as a regime surrounded by his circus of dubious advisors and sycophants. Absolute power equals absolute immunity. Dissenting civil servants were offered impossible alternatives. Sign, or be damned. No questions. No investigating agencies. No public opinion. Everything was hushed and easy as pie.

'I have been given the leadership and I have never subdued people's feelings,' declared Tanik. 'It is a tribal characteristic to speak out. I say, let everyone speak. I have called many meetings to sort out differences, but people clandestinely join other parties and try to dislodge the government. Who can tolerate such a thing? And now you see this attack. They were trying to topple me but they failed. An impartial enquiry will be conducted. *White ko white black ko black!* It is a good turning point to scrutinise criminal activity in our state. Now they have done this, it is like spitting at the sky. The spit will fall back on them!'

The APCOCA diaries

A week after the incident, the controversial Bill for Control of Organised Crime Act (APCOCA) was passed in the state legislative assembly amidst tight security. A group of protesters waved banners and shouted at the fleet of ministerial cars but police and CRPF pushed them back. In his speech to move the Bill, Tanik was very brief. He said that his government was committed to ensuring peace and development in the state. Aohun, in his address in support of the Bill gave his assurance that the Bill would not violate human rights nor be misused against political organisations, students and media. Our prime concern is to secure freedom from fear for the people of the state, he said. APCOCA's enactment would give a clear signal to the Army and security forces that the state government was serious about controlling the activities of terrorist groups. To withdraw the Bill on the mere supposition that it will be abused would not serve the interest of any party.

'Don't bring tears to our eyes,' said Temat. He was bitterly opposed to the Bill but Aohun had issued a three-line whip to ensure that the Bill was enacted—no one would be absent. All would vote for the motion. And if there was any violation it would be taken up under the anti-defection

Bill. Now Temat said, 'At no point of time were the people of Tirap and Changlang consulted on this Bill. Now it is placed before the house and I have to humbly agree to its enactment. So be it. I am a loyal UNC party man and my only prayer is that APCOCA will not be used against innocent people of my district to harass my beloved brothers and sisters.'

He sat down with a stiff bow to the Speaker. The marathon five and a half hour discussion that followed showed up the ignorance of the legislators on the issue. Some were sycophantic in their support, while others argued that strong customary laws were enough to fight crime.

'Our traditional law says an eye for an eye. It is the same as APCOCA.'

'Bah!' someone else shouted. 'Customary laws to deal with AK-47s?'

'More laws mean more criminals!'

'What do you mean? No laws no criminals?'

'Laws should be harsh on those who want to destroy the fabric of society!'

Lutor sat facing the treasury bench and wondered what would happen now. Temat depressed him by his arrogance and melodramatic mannerisms. He was using words to absolve himself so that later he could say, 'But I was against it. It is on record.' It was true what they said of him, that his outspokenness was based on lies. If only the Tirap leaders had put aside their petty rivalries and worked together, all this might have been prevented, thought Lutor.

Close on the heels of the Assembly proceedings, Aohun's police arrested two boys in Khonsa driving a brand new Maruti Alto. Where were they from? From Dimapur, they said. What were they doing here? They were visiting a friend. A friend, who? There was some confusion. No, they were guests of Sambong, and the minister, they said.

'The minister is in Itanagar. Get out of the car.' During interrogation and examination of their documents the young sub-inspector found that they were active members of the NSCN (I-M) shuttling between Khonsa, Itanagar and Dimapur. He filed a report and sent them to Itanagar where a police case under APCOCA was registered against them for engaging in unlawful activities and obtaining pecuniary gains through their activities.

'Oh yes, I know them,' said Sambong when asked if he knew the two boys. 'I think they are trying to start a business in Itanagar.'

'What business?'

'Oh, how can I know what young boys want? They are better known to Temat.' Temat said he had been introduced to them by a friend from Nagaland, but that was all. He had met them only once, very briefly.

'But they were seen emerging out of your house.'

'No, of course not! They were trying to contact Mankong.' He stood facing the policeman angrily and said, 'I know what you think. You think I am trying to blame Mankong and this is personal rivalry. But you listen to this. I have no bone to pick with anyone. In fact, I am prepared to resign and take sanyaas if it will bring peace. Ask Mankong!'

Mankong was out of station and no one was able to trace him.

'Find out. Find out. Interrogate them!' Aohun ordered.

The name of the tall, fair boy was John alias Jaku Taorin, resident of Purana Bazaar, Dimapur, Nagaland. His colleague Chey was from Manipur. Under interrogation while in judicial custody, John confessed that a personal diary recovered from his possession belonged to him and was maintained in his handwriting. John was a member of the NSCN steering committee and he had come to Itanagar to replace Captain Arno. Who was Arno? He was the outfit's armed wing member stationed in Itanagar before John. John's instructions were to mobilise a signature campaign against enactment of APCOCA and change of leadership of the government that was responsible for getting the APCOCA Bill passed. He had obtained a number of signatures during the month of July and collected more than twelve lakh in cash from certain politicians. John and his colleague reported to uncle Alwin who lived in Dimapur. Uncle Alwin sent them messages. John possessed a satellite phone gifted to him by a friend of Alwin who lived in Kolkata. Sambong had helped him buy the new car. They were planning to drive it back to Dimapur.

Lutor came to the lock-up. He looked at the pale face of John and saw a thin youth dressed in jeans and a brown T-shirt with white lettering: YOU CANT ESCAPE. There was a picture of a fish, and lettering at the back—ME. His friend Chey sat bent and silent, looking down at the cement floor. Dangerous people? How old were they—twenty-six, twenty-seven?

Who did they meet in Itanagar?

'We were introduced to many friends,' said John. Lutor had seen the diary with the names of ministers that John had met in their bungalows and in a hotel room in Itanagar. He knew three boys from Pasighat had also met John in March and pledged to work for the organisation. What he wanted to know was Kasi's involvement. No, John shook his head and said he had never met anyone by that name. Kasi's name was not in the diary either. This was a relief for

Lutor but it left a blank in the investigations on the identity of the two men who had ambushed Rasa's car. The mystery of the girl he had bumped into on Gohpur road had also been cleared up; she was Susanna alias Chanu, a relative of John. There was nothing to tag her to the ambush. If Orin and Kasi had not rushed out in that car, Rasa and the driver might have been killed too. Their arrival had panicked the men. Did the killers think Kellan was Rasa? Maybe Kasi had passed on information about Rasa's movements but he didn't know the killers, thought Lutor, and the killers believed Rasa would be travelling alone. What about John? It was evident he had been in constant communication with NSCN cadre in many cities of the country and abroad, but John and Chey were on a separate assignment and they were not the killers. In the eyes of the young man Lutor saw only disdain. John believed in what he was doing. He had recorded his dream of climbing to the top of a mountain and achieving freedom through obedience and sacrifice. It was the only thing he had known. If you remove me there will be another in my place, his eyes told Lutor. He answered questions calmly as if he already knew that his work was done but the mission would go on and there would always be a replacement.

In Guwahati, Kasi succumbed to his injuries and Lutor realised a chance to find out the truth about all that had happened had slipped away. He looked at Orin's face and knew that Orin had stumbled upon some secret, maybe, but there would be no one to corroborate evidence. They were only in possession of a notebook that recorded Kasi's theories of war and song. It soothed his soul, he had written. One day he thought he had heard singing in the forest. That was what had drawn him, the singing. It happened when he was visiting Kellan in Tirap and it had been a stroke of destiny that Kellan had sent him out to buy candles. 'Just get candles and come back,' Kellan had said. Kasi was very happy. He was in awe of Kellan—his quiet, intense nature, and his kindness. Kellan always hailed him with a smile and treated him as an equal. He could feel it. The man was good. The shop was almost closing but two men were there, talking to the shopkeeper. 'Is it ready?' One of them was leaning forward and asking.

'Oh yes, of course.'

It was just at that moment that he, Kasi, had stepped in. 'Give me a packet of candles,' he said.

The shopkeeper shuffled towards the back shelves. The two men and Kasi stood waiting. One of them, the taller one, was staring at him and Kasi said hello. He didn't reply. The shopkeeper was coming back. How many packets?

'One, okay give me two.' Kasi pulled out his wallet.

Are you living here? It was the taller one.

'I'm from Pasighat,' Kasi said.

'Oh.'

'But I live in Itanagar,' Kasi said.

'Where are you staying here?'

He told them. The shopkeeper counted out the change slowly and the taller one said, 'Why don't you join us, we are going to a friend's place. It is nearby.'

That was the way it had happened. He could think of no good excuse except to say that it was getting late, and the two men had said, only for a short while. It is not far. This is our uncle's house, they said, leading him up to a square building. The windows were brightly lit and Kasi heard the sound of singing. A fortyish man opened the door. He was striking to look at, dressed in a dark blue suit and a yellow printed tie and his rosy face was beaming with happiness. Kasi felt a strong hand clasp him and draw him in. 'Come in, friend,' the man said.

The evening passed. He drank fruit juice and he might have talked a lot, he could not recall. He had never felt so welcome anywhere else before. He had fallen under the spell of songs, rituals, drums. The atmosphere was hypnotic: this meeting, who knows when we will meet again? So, dance! What does it matter that the decorations are now tufts of grass or wool dyed red? Our blood is still the colour red. Our hearts are pumping the same blood, the blood that ran in our forefathers. The song was an invocation. The song was a roar. Arise. Awaken. Go forth. Our naked feet are the weapons that carry us into the jungle, across the hills, into new territories, up into the mountains and into the heart of war, sacrifice and freedom.

He remembered a young woman sitting beside him who said she was a relative of the tall, fair man. His name was John, she told him, and she was Susanna from Dimapur. They had a small shop there, but business was very tough. We want to start afresh in Itanagar. Would that be very difficult, she wanted to know.

No, many people were doing business in Itanagar, Kasi said.

John said 'We are the same people. We are like brothers. We will meet again,' and Kasi had said yes, they would. After that John had contacted him, once, in Pasighat. Then John made a number of visits to Itanagar and he and John met in the Sochi hotel right in the centre of town. They drank rum, triple XXX, and ate greasy omelettes. Uncle doesn't like this, John told him, he was afraid of uncle, but he is not here, ha! Ha! Cheers! John said he needed some things and gave Kasi money to buy blankets, medicines and envelopes. Once they had gone out together and John had bought a waistcoat. Several times in a month John went away to meet his uncle and once he had returned with Susanna and the other man Kasi had first seen in the shop. His name was Chey, John told him, he was here to assist him because he was not well and the doctor had advised him to rest. 'My blood pressure shoots up, even though I don't feel anything. That's the dangerous part,' John said.

'What work do you do,' Kasi asked him again, curious.

'Oh, I am entrusted with so many special duties,' said John. 'I have to meet so many people. Do you know…?' He named many politicians.

No, Kasi did not know them except by name. He knew Lutor and sometimes he saw Mr. Aohun, he said.

What about a man by the name of Rasa? Oh yes, he had met him at Kellan's place in Tirap. Why, do you have to meet him?

'Yes, I have some work with him. Will he be coming to visit Itanagar anytime?'

'He will be coming to Itanagar soon.'

'Mr. Rasa is coming to Itanagar?'

'Yes. He is likely to be here soon.'

The notes trailed away after this. John bought a heater and had watched TV most of the time. One mysterious entry was a line that said, 'Oh, the news is that X has betrayed…' but there was nothing else to go on. The last entry said: *Nobody boasts even if he catches many fishes. Those who want to live, he lives according to his own wishes.*

Who was X? Was it a reference to Rasa? Lutor wondered. Rasa had hinted at a larger plot to create political instability in the state and install a chief minister who would do their bidding. By and by the state government would agree to a token referendum for Tirap and Changlang and the Centre would bow to the people's vote by which the two districts could be bargained away for the larger interests of peace in the region and an end to the Naga insurgency. But there were red herrings everywhere. X could be anyone. Everyone was in connivance with someone else for something. Lutor knew many people had met John and Chey in a hotel room one evening. Everyone was listed in John's diary. Thank god, he thought, that he had seen it before it disappeared as classified material. Lutor's first reaction was to confront Tanik.

'Drop your ministers,' he said. 'Drop Mankong and Temat.'

Tanik looked shocked. 'Why! What is this?'

'Drop them if you are serious about finding the killers. Drop them. See what happens. Take action!'

Tanik looked at Lutor in an uncomfortable way and said if there was evidence he was ready to drop anyone. 'But they have not done anything anti-national! I will also resign if anyone in my government is guilty of harbouring criminals. But let us wait for the police to do their duty.'

Lutor turned to Aohun. 'They can be axed. Drop them, both of them together.'

'I can't. On what grounds?'

'The car! Sambong helped them to buy the car, didn't he? There's something here. He's Temat's man, and it's aiding and abetting criminal activity. You can expel him from the Party. Mankong paid money to John. That's wilful funding of terrorists. It's an offence.'

'But everyone has paid money!' Aohun exclaimed. John's diary was full of accounts of who had paid how much, but as usual it was a security issue and Aohun was trapped by the need for secrecy. In a token gesture Sambong and Temat were arrested under APCOCA, but were immediately out on anticipatory bail shouting they were not guilty of anything and they would turn State Approvers if that was what the government wanted. How dare anyone accuse them like this!

'I have done what I could,' Tanik said, and left the field open to Aohun who faced the brunt of public protest over the APCOCA legislation that was now viciously criticised as a useless, discriminatory piece of law that made a show of arresting political high-ups only to release them immediately on bail. Lutor was equally angry that Aohun should have fallen into the trap of Tanik's manipulative politics. 'You should have dropped them. Expelled them from the Party!' he shouted at his friend.

'But you see Tanik didn't! It wasn't in my hands!' Aohun shouted back. He was hot and angry. It had been a long, heartstopping summer full of political unrest and hateful allegations but Aohun was a fighter. In a long, chequered career he was equal to Tanik, and he told Lutor, 'I had a dream the other night. I was in a closed space. I thought, oh! I have made my house in the wrong way. Then I heard the spirit of my dead father telling me, "You should put a window there." I did that, it was a wooden house, and suddenly I saw the sky and flew out! What do you think of that?'

'It means you will become chief minister,' said Lutor, glad to see his friend indomitable as ever.

For people on the periphery, like me, the run-up to the election was a long journey into a forgotten landscape. There were green trees and voices of women lilting in the wind. They were calling me. Many relatives had come from Pasighat and visitors filled the hospital to meet Orin. Bits of ginger were scattered around the room and Lutor had tied a ridin twine around Orin's wrist. Two metal discs shaped like a cross hung on the wall above his bed. This was the emul, the instrument to make music to call back the wandering soul from the path of death. The rainman had put it there. Lipun came in one day, talking non-stop in a breathless, eager voice. 'Oh, here is the room,' he said, praising the hospital and the ward and the care they were giving Orin. I knew Lipun was frightened and this was his way of dealing with the shock. How old he was—he need not have taken the trouble to come to the hospital, I thought. He had avoided hospitals all his life. 'Doctors will always find something wrong with you,' I remembered him saying, yet here he was gazing about him with perplexed, rheumy eyes. Kampo brought the old man up on Orin's progress, telling him that he would be discharged soon, and I was surprised to hear her gentle, soothing tone. She has a spiritual side, I thought. Kampo, the spirited, rebellious girl was talking to Lipun as if to a child who needed consolation. Lutor is right, I thought. Our people are the salt of the earth. In fact, it was I who was struggling to keep up, still feeling shaken by the Gohpur road ambush and how anything could happen in the blink of an eye. Gagil had marshalled forces and many young relatives had arrived from Pasighat. Kampo and they took turns to keep watch over Orin. 'The other night I was fast asleep when I felt something cold on my left arm,' one of the boys said. 'I thought it was a ghost!'

'Ha, hai! What happened?'

'It was the nurse. She thought I was the patient and she was going to give me an injection. I screamed.'

Ha ha!

Another evening, when everything was quiet, I felt a warm hand on my shoulder. I was tired and dopey. 'Are you asleep…?' It was Kamin. 'I am so sorry,' he whispered. 'Is there anything you need?' He was pushing my hair back. I thought his hand was trembling and I shut my eyes tighter, feeling, for no reason, as if I wanted to weep.

Book Five

THE DIE IS CAST

Elections

No other animal tries to hide his inherent nature except man. In the massive exercise of an election the entire state with its rocky, pot-holed, unkempt facade of development was bedecked with flags and banners and overnight, sour, scheming politicians wrapped in layers of camouflage turned into smiling benefactors who gave people what they wanted. The electorate was the beggared mistress they returned to every time and they were courting her again with a heady cocktail of culture, promises and money. They slaughtered mithun and filled every house with money, blankets, and crates of whisky. The lucky ones got motorcycles and new cars.

'Everyone is having secret meetings,' said Kampo. At the end of the year feverish underground activity had gripped the citizens. No one slept. All the talk was about elections and money. The Banderdewa police checkgate made news when they found stacks of money in a fake coffin carried by weeping women holding agarbattis. Where did people get so much money? It was unbelievable, the amount of money people today could whip up just like that.

'In the past people made money from earth cutting and tree felling, the two major industries of the state,' said Kamin curtly. Now it was a different ball game. There were new sources and a candidate could spend a million rupees on nine thousand voters and yet be defeated because his opponent would spend more. Obviously, the cost of electioneering was going up all the time.

The UNC and AINA offices were lit up with coloured bulbs and it was apparent by the number of parked cars that they were busy. Women were very visible too, riding motorcycles and driving Maruti cars with a record number of them vying for party tickets. For the first time nine Independent candidates were also preparing to file their nominations. There were meetings, appeals, rallies and reports of huge pay-offs, and with the call of the student's union to boycott Statehood Day celebrations in protest against APCOCA and the government's failure on all other counts, the wooing of the electorate began.

After the press conference Tanik had said nothing more. The hunt for the killers was still on but no fresh clue had surfaced. Lutor stood by his friend and he and Aohun faced the brunt of student agitation and angry protests. There was speculation that Aohun was a stooge of the NSCN and he wanted to stop Rasa from giving evidence against them. It was not clear which faction they were referring to but letters were floated saying Aohun would be tried by the court of the people. Aohun was furious. 'What court of the people?' he shouted. 'Why are politicians blamed for everything? Why are only *we* representative? We are all representative and equally responsible! What's wrong with these people?'

Lutor knew about elections and public panic and predicted more rumours and mudslinging yet. It was a complicated game but he was ready to press on. 'The accident was a personal tragedy for me,' was all he said. It was a cruel public. Kijji Ongo started a story about Lutor's love interest, gossiping that Lutor had been so busy that he had failed to protect the brother of his sweetheart. Lutor looked at Kamin and said, 'Tell Kijji I will kill anyone who brings me such gossip.'

Lutor did not show outward panic but sometimes even he despaired. Everything was equally true or untrue, and everyone was equally captive, even though he wanted to say, 'No, no, look here, this is not what it seems. This is how we were. This is not what we want to be. This is the way we are. This is what we are trying to do.' But who would have the last word? The changes seen from within, as insiders, these things could not be expressed nor understood in the way it was meant. Everything, it seemed, was only in the moment.

Money, money money! 'Money is the key,' said Kamin. The other parties carried briefcases and drove in shiny vehicles. They began their campaign with well-printed pamphlets, multi-coloured and arrogant.

'Yipes, poor creature,' said Kampo when she saw the ANP manifesto with its election symbol of a black mithun.

Orin glared at her. He had a slight limp but his leg was mending, and he was back at work. Everyone was struggling to help, in one way or another, and some opted to sit with Orin in his office, thinking of words. What are the words to woo the public and appeal to voters? Kind words? Hard words, emotional, provocative words?

Lutor struggled with a typewriter, sitting on a low stool hunched over the machine and typing with hard, slow punches.

'What are you writing?'

He had thrown out his arms and said, smiling and stretching back, 'I am trying to draft the Party Manifesto.'

Words, words. 'It has to be done, you know, and then it goes for printing.'

Who uses a manual typewriter in these times? Lutor had said he had tried his hand at a laptop but felt that it was so small it would fall apart in his hands. I can hardly see the arrow, he exclaimed, and once or twice everything had disappeared, just like that. Paperwork, he hated it. Yet he wrote everything down in longhand and fussed over words—he did not want 'alleged,' he did not like vicious words, but he wanted facts. Sometimes, watching him had been like seeing someone tapping out his heart. He was always struggling to gather the hills and villages with arms wide enough to take it all in and bring it together to merge into a balance between an interior and exterior landscape. He cared, and that made him vulnerable, and, according to Kamin, it made him weak.

Now he said, 'best to be direct and honest,' as if this was the easiest thing in the world. 'Talk about policies. After all, what can a government give its people? It can give good policies.'

'It won't sell, not without money,' Kamin insisted. He moved around more than anyone, into people's homes and the back alleys of shops and small huts of workmen, rickshaw pullers and petty traders. In Pasighat he said the aying vote would count for a lot, tipping the balance, and he knew how Tanik's hatchet men had already captured them with money and threats.

'I can take anything but this asking for money is too much,' said Lutor. 'I can't stay in the house. Any time of day or night and early morning someone will barge in, all talking about medical bills, fire victims, widow, food, fuel, accident. My pocket is torn, empty! One man said to me the other day, money, money, money!'

'Tanik is distributing money to everyone.'

'Let him' Lutor shouted. 'It's easy money! Who funded the dissidents when he came back to power? What held them together? It was money, nothing else. Everyone should know about his money. Politics in the state is a distribution system for easy money. Talk about terrorism. Look at the extortion racket. Those who pay are assured of political success for the next six years. No one will be allowed to contest against them. How long will he carry on like this?'

Kamin slumped back in his seat and compressed his lips. He was impatient with all that was happening. He found Lutor's words weak and clichéd. Easy money, so what? The whole world was on to it, why not us? There was no time for high-sounding arguments. Politics was about winning and without money no one could win. Not even Lutor, not any more. The times were different. People were different. The consensus theory of Lutor was outdated. One could impose consensus. If people could not read and write then someone who could would have to take over. If destiny was favourable he would be a good leader. This was Kamin's argument. Immediacy was what mattered. Grabbing power was what mattered. Power was what mattered. One could start from there, and then if it was in your power one could begin giving back to the people.

'We don't want to make the same mistakes!' Lutor would not let up. 'We talk about the failure of elected leaders. Are we a failed state? What is wrong with our state? What is lacking today for our young people? You tell me. There is no inspiration. This is what we must change. Bring back inspiration. A new image, self pride, hope!'

'Not in our lifetime,' Kamin said despairingly. 'If you keep thinking on those lines there'll be no government. We might as well pack it in.' He had assessed the party positions and concluded that AINA was mounting a strong campaign. 'I think they are going to get nine or ten seats. We could work together to overthrow Tanik,' Kamin said.

Lutor refused to respond to these discussions. 'We are already working on that,' he said.

Lutor said this, but his days were restless with people coming and going, hopping from one camp to the other as if election time was a festival of money and liquor. It was easy to lose track under the sheer weight of people pressing in on you as if they wanted to see how much you could withstand. Nothing was sacred. Everything was open—house, hearth, your pockets, toilet, travel, your car, everything. In Pasighat, the rainman's house was crowded with people from morning till night. Everyone wanted to meet Lutor. 'Lutor, it's me! I have come early before the crowd.' They would shake his mosquito net and call out loudly, 'Where is your cook? Tell him to make some tea—since you're not serving apong.' A group of people stood smiling at him the moment he opened his door. 'It is my fate,' he joked sometimes. He tried to attend to everyone—it was his nature, but with all that had happened he was irritable and sometimes he felt wearied to death. They drank tea, chewed paan and stayed on for meals. After that it was favours, employment and requests for medical bills to be paid. 'If they elected me only to dole out money then they are mistaken,' he exclaimed in exasperation. Every year he had seen it grow worse, the electorate turning into a swarm of flies alighting on anything that carried the scent of money. He was comfortable with people in the village but the new Arunachal of shiny suits and dark glasses made his blood boil. One day a woman came in and sat down gingerly on a stool. Lutor felt his skin prickle when he realised she was a friend of his ex-wife.

'Hai', she smiled falsely. 'I thought I was family but it seems I am not…' She burst into tears.

'Why, what's wrong? Stop it! What's the matter with you?'

'I am so ashamed. Hai! You have put everyone into some Works Department. What about me?'

'But you never asked me to!'

'Does family have to spell out everything?'

'But those people I helped with jobs were already working here. They look after the house and they are needy people. I never saw you and you never mentioned wanting a job.'

'But you never asked me,' she insisted.

'Does family have to dole out everything?' he retorted now, angry and sick of everyone, especially this woman in her bright gale, shining Rolex and wearing bright lipstick to match.

'Hai,' she wailed, 'I am helpless, what shall I do? I could commit suicide!'

'Go ahead! Lutor wanted to shout. 'Shall I buy you a nylon rope, you stupid woman?' He was incensed that she should dare demand money and a job when all the time husband and wife were probably being paid by Tanik. My god! These people, insufferable!

He was rescued by the phone. 'Yes, yes, I am here…' It was Rudar asking something about his programme. Yes, yes, he shouted, angry at the weak phone and the dim lights and the long journeys on bad roads that he knew he would have to make a hundred times in order to move his Party forward towards electoral victory. He looked at the woman and said, 'I have to go. I'll see what I can do.'

She gave him a knowing look and murmured, 'Don't forget, after all, we are family.'

Outside, the air was cold and fresh. His meeting with the woman had disturbed him and he wanted to get away somewhere and be alone. Umsi had disappeared into a deep silence and he was worried. Why was she not responding to his phone calls? He wanted to say, don't run away again. Don't leave me! This time I will not survive. But he was afraid. Maybe she had not forgiven him for Kellan's death. If only she would speak to him again!

There was another thing worrying him. A few weeks ago he had seen Lipun and found the old man tired and flushed. He was coughing badly and Lutor had suggested a check-up. Lipun had balked. 'I don't need to do that,' he said. 'I am quite well.'

'I think all that has happened has hit him hard,' said Rudar, meaning the violence and bloodshed on Gohpur road. The state has changed so much, it must be incomprehensible. 'Say, why don't we do a trip to Guwahati for a check-up? It will be a change for the old man and for us. We'll go there and drive back in a couple of days.'

The end of an era

There was something familiar about clinics everywhere that made Lutor feel tense and vulnerable. He saw the chequered floor of the OPD cash counters, the row of rooms with numbers and people waiting, lined up or sitting on benches, just outside the closed doors.

'Tuck your feet in,' he heard a man say to his wife.

Everyone was impatient; everyone was asking each other their number on the list, who was ahead in the queue, is the doctor in.

Rudar and Lutor were in a clinic in Guwahati where they had brought Lipun and much to their surprise the doctor had said that Lipun should be admitted immediately. Now they were waiting to meet the doctor. 'Ah, here it is,' the good-looking doctor was holding up a big, shiny X-ray and saying, 'the left lung is totally white. He must have had an earlier case of tuberculosis?'

Rudar wiped his mouth and looked at his friend. This was unexpected. How could this be? Lipun never talked about illness. But that was the thing about Lipun. He would not talk about himself. I have nothing to hide, he would say, and Lutor would be defeated by his utter simplicity. Say something! Tell me something! He wanted to shake his old mentor and make him spill out words, advice, love, hate, anger, anything, but all he got was a simple, puzzled look that broke his heart.

'Did the patient complain of chest pains, congestion?'

No, Lutor did not know anything about that. He remembered some hot sunny days when Lipun coughed and sat with a flushed face on his folding chair. But that was such a long time ago. Once, only once, had he mentioned being quite ill in his young days. It was during a time when Lutor had been sick in one of those remote outposts and Lipun had mentioned it just then, as if talking about someone else's illness might somehow ease Lutor's depression. 'I was stuffed with medicine for a whole year,' he had said. 'Since then I have never taken another medicine.'

'What happened?'

'Oh, coughing, weakness. Maybe it was malnutrition, ha ha! That's why I say we should drink milk even though our people resisted dairy products until settlers brought cows and goats.' And that had been the end of anything Lipun said about illness or health.

'What is the treatment now?' Lutor didn't know what to ask the doctor.

'He needs to rest,' the doctor said. 'You should have come sooner. We'll give him a course of drugs, but he is very frail and we don't want to provoke nasty side effects. Give him proper food. Let him rest.'

Bring food! Lutor told me as I prepared to travel to Guwahati. He wanted me to carry a bag of rice and smoked meat and fish on sticks so that Lipun would be happy and regain his vigour. The man's appetite was waning. He was thin as a stick, he said, but when I arrived Lipun raised himself up on the bed and exclaimed over all the things I had brought. The room was so small, there was not enough space to put everything. I had also spoken to Umsi from Itanagar and her response had been immediate. She would join me in Guwahati. She had suffered a bout of dengue fever—that was why she had been out of touch all this while.

'We will ask for a bigger room,' said Lutor. He was finding it difficult to deal with the doctors and nurses whispering all the time in low voices as if they didn't want him to hear what they were saying. He wanted Lipun to recover and he wanted to lift him in his arms and carry him back to the hills. Ah! The hills are safe for us. Was that not what Lipun had always said?

The new room was brighter, with a big window and Venetian blinds but all one could see was the end of a busy street crammed with small shops selling food where autorickshaws spluttered up and down carrying sick people to and fro. Lutor didn't look out and I could sense how he hated the city, its streets, flyovers, the noise and the mud. He hated the big river flowing endlessly, so indifferent to the lives of men. The distant hump of the hills across the river soothed him but his heart was ill at ease. He was reminded of Pasighat, of his long wait by the river, waiting for Lipun to return from his tours, waiting for Umsi, and of that waiting time when he had wanted to wrench the river dry when he lost his son.

'What are we going to do now?' Rudar stood by him and looked out at the street and the line of cars standing still in a traffic jam. He was thinking about elections and all the work that remained to be done. 'You should let Umsi come here. You told me she was ready.'

Yes. Lutor kept staring straight out. Yes. What are the things we want to do? They say what is desirable is different from what is feasible. What is desirable? One life! Say we have time, we have time to do whatever we desire! He knew he should be back on the campaign trail but he wanted to stay with Lipun.

'You go back to Pasighat,' he told Rudar. 'I'll stay on, maybe another week, let's see. We'll stay in a guest house, it will feel more homely.'

Umsi came up on the next flight from Delhi and took charge of the rooms in the guest house nearby, and did the cooking for all of us. She made soup for Lipun and he seemed to be enthralled by her presence.

'I remember your father,' he told her. 'Do you know, when we were in that Tezpur camp when you were a small girl, we were held up at the bridge by the Indian army?'

'No. Why was that?'

'Because they thought we were Chinese! I was running from Bameng and your father from Dirang, we were running for our lives fleeing the Chinese and they thought your father and I were Chinese!' Lipun shook his head in wonder.

Watching the two of them I felt I could never feel more grateful to anyone in my life than for Umsi's presence at this time. She was calm and soothing. Lutor was happy too, relying on Umsi to be the conduit between Lipun and him when both of them were so inward, silent and similar. In the evenings Lutor insisted on keeping keeping watch over Lipun. Sometimes he returned to the guest house and talked quietly with Umsi. They talked about everything. They talked about food, music, medicines, bone ache, books, and they talked about politics, justice, other countries, and foreign exchange. He thought he knew her but he was discovering another Umsi who was comfortable and wise, he said, making her laugh.

'People expect us to leave our doors wide open now,' he said. 'But I want to shut it and make love to you.'

'Be quiet. We are mature elderly people.'

He grinned at her. Maturity? In the past, for so many years he had started up determined to carry out his Operation Find, searching for her. But the obstacles had been too many and too confusing. Yet just when he thought it was over suddenly, time itself had decided they should meet again.

'Mature elderly people just like our parents whose doors were always open as though they had nothing to hide and never did it anymore…Hmm…As if we are old enough, when actually I am full of desire!' he repeated.

Sometimes he fell asleep stretched out on the chair and Umsi drank tea and watched him. She liked the way his mouth became crooked when he slept. He was sleeping peacefully, without his eyes flickering restlessly when he used to dream about wild birds and drowning rivers. It is a fine face, she thought, filled with tenderness. His hair was greying at the temples. She touched his face and he peeped at her and lifted his chin waiting for her to run her fingers down his throat. It made her smile. In the past he had been so strong and wild. If he did not like something he would not say so, but sooner or later he would get up, look around, and without another word squash the obstacle from his path. This kind of behaviour had resulted in a lot of situations. People said, 'Who does he think he is?' when he had lifted one of his workers and threatened to hurl him out of the window. Imagine! Just because the poor man had said that he should patch up with Tanik and get a ministerial berth so that his supporters' hard work would not have been in vain.

'Never. I will never go with Tanik!' Lutor had said, and that was that.

He's too proud, you can't be proud in politics, they said, but secretly they admired him. He was the only one who had stood up to Tanik, everyone knew that. But to hurl someone out of a window like that? They shook their heads. From his house perched on the hillside it would have been like falling five floors!

'Nah! He would have clung to a bush,' Lutor had said.

In the midst of chaos, in between waiting in bleak hospital corridors with the hushed footfall of doctors and nurses, this interlude in a city guest house was a time for Lutor and Umsi to discover another aspect of each other and make their decisions. It was a trying time, no doubt, but maybe, I thought, it would turn out to be that second chance that those who struggled and loved believed in.

In the clinic, Lipun lay awake with a heavy, cold sensation that curiously made him sweat. The hospital bed was high and narrow and Lipun felt he wanted to get up and walk about but he was afraid his feet might not reach the floor and he would have to call for help. He lay still and crossed his arms over his chest to ease the discomfort. He didn't like this place and he wondered why Lutor had brought him here. Perhaps the boy was worried he was really sick. There was nothing wrong with him, just a feeling of weariness. He felt tired. Tired…that was it. A scent of summer, a smell of earth and flowers was creeping in though the open window filling him with a sense of deja-vu, as if he was trying to remember something he had known intimately. Ah…all those years of walking through jungle was catching up now. And about time too, he thought. He was seventy-nine, almost eighty! He couldn't believe it. He had never been sick in his life so it was alright to feel a little tired.

Lutor looked in at this moment and saw the smile on Lipun's face. It was a smile of such sweetness that Lutor felt he wanted to weep. I must take him home, he thought. He will recover faster. He can have his garden back, sit in the sun or start stacking twigs and leaves again like a beaver piling them into a neat mound to be burned later. Maybe the doctors could release him soon. Hospitals only made one feel more ill. 'Is there anything you want?' he asked.

'Oh no, no. I have been doing nothing but eat and sleep.' Lipun was holding a small orange in his hand. 'When will we be allowed to leave this place?'

'Soon, soon,' Lutor said.

'Ah.' Lipun closed his eyes. Home! After all these years he allowed himself to remember Nefa and how bitterly he had mourned her death. He remembered the wilderness of those years. How he had struggled to be a good, smart officer and how many files he had handled and all the words he had said. What did they amount to now? He thought about dying. What was it? Dying should not be so difficult if one was sure the image would survive. The image of what? He had no children. But there was Lutor, like his own son whom he still saw as a thin boy following him up and down hills. So many images. Dying should be like taking a long walk, and then walking off the edge of the world, just stepping off, like that. What was wrong with that? Nothing, except that one would be doing it alone. It was like a child leaving home or being sent away without his parents. It was a lonely feeling. That was the frightening part, he thought. Alone. The loneliness of dying. He sighed and a cough escaped his lips.

Lutor and Umsi looked in at him again. He was lying prone and he raised his hand. It's alright. Go back to what you were doing. They were sitting facing each other and he could see Umsi's face slightly bent to one side listening to something Lutor was saying. What was the boy talking about? He used to be so silent, curling up on camp beds wherever he had led him and falling asleep immediately. He saw big white parachutes sailing down to earth and heard the rainman saying, this is the end of solitude. It had been such a confusing time. Perhaps they should never have let the government come in, bringing change so rapidly. But it was his work to open up the land so that food and salt could reach the tribes. Perhaps things could have been worse. How much worse? He felt too weary to think now. How they had struggled! Ah! If they had failed it had not been for lack of trying. Frontiermen used to say that they knew pain because they had loved the land so much. It was that kind of love that had made them surrender their youth and energy all those years ago. Love!

Suddenly Lipun recalled the face of his friend, Umsi's father, and saw his big, furry hat looking smart in a patch of sunlight.

Now the faces of Dinu and Lomey seemed to be standing next to him and he saw Nefa, his young wife, standing near a swaying cane bridge. Were those hills in the distance? Astounding! Look at that! Nefa seemed to be smiling at him and all the sweetness of the years poured out of her eyes as a tear fell from his own and coursed down his cheek. After all these years the relief of tears! He was walking and laughing, and through his half-closed lids he could see the whole world again, the villages emerging out of the shadow of great trees. There they were! The days of his youth! He could hear the rustle of leaves, the wind was scattering leaves everywhere, and he heard the crunch of stones as he walked on straight into the heart of a swelling, mysterious current.

Lutor and I were sitting in the canteen just outside the block when Lutor's phone rang. The mornings were very cold and I was warming my hands holding a paper cup of coffee. Umsi had returned to the guest house to make soup for Lipun. The clinic was quiet and ghostly when we entered the corridor again. A nurse was waiting for us. 'Please come,' she said.

I looked at her face and saw fear and hesitation. What is it? I tried to keep my voice calm but felt as if I had stopped breathing. The nurse was talking to Lutor. I heard words—I...uh, sorry sir, I was trying to inform...I...Was trying to telephone. The doctor will speak to you...

'What is she trying to say?' Lutor brushed past her shouting in a loud voice. 'Tell her I cannot understand what she is saying. Tell her to shut up! I don't want to hear!'

Lutor's angry words—hearing him shouting and seeing the nurse trembling and almost in tears, it shot through me like a searing flash that Lipun was dead. He had passed away! Those were polite words, and Lutor knew, but he was refusing to accept it.

'Get out of my way!' He was shouting at someone by

the room door. A young doctor was standing aside. There was no one blocking his way but he was standing there and looking back at me with a look of utter terror on his face.

Rudar arrived the same evening, driving non-stop from Pasighat. He gripped my hand. What is there to say or do, but to honour a great man with a decent burial? Umsi was silent and focussed. Rudar knew she was strong. He had heard her talking to Gagil on the phone answering the old lady's questions in a calm, detailed manner. It was Lutor he worried about.

'He fed me! He clothed me!' Lutor wept. 'He carried suitcases and climbed up mountains. So many times we almost died. How can he die now?'

'No more, no more,' Rudar said, holding him back. His own face was crestfallen and lined with sorrow. 'We will carry him back to Pasighat.'

The mention of Pasighat seemed to revive Lutor. He began to call everyone and he contacted Tanmut and his uncle, the rainman. 'Yes, bring him home,' his uncle said. He rang Aohun to demand helicopter service for Lipun. He gathered all the medical reports from the hospital and packed Lipun's transistor and his slippers into his suitcase. 'We will leave nothing here,' he said. 'We will carry everything back.' He collected every scrap of paper in the room and wrapped up the small comb and soap and toilet things into a neat parcel for Umsi to pack.

Now I am losing him, Umsi thought, gazing at his face. Lutor had forbidden her to come with us to Pasighat. Too many deaths, he had said. Her daughter and Kellan's son were alone in Delhi and she should go back to them. He would talk to her later. He was distant and aloof, as if he was coiling into himself and holding Lipun deep inside him. How could she climb through his barrier of grief? It was a frightening experience for her but Rudar said it was a matter of time. Lutor had an election to fight and he would come out of it once he saw his people again. She wondered about this and braced herself when she came to the airport.

Officials were running to the helicopter to complete the final formalities and Lutor was standing on the tarmac mopping his face with a big kerchief. She embraced him impulsively. So what if anyone saw them. She might never see him again. He surprised her by holding her close and kissing her on the forehead. Then he nodded and the coffin was lifted into the aircraft and we climbed in.

The old hometown of Pasighat was invisible beneath a blanket of fog. The aircraft began its descent, circling slowly. There was a flash of arcing bamboo and the broad shoulder of a green hill. Patches of land laid out in random squares and oblongs appeared, and then vanished. We were dropping down, down, slicing through the white band of mist, until suddenly we were clear and I saw a sea of people. The small airfield was covered with people waiting to receive Lipun.

'Oh my god! What shall we tell them?' Rudar gasped.

It struck me that Lipun might have made his first journey from this small airstrip in the NEFA days. Now he was returning to this very spot. I heard Lutor saying, 'Tell them he was good. Tell them he was great. Most of all tell them that he was a simple man with a pure heart and a smile of great sweetness.'

A sigh went up as the pilot negotiated a landing space amidst the throng of people. I saw Kamin and Lutor's party workers holding back the crowd with their linked hands. Lutor nudged me gently to step out first. 'I'm right here,' he said. 'Everyone is here.' Then he faced Kamin and the row of faces pressing forward to reach him. 'It's alright,' he said. 'Everyone will see him. Wait. Please be patient. He has come home. Your son has come home.'

In the hot sunlight the old women of the village were full of thoughts. They looked at the fields and they talked about the dead. They touched the leaves of trees, cleared the undergrowth, and while lighting fires in the garden they talked about the preparations for the dead. 'This will be a good burial place,' they said. 'Here the sun falls in the morning and that is good.' People from all the surrounding villages had arrived on hearing the news of Lipun's death. Lipun was a beloved son. Many of them had not seen him for many years but everyone remembered the stories of the first officers and how they had grown up in this very town, throwing down their books and running across the open fields instead, chasing cows with sticks, while everyone said how clever they were.

All the men were sitting in the sun. Tanik had arrived with many of his colleagues and tea and biscuits and betel nut were being passed around. Everyone hailed one another. 'I am your aunty, I am your uncle,' they said, clasping my hand. 'I am your elder brother.' An old woman with a shock of white hair told Kampo and me, 'I am your uncle Tanmut's friend. I have ten children and forty grandchildren. That boy is my son. That girl is your uncle's daughter.' At one point I saw Tanmut trying to slip his old watch on to Gagil's wrist and saw her patting his hand away and saying, 'Later, later. I don't want to know the time now.'

In this ambience of kinship, I realised that this was what the end was about. Family mattered, and the lives of children, the small boys and girls looking around with clear eyes, not understanding everything but trying to behave as their parents instructed them—they mattered. Their mothers said, 'Shh...Don't make such a noise.' Fathers led their sons saying, 'Shake hands, shake hands.'

For everyone, family and visitors alike, it was the children who mattered. Every adult sitting in the sun knew death could not be postponed. Everyone thought after they were gone the children would still be here, dancing and twirling in the bright sunlight.

Lutor and Rudar, the rainman and two elderly villagers carried Lipun's body and Lutor made the symbolic slashes in a gadu, a white woven blanket, before placing it over the coffin to keep the old man warm.

'Slowly, slowly, careful, careful,' he said. He was wearing his eyok dao slung across his chest and he looked tired. An elder grandson of Tanmut and Gagil fired a gun and the shot reverberated across the tall trees and the clear sky. The women began to cry in response. 'Oh, we will never see another one like our Lipun again,' they wept. 'Only the gods know what it is we should pray for, give us that, we pray! There is the wind, sky, heaven's light, the faces of men and women and children who gave us joy. Pray to remember, and never forget.'

'I never thought I would feel like this,' said Kampo, pressing close to me. Her voice was trembling. The curving past was completing its circle of images and I saw how all our lives intersected at this point, so suddenly and so sharply. It was just a short time ago that I had been here, celebrating the start of the New Year. In the end this is what our lives are about—unknown little stories, stray bits of information that we show to someone sometimes, someone to share it with, if we are lucky. This is what happens between families, I thought. We know each other by intuition. It is what makes the ties so binding, so anguished and sometimes so unacceptable. We turn away, yet later we return, seeking this little consolation of family because we realise then, somewhat unwillingly and almost always belatedly that this is where our story began, and that it is the sharing that gives meaning to a life—a testimony, a kind of perplexed witness that we have lived.

The salt of the earth

Tanik stood close to Lutor and expressed his sadness. 'Lipun was like a father to me,' he said. 'He helped me so many times.' Kijji nodded in agreement, remembering the times he had visited Lipun when Nefa was alive. 'How the time goes! I was a young man too. Everything was there before us. Now look at the troubles we are facing,' he said, spreading his hands. 'We should work together for so many things and start afresh.'

It was a veiled offer. Kijji was sure Lutor would never throw in his lot with Tanik and him. Why this was, he could not understand, but at this moment it was worth a try. 'If you have money you can do anything,' he had told everyone. How can you play politics without money?'

'Let people take from Tanik,' said Rudar. 'It's their due and he owes it. Just make sure you keep Kamin close. I don't trust Kijji.'

Lutor looked at his friend. 'Why, what do you mean?'

'It's just a feeling. I get these feelings, you know.'

Lutor listened and thought about election gossip. Every election time unusual happenings and strange stories circulated as if the frenzy of the electoral exercise made men's minds extra sensory and a bit demented. If people like Kijji started rumours there were stories circulating about Tanik too and a strange fire that had broken out in a village after Tanik had visited the place. A marriage party carrying utensils and seeds of foodgrain had escorted the bride to the groom's house. A mithun had been sacrificed in honour of the occasion and a big fire had been lit in open ground for the nuptial feast. Everyone swore that there was not a breath of wind. But a fire had begun to whirl upwards like a white spirit and landed on the roof of another house. As people screamed the mithun they thought was dead had lowed three times and its fur began falling off in big chunks. The fire leaped through the village and sixty-seven houses were gutted. The fire destroyed tin, metal, wood and even the fruit trees full of green sap. Two girls standing high above the village on their way back from the fields testified to the unbelievable way that fire had moved. It zig-zagged across the village, they said, leaping over some homes and alighting on others right down to the last house where it fizzled out in a stream. All the houses that were gutted were supporters of Lutor. How could such a thing happen?

Lutor did not attach importance to these tales. He was superstitious, but it was election panic all over again. He knew Tanik. He had known him in high school and they had been through the same initiation from student leaders to young politicians in full-fledged state politics. If Tanik was smart, conniving, lucky, people said Lutor was truthful, courageous, and impulsive. All these years they had jostled side by side and in his heart Lutor felt no personal threat from Tanik. The danger came from the man Tanik had propped up to fight him in his Sirum-Pasighat seat. It was Tasong he was wary of because Tasong was the older man, full of command, and a real force in the ancient way of warriors with an impassive, implacable will.

At night Lutor lay awake and listened to the wind. As soon as darkness fell he would feel the first stealthy rustle of the notorious night wind of Pasighat as it began creeping down the gorge, whistling and flinging sand against the doors of houses facing north. By midnight it would be throwing a tantrum, moaning over the town, rattling the tin roofs and shaking the trees. It retreated before daybreak, curling back into the gorge with a sigh. Where was solace now and the happiness to carry on? Where was that quiet, unalterable state that he could turn to? Where did it reside? These were the questions Lutor asked himself a thousand times. Whenever he looked at the land he knew its physical features, yes, but more than this, he knew it as a living relationship with its myriad strands of desire, dreams, sleep, terror, bubble of laughter, hope. He thought he knew this by a feeling of wellbeing, by a conviction that everything could be achieved or rearranged by this understanding, a feeling akin to love. But now, suddenly, without the slightest warning it seemed to be slipping away. Hell is when you are losing control. He could feel it. Everything was spinning away, reeling out of his hands.

'Now we have an election to fight,' Rudar said. 'Get out of it. Come on!'

'Yes. Yes,' said Lutor, but it was a heavy, painstaking process for him to think about facing people again and saying words that he no longer had any wish to say. Look, he remembered how Lipun was always pointing, and he was still looking. So many things had happened and everything was still unfinished. The past outgrew the present and life moved back and forth like his thoughts until their sedulous intermingling fooled him into thinking that everything was the same as before. What had happened to his life? It was neither present nor past. All that he could analyse now was that he had mixed up infinite worlds so well that he had created chaos. The unbearable thing was that he was no longer a part of it. The maelstrom had pulled itself out of his hands and he was now only a helpless observer. He wanted to talk to his uncle but the rainman had gone away to visit a far village.

Yes, he thought over and over again, the things we allow to happen are the signs of our acceptance. Memory is only good for luring you into acceptance. It is better to keep it locked away forever if the aim is to survive. The Anti-terrorist Act floated before his eyes, a dozen printed pages of law to bring peace and security, and see what had happened! He slept badly and was shocked that despite Lipun's death and the terrible killing on Gohpur road life was going on. People were pouring into his house and they were eager and excited as ever for the election and his success.

One day just before dawn he woke up with a start. He thought someone was in the room. There was a strong odour of crushed fern and wild chestnut. Like a flash he remembered his vision of the flying fox seated on the chair one rainy evening long ago. His heart was thumping madly and he turned to look at the wooden chair. No, there was nothing there. But he felt the golden eyes of the animal looking at him. He jumped out of bed and pulled back the curtains. Everywhere he looked he saw clouds piled up solidly over the mountains as if determined not to be moved. But slowly, slowly, he felt a stirring in his heart as if he could feel the eyes of the town people straining for a sign, a signal of something bright and new. Just now we are waiting, he thought, even though it appears that all our tracks have been erased. But beyond, there somewhere, just beyond the limit of sight there is more! The features of the land were breaking through—clear, sun washed, and like a voice from the past he was reminded again of the idea of home and a place among his own people.

The All NEFA Peoples Party began its election tour on a cold, windy, January day. First Lutor travelled to the aid of his candidates in the districts and he travelled twice to Kolkata to get funds for the party from business friends who supported him. The demand for money grew daily, but Lutor was undeterred.

'I want to tell a story,' he said. 'How shall I begin? Where is the point of illumination?' He travelled everywhere and spoke in open fields, auditoriums, universities and village mosup—longhouses. And everywhere he went people turned out in thousands to hear him speak. There was sorrow and there was passion, and slowly, day by day Rudar looked at his friend and sighed. He had heard Lutor speak so many times before but every time it was different. He spoke about election issues, about health and education and labour wages and law and order, but most of all he spoke about the land. The life of it, the blood of it, the best of it.

'If you love the land then you will feel your life belongs to you,' he said.

Times had changed, he acknowledged that, but Lutor continued to believe and live in anticipation. He would never abandon his image of silhouettes and the dream of pan-Arunachal unity. The end result was a new image. It was the imagined thing. A new birth that had grown its own wings, traced its own features and selected its lineaments and now spoke in new words asking for a return of love that refused to believe in the worst and only hoped for the best and loveliest.

It is the way he expresses it, thought Rudar, looking around quietly at the crowd. He saw the furrowed faces of men and the faces of women turning thoughtful as if touched by a shadow of grief. He looked at his friend and saw him dressed in his work day clothes, a big, untidy man in brown shirt and trousers creased and crumpled with travelling, standing before the crowd day after day and talking to them like in the old days of village kebangs when men believed in what they were saying.

'Lipun has shown me the meaning of virtue,' Lutor said. 'Our people are the salt of the earth, and all that we can do as politicians is an affirmation of this belief. A leader will lead, but it must be in the right direction. For this we need to hear your voice and receive your mandate. This is how we should look at each other. Every moment history is being written. Every day it is being written by our thoughts and actions, by the hopes of men and women for a better life, and this is the source of our effort and inspiration.

'Some of my friends tell me we should pack it in. Or compromise. But why? Because we are too poor to be politicians? What will we achieve by that? Victory? But it will come with a price that will be higher than I can pay. So don't tell me about funds. This kind of talk only makes people run after money and we are creating a new slavery. Once we wanted the same things, remember! Now it seems we have become mere imitations of a world that has no relevance to our present circumstance. Promises are made, but who will keep them? I once asked if we are a peaceful state. Sometimes it seems an impossible dream when we talk about conflict and death and fear. The terror of mistakes makes us indecisive and wavering and we cannot move forward. Our inability to return to what we were haunts us like silent tears. But deep in my heart I know we are a strong state and like this land we will survive and remain bigger, better, stronger!'

The die is cast

In another house another group of people were eating, sitting all together in a row. It was raining and a fine mist covered the land. There was sweetness in the land when the rain drummed on the roof and mingled with the aroma of spices and gravy and meat bubbling and sizzling in the pot. The workmen ate, looking at the rain and almost wept with gratitude for the joy of eating such delicious food. It was the last pre-election dinner in Tanik's residence and the kitchen was teeming with people. There were daughters and young girls, food on the table, the loud conversation of relatives and well-wishers wishing him success and continuity and grandchildren. In the garden there were more women sitting in groups, or simply moving around supervising food, pouring beer, and talking.

Tanik was always fascinated by this remarkable quality about women sitting together and talking. They were a force to reckon with. His eyes took in everything and he saw Kijji Ongo seated at a table. Kijji had a way of eating as if he was being blown about by a small wind. First he cut meat into small pieces and then popped one into his mouth. He swayed to one side as he did this, tackling his food as if it were an operation set to music. He raised his eyes only when he popped food into his mouth. Then he was looking down again and moving his upper torso side to side in rhythm with the cutting and shovelling of rice and meat into his mouth. It looked like he was engaged in a dance of happiness.

Kijji had been with Tanik all these years yet today Tanik felt he still did not know the man. When they had started together as small-time timber agents in a nearby town, Tanik remembered how Kijji had overwhelmed him with his lust for life. He brought him women and had introduced him to his second wife, whom he had taken even though he was already a father of two at the time. When the second woman appeared his first wife had fought like a wild cat. Why, she demanded. What will happen to the children? A fine example you are setting for your children!

The new woman had slipped into her place quietly. She bore Tanik a baby girl and lived with her sister, waiting for his visits and trying to win him with coy looks. She whispered sweetly that she would respect his wishes and that if her presence made trouble for him with his elder wife perhaps it would be better if she left. No, he had cried. He was awestruck by her spirit of sacrifice and gentleness. What a difference from his first wife who hissed and cursed the other woman openly.

'Don't you see how sly she is?' she shouted at him. 'Why did she come to you? Because no one else would have her, you stupid, greedy man! I never thought you would do this to me. Why?'

The younger woman wept. She was well aware that a man would succumb to tears. She said, 'Why did you come to me then, why?'

Tanik had listened without saying a word. The deep summer sunsets and the fragrance of river and mountain made him feel restless. Life was so big. Relationships were ruled by mistakes. Harsh words were spoken. And if unspoken, they were stored away to poison each moment that their eyes met and when their hearts remembered. What hate! What ferocity!

He longed to love a woman again, quietly and simply, without war and such turbulence. Neither of the women meant anything much to him anymore. They had given him sons and daughters. His opponents did not rake up his personal life, and sometimes he felt he had become invisible, nonexistent. But so what, he told himself, secretly afraid. I can no more resist than a block of wood can fight against the tide. He was hoping one of them would leave him in disgust but they both hung on, determined to drive him mad. They watched him and he began to dread the feeling of guilt that they poisoned his life with.

He stared at the bark of the old tree and felt his life burnt out and flaking away. He felt tired if he did not rest in the afternoon and his digestion had become acutely sensitive. Sometimes a curious allergy made him want to draw blood. 'Everything will still go on. Other people will do as I have done. But I won't be around anymore. And it'll still go on.' This was when he thought life was big.

Snap, snap—click! Someone was taking a photograph. A family photo. Let's all stand together. Look! There's so many of us! Tanik stood up, feeling saddened by his own thoughts. He was secure, settled, at the height of power. But the thing was he wanted to live on the edge again. His elder wife loved these days full of people, mothers and babies. He smiled at her, feeling a little frightened by her happiness. A big, well-fed, extended family gave a woman status. At her age now she had nothing to fear. And neither did he, for that matter, but there it was, that little worm of doubt. Security. Family. The lives that would live on after him. All this frightened him now. It was terrible. Just when he wanted peace and quiet his old self seemed to be waking up and mocking him. What happened to you, huh?

He remembered his mother weaving by lamplight. Ah… mother! He wanted to whisper her name and hear her voice again…If only she was alive! He remembered her great strength and resilience—what dreams she had spun for him! If only he could get to the heart of this feeling that was taunting him, he would be prepared for a momentary flash, a burst of light, then oblivion! He looked up and the sky appeared cold and higher than usual, as if everything was moving further away. He wished he could have the old days back again, before he was entangled in this endless relationship of men and women and politics. But the die was cast. He had climbed down from the mountain, from the place of cold winds and unlimited vistas and the years had dropped behind. This was the tapestry that had emerged. So be it, he thought. He was a politician and a ruthless one. I will mow down my enemies!

He was jolted out of his morose thoughts when he saw Kijji Ongo coming towards him followed by Kamin. Kamin! What was this? Was he not a close aide of Lutor? How had he come here?

'I have brought a guest,' said Kijji. 'He is a very busy man. But we're celebrating and after all he's more than a guest. We are family.'

Tanik marvelled at Kijji's astute ways. He was like a fox. He had heard about Lutor's campaign and how people were flocking to hear him. He will win hands down, everyone had told him. And Tanik had no reply to this except to think that maybe the rainman had worked some magic again. And where was he? No one knew. The rainman could disappear just like that and no one in the length and breadth of the land would have a clue to his whereabouts. He could be a tiger running through the forest or sitting on that rock watching them, and they would never know.

'He has gone to Pemako,' Kamin said, 'to find out about the missing children who disappeared after a fire engulfed a hunting shed. People begged for his presence because they fear a great calamity is about to befall them.'

So that was it! Tanik felt rejuvenated. Here was deliverance! The fire, after all, was not what Kamin had come about. Fires and funerals happened all the time, especially during election time. Marriages were also celebrated at this time, and house building and drink parties.

'The spirits of the mountains must be propitiated to protect us from unknown dangers,' he said. 'Come, you are most welcome. We are honoured indeed.' He held out his hand.

Kamin hesitated for a fraction of a second and then clasped Tanik's extended hand. Across the room he saw a tall, thin, unsmiling man looking at him and felt a shudder as his gaze met the humourless eyes of Tasong.

'A drink, hey girls! Bring us a drink, will you?' shouted Kijji. Then he turned to Kamin and said, 'Life once lost cannot be taken back. But the poor may hope to have a house of their own…' He stopped in mid-sentence and rolled his eyes. 'We want to see you get your rightful place.'

Unstoppable journeys

'We are organising a rally,' said Mentiri. 'You should join us.' Her long, lank hair was pulled up and her movements were brisk and angry. 'Look, I am in the open now,' she told me. 'We are going to protest APCOCA and army operations in Tirap. It serves no purpose. The Army moves in and what happens? It's women like us who suffer. You go to fetch water, you get raped. You stay at home, the militants want you to cook and clean for them. The men are silent or they have all run away. What has Rasa done all these years? Is he not a representative of the people?' Her voice broke a little and her movements became more agitated. 'We want to press for something different. No more frontal organisation and hanging in the wings. We want equal representation. Our towns are no longer safe, there are bomb blasts and murders and not a single culprit has been caught so far. We can play a vital role.'

I knew Ongat and many other women were joining these rallies. Everyone was angry about the Gohpur road incident. The tide had turned against Lutor and Aohun, but it was coming from the most unexpected side. It had turned me around too, but in another way. I had come to pay my respects to family before leaving Pasighat once again. More than ever, I wanted no part in politics now. It was a game only some people could play, but one thing I had never realised was the heartache it could bring. Day after day I saw Lutor struggling with the electorate and giving them his heart but sometimes they went away without any concern or understanding of what he was saying.

And now Mentiri had swung to the other side. 'Of course I love Lutor,' she said. 'We all look up to him, but he can't do everything.'

In Gagil's house the old lady said, 'I think the Nationalist Alliance is going to give Mentiri a party post on compassionate grounds.'

'Hai, she always wanted to be in politics. When the men are so bad at it maybe women will be better,' said Tibul.

'What about you, are you going to campaign?' I asked her.

'I have always been in Lutor's camp,' she said. 'He comes. He goes. But actually he never leaves us. I know that man. He's too good. That's why it's so difficult for him. I won't be changing sides now.'

Gagil sat nodding silently. 'You know this is all a set up by Tanik. He is wooing women voters. It's the same with all politicians. Let's hope something good comes of it. What about you?' She turned to me.

'Oh, me, I'll get back to work. Wait for the elections to be over, let's see.' Now no one asked me about my work and whether I would be returning to Delhi, but even if they had I would have had nothing to tell them.

'I'll get back to work too,' said Gagil rising stiffly. 'No no, no politicking for me. Rice in the bin, meat on the rack, more than enough! The house, the kitchen, the fields!' She smiled widely. 'I still believe we have time and that women can be good at everything.'

When I left Gagil was standing under the familiar frangipani tree. She was still in robust health but I thought she looked frail and lonely under the wide sky looming with big clouds.

The tempo of campaign rhetoric was at its loudest and most acrimonious in the capital constituency. The national parties predicted the imminent fall of the other. 'Coming events cast their shadow before them. The UNC has alienated the North-east. Our first aim is to finish their rule. It is a demon!' And as if to rub salt into an old wound they called for a disbursal of refugees and illegal settlers to other states, and promised to extend the timber ban all over the country. Why should the North-eastern states suffer like this, they cried, and one state alone bear the influx of outsiders?

The UNC issued hundreds of press releases and demanded front page coverage. Never in the history of the state was the run up to Assembly polls more confused and garbled with a total of 165 candidates fighting for the sixty member state assembly. Everyone was involved—wives, brothers, uncles, friends, relatives, officers, labourers, and the state observers and organising secretaries moving in and out of the state with businessmen and national media following the campaign trail.

As polling day approached, politicians concentrated on wooing voters through clandestine meetings and house to house campaigns. Who would ever know what the players succumb to, and why? The ordeal of meeting people day after day, night after night, began to tell on everyone's nerves. The fickle nature of political alliances forged at the last minute left little time for questions and answers and in the mélee even the insurgency menace in Tirap and Changlang was overshadowed by a series of communal flare-ups and violent incidents that rocked the state. One night the city UNC Youth office was burned by unidentified miscreants.

Sitting in Orin's office it seemed to me that we were the only non-participants watching this frenzied exercise. Busloads of people had already left for their home districts to cast their vote. 'Kamin has also done it,' he said. 'He has made a pact with Tanik, you know, as an Independent candidate for Duyang assembly constituency. If Tanik keeps his word there will be cross voting and Kamin will win against the UNC party's own candidate.'

I remembered the way Kamin used to tilt his head back and look at us with narrowed eyes, and felt a deep sense of embarrassment at the way he had betrayed Lutor. But Lutor had said, 'Let him do what he wants. It's his choice. He's a politician,' and Kampo had said something about the hypocrisy and the nauseous herd mentality that summed it up for me. 'Politicians! Everyone is beginning to resemble each other. It's the punishment they deserve.'

The phone rang constantly and news floated in from the districts.

Hey! So and so is going great guns, no, he's fallen back. The election material got lost, someone tried to snatch away the EVM, a UNC candidate has been kidnapped, ten motorbikes got stolen, the AINA candidate is missing, the bazaar welfare committee has banned the sale of marbles, what? Yes, it's used as catapult ammunition. What? Yes, government offices are open, no, Lutor is travelling, Aohun looks safe, bad weather is making things hard, they're trying to squeeze the opposition dry by witholding fuel, Tirap is unpredictable, and the indigenous priests association is having a meeting to discuss their political affiliation.'

With less than a month to polling day, Itanagar was girdled by a ring of fire. Forest fires burned on the hillside night and day. Bamboo exploded and great sparks leaped upwards and reddened the sky. The traditional practice of jhuming had taken on a new meaning as settlers cleared the land for farming at will. At the same time, the government announced that it would pay twenty rupees per rat tail to villagers in a ploy to enlist public participation in curbing the rat menace that followed the bamboo flowering in some districts of the state. In response wild rodents were trapped in overwhelming numbers and sold in the local bazaar, grimacing in huge mounds of crinkled grey fur. The bamboo flowers once in its life cycle, and then dies. The rodent population multiplies as it feeds on the pods and seeds of bamboo, then in a feeding frenzy head for towns and villages to destroy crops and the food in government storehouses. It was happening just now, just as there was a report about the revenge of the insect tari. It started in Pasighat where people were falling prey to their addiction for a river beetle that arrived at this time every year to hibernate in the dry river beds. It was a delicacy, but the insect contained a potent hallucinogen and the report said several politicians and their wives were suffering an overdose of tari.

'People don't die, they just act strange,' said Orin. 'They start fluttering their hands and try to crawl under wooden blocks and beds. They want the dark, they want to hide under a stone and snuggle under a pile of clothing, taking on all the characteristics of what they eat.' The madness had struck all the districts of the tari-belt, and there was a rumour that Kijji Ongo had also suffered an overdose and that he had grabbed his wife's hand and tried to eat it. When relatives tried to pull him away he wrapped himself round her in an embrace hard and stiff as rigor mortis.

'It must be true,' said Kampo, laughing hard. 'Imagine the taris whispering—let's give them a dose of poison!'

'It can't be true,' said Orin, 'because the man is climbing and I think he's going to come back.'

'Keep fingers crossed he doesn't. Maybe he grabbed Kamin's hand,' said Kampo.

'Yes, that he did,' said Orin vehemently.

On the eve of polling day, the city was very quiet, like the calm before the storm. Party vigilantes kept watch all night over their voters to prevent a last-minute swing. This was the most dangerous time, but who could keep their eyes open all the time or their wits about them at a time like this? Only politicians work while others sleep. They glide around in the dark turning up in the most unexpected places, meeting at unearthly hours like an all-seeing eye marking everyone, hearing every footfall; and the clever ones, even when they are eating and drinking never say it all in case a friend turns into an enemy the very next day. In Pasighat many people swore that they had a seen a tall, thin man hunched up in an autorickshaw whirling around every nook and cranny of the town in the middle of the night. Who was this man, no one could say for sure. Some said it was a woman, but many thought it was Tasong. On the eve of polling day he had circled the town like a silent ghost distributing money.

It was on the day of counting when I stood with a crowd

of people in the grounds of Nirvachan Bhawan that I felt the full import of this great exercise that had kept us so unaccountably busy all these days. My stomach felt tight and constricted. Results! Had we worked hard enough, had we done everything we could? What would the results be? Suddenly I felt there was no guarantee of anything. Everyone said Lutor would win but what if, just by a freak chance, he didn't? Anything could happen at the last moment. No, it was alright. In Pasighat Lutor was leading by 164 votes. Orin emerged and grinned at me. Then he went back in again. The Election Commission issued a single pass per newspaper. In Itanagar Tunar was leading but the UNC had already won three seats unopposed. The results were being flashed out and announced over the public address system almost simultaneously with the round-wise results announced by the returning officers in the district counting centres. A big crowd near me suddenly burst into jubilant shouts and clapped loudly. I looked at them feeling the sweat trickling down my back. If only it was over! I had never expected to feel so much tension. As the day progressed everyone became restive. People were milling around asking, 'Who, who? How much? What about him, what about her, hey! How can that be? Aah, impossible!'

117 votes…Lutor was trailing. I held my breath and concentrated hard willing a new number. The counting was not over yet. Hang on! Hang on! This became two hundred, and as if the counting process had suddenly speeded up at final count while my breathing had slowed and almost stopped, I realised that Lutor, the leader of the ANP, had been defeated by Tasong by a margin of 206 votes. It was unthinkable! The clear, bright day seemed unreal and I wondered if there would be a re-counting? Orin came out

red-faced and sweating, shaking his notebook. Curious faces in the crowd looked at us and I felt like crying. It was impossible to imagine that Lutor had lost, in Pasighat-Pigo!

'Come on, let's get out of here,' said Orin.

The streets of Itanagar looked the same. There was a traffic snarl up near the secretariat building and Orin shouted at some pedestrians as he reversed the car angrily and we sped away. Across the hills sunlight was spread out like a warm, golden web, unbroken, lethargic, heavy. A line of young bikers carrying flags were speeding through the town but for me it all seemed meaningless now. How strange it is, I thought, that after all the work defeat should creep up like this, like a sly thief and leave us breathless and uncomprehending. For so many days I had lost track of time, faces, memory, and awareness of life itself. Now it was simply as if the year that vanished.

What happens at the end of elections? The birth of desire! The answer was obvious as the capital was suddenly full of shiny new cars on the roads, the sound of crackers and people talking at the top of their voices. Everyone was rushing to meet someone, full of anticipation and desire. They had fought, lied, spread rumours and spent all their money in a bitter, taxing battle and now everyone wanted a piece of the pie. Everywhere politicians and their workers were celebrating or cursing the electorate. Everywhere their homes were full of people waiting to meet them. Sometimes they answered and sometimes they instructed their personal secretaries who said, 'No, *honourable* is not in. He is in a meeting,' and drew the curtains as if to shield the harassed politicians from the gloating eyes of the public.

The UNC party was victorious but all was still chaos and turmoil. Just as Kamin had predicted, the Nationalist

Alliance had won nine seats and Tanik had to contend with thirteen Independent candidates including Kamin, who had scraped through by a hairbreadth margin of thirteen votes. In Tirap and Changlang the old guard had been thrown out by a new breed of young leaders and in Itanagar Tunar of the ANP had crushed his opponent. Now the battlefield was set for a tug of war between the Tanik and Aohun camps for party supremo in what Orin reported as the clash of the titans.

'Hai, now it seems there is no room for laughter. Our politicians are weeping when they lose. In another election they win and they weep even more than when they lost! What is the meaning of this?'

Someone was singing loudly and everyone was smiling and clapping. 'They are like the ngopi-fish, scrabbling to rush upstream. The people of Arunachal have begun to shed tears very easily,' continued the singer.

Lutor's defeat was a death blow for the ANP and he had wanted to travel back to Itanagar immediately but the rainman had intervened.

'No,' he said. 'Not yet.' There were rituals to be performed for victory, and for defeat. An electoral defeat is devastating. A man could turn against his friends or against himself seeing defeat as the result of betrayal or a sign of his weakness. For this it was necessary to perform a ritual to regain trust and prepare for the future. No harm done if the tide turns against you. Win or lose—what we do after is equally important, said the rainman. In fact, it was necessary to celebrate the love and efforts of the candidate's workers and his family and offer sacrifice to thank the guardian spirits who had protected them all and ask for their continued affection.

Orin explained this to me and Lutor had also telephoned, calling us to come to Pasighat. By late evening, the Gagil house was full of people again. Lutor was standing in the middle of this gathering, nodding his head up and down. His face was sunburnt and he still wore his brown shirt but he had put on a black, embroidered galuk over it. Rudar was wearing a tie and hat and he was regaling the audience with anecdotes about an old man in a village who was regularly visiting his equally aging lady love. The wicked villagers knew everything and wanted to play a joke on the lovers. Hoosh, hoosh, they said, the chickens are really going for that corn! And what happened then? The alert old man rushes out wrapped in his lady's crimson ga-le shouting Hoosh! Hoosh! to chase the chickens away!

Lutor laughed to hear his friend talking so much. Nothing surprised or defeated Rudar and since the time he had jumped into the water in aid of Lutor against Kellan and his gang, he had always been around. He was thinking this when his phone rang.

Hello? He heard Umsi's voice. 'How are you?' Short pause…and then, 'It's alright you know, politics is like this.'

He smiled, listening to her trying to console him. 'It's a knock out,' he said, 'like losing in the boxing ring.'

There was a long pause. Then he heard her laughing softly. 'Don't be silly, you. Who is there with you?'

'Everyone is here,' he said. 'We are eating chicken liver and ginger.'

She was laughing some more. He handed the phone to me, maybe because he thought I was looking a bit woebegone. 'Here, tell her,' he said, 'say Rudar is gnawing a bone.'

'Tell her it's over, thank god election is over!' Kampo

shouted from the kitchen where she was shaking out packets of food stuff as if she had already forgotten the meaning of boredom. She was grinning at Orin and reciting an election joke, 'Yep yep,' she said, 'it's over and the Party will take care of our f-u-t-u-r-e and also our p-o-st-erior!'

Lutor was holding the phone again and he was saying, 'yes, yes, okay,' frowning and smiling at the same time and trying to look calm and unperturbed. Lutor had a journey ahead of him. He had a tentative plan to go to Delhi. It all depended, on what, he didn't quite know, but he hoped something would occur and the decision would come of itself. He thought he could hear the voice of Kellan's young son reading about the big land. So big, ah, but I thought it was bigger! It was bigger than one could ever imagine. There were places where he had never been. Maybe he could start again, travel to different places and start looking. Looking for what? Well, he could just look. Look at the hills, that mountain there like the reclining face of an old man with a protruding chin lifted up to the sky. Look again, and there would be something to find. How hard he had struggled and scraped at the mountains right from the NEFA days and what had the mountain given him? He squinted his eyes. Maybe the mountain had given him a piece of flint.

The last rite that his uncle, the rainman, performed was simple. He took Lutor aside. In his hands he held ridin thread and he said, *I claim these limbs, face, eyes, mouth, nose, ears. I claim this body, heart, hair, head. May no harm come to what I have claimed.*

He tied the strong vine around Lutor's wrist and knotted it firmly.

The tea bushes were a green carpet glistening with heat and light. Deep drainage canals ran between the closely spaced rows and the sun was burning through the shade trees. Small whitewashed houses with blue windows and rusty brown tin roofs flashed past. We were following Lutor in a convoy and returning to Itanagar. Somewhere, a thin sliver of moon was rising, floating above the world again after the period of darkness that people believed was the time when the moon was swallowed by the sky, or a frog, and died, before it was born again.

'This is the time one imagines being something else, like a tree, full of murmuring leaves and branches,' said Kampo.

'Why one tree, you have inherited all this,' said Orin, sweeping his arms out.

'What was that about the green enchantress?' said Kampo. 'Look at that!' We were driving on a high bund surrounded by green paddy fields running parallel to the railway track, and beyond we could see a white veil of evening mist spreading across the hills. 'The green garb,' mused Kampo. 'We try to be different in so many ways but this green garb does not fall off. I guess we'll carry it to the grave!'

At dusk we crossed a river looking so blue and shimmering, it was merged with the skyline as if its heart was pressed to the earth with arms outstretched, lying flat against the earth. So what if we never climbed those mountains, I thought. So what if we did not anticipate what was beyond the bend, or the meaning of the water's journey. It is all one and the same if we lie pressed flat against the earth like the river. Your heart is where you have laid it, but the river flows on through it as if all movement, the beginning and the end were running through your soul.

Just before we had left, Kamin had come to meet me. I was angry at his betrayal but in a way I could understand his dilemma. So much energy and thought revolved around an election—you play to win. He had won, but I knew there was guilt lying in a corner, and he was ready to rebel if anyone said anything.

'Tell me, what are your plans now?' he asked me. It seemed like a hundred years ago that we had played the numbers game so avidly and now everything was changed again.

'I haven't decided,' I had said. But I knew it was still the city for me. Maybe an elder, like the rainman, would say, 'you cannot buy time.' Neither can we exchange lives saying, 'You take a portion of my time and I'll take yours—see if it suits you, see if it makes sense.' There was my small flat in the city, not posh, not spacious at all, but familiar and intimate nevertheless, with books and clothes and shoes, and my hairbrush on the table and keys on the shelf. In a way it would be getting back to the place from where the unknown versions of my floating self could emerge, breathing in the scent of oceans and continents and, time and will permitting, go hotfooting again across the wide open map of the world.

'You should have stayed with Lutor,' I said. 'You really let him down.'

'Don't talk like that. If you don't have anything to say don't say these things.'

'Well, it is over now.' I stared at the mountains thinly veiled with mist. Air and water, but the elements remained their separate selves.

'Not over. Never say over,' Kamin had said. I had stayed silent. There were no answers to be pulled out of the air, placed on the table and studied like a map of alternatives.

But it was true. All was not over yet. In Itanagar there

was still a great deal of activity. Tunar said that Aohun's supporters were preparing to meet the governor to stake their claim to form the ministry. The Independents might merge en-bloc with Aohun's Congress to forestall a move by the Tirap and Changlang legislators to break away. Everything was up in the air, but one thing was clear. Tanik was out. He had lost all credibility and another group of legislators would withdraw support if Tanik did not step down as party supremo. It was amazing. Everything was the same and yet so different. What had happened? Somewhere along the way Tanik had slipped up. That was all. He had been summoned to New Delhi and the rumour was that he was being asked to step down gracefully so that the Centre could close this tug-of-war within the ranks and give the nod for ministry formation to Aohun as the strongest contender for CLP leader and chief minister.

'What gives anyone the right to do that,' shouted Tanik. 'I will never step down. I have the full support of my legislators!'

Politicians know how the anxiety of losing power could affect a person. A person hangs on, even if only by the nails and agrees to do anything, begs, weeps, dangling over the edge of the precipice because no one wants to fall into that abyss of oblivion, to be broken and unidentifiable. But pressure was mounting and in the grey wet weather, helicopters whirred overhead as politicians flew to Delhi to convince the Centre, and flew back to be in time for the swearing-in ceremony at the Raj Bhawan of a new chief minister of the state and a new cabinet. Everyone was confused and agitated. At night miscreants staked a claim on a ministerial bungalow by breaking all the windows and uprooting the garden. No, nothing was over. Kellan's killers had to be tracked down. There was the parliamentary election for Rasa to fight, and Lutor thought about Kasi's diary. There would always be politicians playing the same dangerous games. Perhaps APCOCA would be scrapped. There were many things still to be done, or undone.

A man could play politics over and over again. The struggle was never over, but there was one thing he needed to do that he knew he could only do once. He had staked his life on it and it was something that filled him with even greater panic than any election. One moment he was seized with fear, the next he felt determined as an ox to bulldoze his way to the city where Umsi lived, come what may. And all the time he sweated in fear and anticipation knowing full well that time was ticking away and he would have to take courage in his hands and start his journey right away. He thought of cancelling his flight, not showing up at all, just staying still and seeing what happens. They said there was an Assam bandh—that could be an excuse. 'I can't move. Bad weather! Bandh call!' But there was no escape. Instead of driving to Guwahati he had opted, on Rudar's advice, to take the flight from a place called Lilabari. 'It will be better than taking the helicopter,' Rudar said.

Lutor hated the helicopter. After Lipun's death he never wanted to fly in one ever again. He was afraid of flying anyway. Maybe the flight would be cancelled, but it was too late. Rudar was already waving goodbye and he was walking towards the security gate for the connecting flight to Guwahati.

The seats were red. A smart hostess in a red jacket and skirt pushed a trolley and handed him a bottle of water. No, he didn't want anything to eat. He leaned towards the window and tried to look down. They were flying over clouds and he caught a glimpse of glistening snow mountains on his right. Our mountains, he thought.

Something tugged at his heart. Goodbye to the hills. What would his life be like now? He shut his eyes and couldn't concentrate on anything. I want to bring Umsi back to these hills, he thought suddenly. Why should she be living so far away from him? Why should she be living in a strange city?

I will ask her, he thought, feeling a bit refreshed now. A brief stopover in Guwahati, then onward. There was not much time after all, but his mind was made up. The aircraft clacked and hummed and the pilot announced their approach into Guwahati. Whew! Now he could see a landscape of hills below him. Something about the landscape, the colour brown, mud, rusty tin, plastic curtains, cycles on narrow, dusty roads, all this was so recognisable. No shine. No affluence. Yet a bright moon shines over it and one was filled with love and yearning! In the end perhaps it is not about what you have done or not done, he thought. These things belong to everyone, missing something or showing some achievement. It is about feeling. Did you ever feel this way?

In the bright city Umsi laid the plates around the dining table. She placed the cake in the centre and covered it with a round wiremesh fly protector. It was a tradition, something she had made for Lutor. Her strength and suppleness were not what it had been but then it was more than fifteen years ago that she had started this stirring and chopping and baking chocolate walnut cake. Her daughter had stared at her labouring over it and laughed before she rushed off to meet her own friends.

One more time, just one more time she wanted to feel the taste of love again. He was coming to see her! She closed the windows and drew the curtains. Then she pulled them open again and left only the thin white drapes in place. Like this she could catch the glow of lights. She hummed a little and smiled to herself thinking how strange life was. Strange, yes. Mysterious! Miraculous! She slumped down in a chair, musing.

Who says anything disappears? She remembered the words of the rainman. Our hearts are taken, given, mistaken, lost; who knows why. But what is never lost is the original obsession that was a dream of love, of finding your place in life and fulfilling your destiny with understanding and happiness. What to do now?

Travel to and fro to the hills was not as arduous as it used to be. When she had left it was on the train chugging slowly through unfamiliar stations. Now there was air travel, so many flights and feeder airlines. Lutor had told her he was flying out of Lilabari. This made her laugh out loud. Imagine! A man was crossing mountains and rivers to catch a flight, eager to reach this city that he had told her he disliked. He had never seen where she lived. He said he might lose his way and turn into a piece of machinery in the terrible traffic. He said he might have a nervous fit and collapse on the street, but she knew he would find her. His instinct was the same. His will was the same. Her heart was the same.

She calculated he would be arriving any moment now. She jumped up and dashed to the dining room to look at the cake again. Marvellous! She thought she heard the familiar clink of someone opening the gate. Someone was opening it! She dared not peep out. Everything would be as it was to be. Kellan's son was running around somewhere. Suddenly she heard him shouting in a loud voice:

'Ami ko adak! Someone is coming!'

Acknowledgements

My sincerest gratitude to Ravi Singh for his patience and encouragement through the setbacks of pandemic times, and to Sudeshna Shome Ghosh for her valuable inputs and generosity in the editing and production of this book.

And to my family and friends, as ever, for their love and support. I am deeply indebted.